A NOVEL

WINNIE FROLIK

ONE IDEA PRESS PITTSBURGH

Printed in the United States
ONE IDEA PRESS
Pittsburgh, PA
OneIdeaPress.com

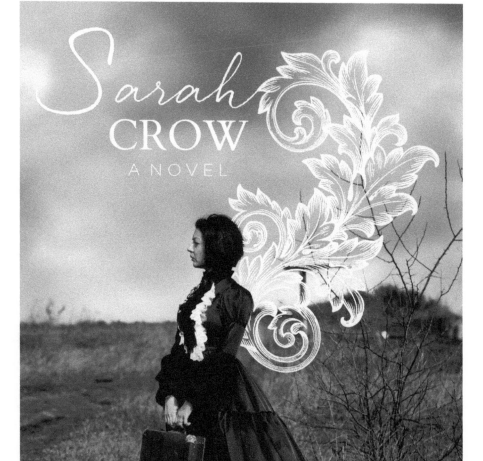

Sarah
CROW

A NOVEL

WINNIE FROLIK

Sarah's Journal

The first time I hurt myself was the day of the funeral, when my mama, papa, and dear little William, the baby of the family, were finally buried. I remember everyone from the village was there that day, even the poorest cottagers. Many of them wept. Everyone came to tell me what a loss it was for Walnut Hill, what good people my parents were, and how they'd be missed. I also heard whispers in the crowd wondering about what was to happen to me, the little beggared orphan child.

I also remember it was a very fine day, sunny and bright, and how wrong that seemed. Funerals should be held on cold days with rain and darkness. This was the sort of day you wanted for picnics and market days. How, on such a pretty day, could three souls be sent into the Earth to rot? It seemed utterly ridiculous to me, and unreal. Everything about what happened was unreal. Only a couple weeks before, I'd had a home. I'd had a mother, a father, and a brother. I'd had a place in the world. Then, I had no one and nothing. The world no longer made sense. I wondered if it was all a sort of dream and any minute I'd wake up and everything would be right again. But, of course, that didn't happen.

I found I didn't just feel a need to cry. I'd been doing that all day. I'd cried until my eyes felt sore. It wasn't enough. I felt a need to do something else. Something violent. Then, I saw the cheese knife... and I did not even think. I just did it. It felt good! It hurt, but the pain was somehow a relief. A release, as it were. It calmed me. I tied a handkerchief around the wound as a bandage, and no one ever knew.

One

"There is no grief like the grief that does not speak."
–Henry Wadsworth Longfellow

Whenever a child is left orphaned in this world, all surviving relations are immediately thrust into a dispute over who's going to be burdened with that most unwanted encumbrance: the poor relation. When Reverend Richard Pole, his wife, Hannah, and seven-year-old William were all taken away by fever in a week, they left behind only a daughter, Sarah, at age twelve. Richard's brother and only living relative, John Pole, was a Naval officer stationed in Majorca, and he was safe from any presumption of responsibility. However, maternal uncle Harold Embry and maternal aunt Penelope Cleary, being both very much in England, were at risk. Their new young charge, Sarah, did not impress them favorably. She was a plain, bony child with sallow skin, dark hair, and eyes rimmed red with tears. She almost never spoke.

Negotiations between brother and sister began over tea in the parlor of the soon-to-be vacated vicarage after the funeral. The uncle, with a receding hairline and weak chin, and the aunt, with a firm jaw and determined eyebrows, were so involved in their discussion that neither thought to lower their voices, nor did they notice the shadow of a small figure watching them from the adjoining room and listening to their every word.

"How long will it be before she must be moved out?" This was Penelope's first question.

"A week, perhaps two," Harold noted sourly, "but the vicarage estate has already been sold. Surely the new parson will want to move in sooner rather than later, and I doubt he'll want the previous occupant's firstborn child as a souvenir."

"And is there really no inheritance for the girl at all?" Penelope sounded incredulous.

"Blame the bad harvest season," Harold replied. "1816 is looking to be a year of record famine in the British Isles and all of western Europe."

"I'm aware the price of food has risen. Lord, all those hideous riots in Ely and Littleport. Thank God Sir Henry Dudley and the Royal Dragoons put things down so firmly and hanged so many of those ruffians."

"Yes, well, Richard Pole was in the camp that insisted on calling for troops and believed in increasing charity to the poor at such times! And he did so out of his own income and what he little had saved," Harold rolled his eyes at the folly.

"Except for some jewelry and silverware that Hannah held for her dowry, the girl will have nothing."

"Blazes! What on Earth ever possessed our sister to marry a nobody like Richard Pole to begin with? He had no money. Nothing but a miserable little country living to recommend him," Penelope pronounced.

"Hannah was a fool," was Harold's verdict. "She always put sentiment ahead of sense. But now she's gone, and someone must take the girl. My dear Penelope, since you and Cecil have no children of your own, how welcome it will be to you both to take this girl in as a daughter." Harold had taken pains to prepare this argument and thought it a winning one. Penelope, though, was not so easily defeated.

"Cecil's health and nerves are most delicate. The last thing he needs is the additional burden of an active little girl running around and making noise all the time. No, a poor invalid like Cecil and his caretaker would be no proper company for a young girl, I'm sure! You and Margaret, though, with four bright and lively children of your own…"

"Soon to be five children. Margaret told me only a few days ago."

"Congratulations. I'm sure young Sarah will welcome yet another cousin. Indeed, she may well play nursemaid."

"But, you see, the last thing we can do at this time is accommodate another child," Harold came to the crux of the matter, "especially a grief-stricken orphan. She, uh… she may not be the most suitable companion for our children, considering her situation." He did not add, but privately thought, how undesirable it would be for his own children to form any kind of attachment with a penniless relation. Good Lord, one of his sons might even fall in love and want to marry the girl.

"Fiddlesticks! Your income is so much greater than mine and Cecil's."

A cunning hit! Harold reeled. Indeed, Harold Embry's enjoyed a far larger income, both from entailment and from his wife's dowry, which had long been a matter of much resentment to Penelope, who was aware she'd had to settle for the less affluent Cecil. They lived only a few miles apart and thus saw quite a lot of each other, which only made matters worse. Had they been on opposite sides of the country or, better yet, different countries altogether, her brother's greater wealth could have been far more easily borne, but every visit to her brother had increased Penelope's resentments. Just looking at the superior state of the furnishings and refinements in Harold's parlor was enough to raise her ire. Even worse, whenever she'd had to entertain Harold and his wife, she'd felt their silent judgement of everything within her own home. Admittedly, Penelope had still done far better for herself than Hannah.

Penelope pressed in for the kill, "And after all, the girl can easily take her lessons alongside your children in the schoolroom with the tutors and daily governess at no extra expense."

"Governess!" Harold gave a start. "There's a thought. The girl can be trained as a governess."

"Well, as a penniless orphan, that's surely her eventual fate," Penelope replied.

"Yes, but aren't there schools for governesses? Surely, we can find some reputable, but reasonably priced, establishment to board and educate the girl until she's ready to go off into the world. That way we can split the fees! We may even get John to contribute."

"I wouldn't hold out much hope there, given the distance, but the expense borne between the two of us would certainly be easier. It doesn't seem likely she'll grow into a beauty."

"No, it certainly doesn't," Harold agreed. "Surprising, really. Hannah and Richard were both good-looking enough, but their daughter is quite a plain thing, isn't she?"

"All the better then she should be trained to teach," Penelope pronounced. "She's no chance of marrying well, I'm afraid, and considering her prospects, it's for the best if she isn't raised in a stately private family dwelling. It would only make her discontented with her future station. Really, it would be far kinder to accustom her to the schoolroom sooner rather than later."

"Undoubtedly. Suppose it's all for the good she's only grown up in Walnut Hill so far," Harold looked around the modestly decorated vicarage with a marked expression of distaste. "She won't have developed any expensive tastes here, I'll be bound."

Penelope and Harold immediately made inquiries. By great luck, they found a newspaper advertisement for a school not so very far away and with seemingly moderate fees.

Penelope soon whisked Sarah off into the coach from the country parsonage to the seaside village of Weberley, more than thirty miles away. The girl had been clumsy enough to cut herself, somehow, and sported a new bandage across one hand, but as Sarah made no complaint of any pain, Penelope did not consider the wound even worth mentioning. Sarah made no complaints at all actually, and rarely spoke the entire trip. Except for an occasional *yes* or *no* in response to direct questions, she might have been taken for a mute. While Penelope found it a bit of a relief, in some respects, that the child was at least quiet and not troubling her, after a while, she began to find the total silence rather unnerving. She had expected—or rather dreaded—a torrent of tears. Yet, Sarah may have been carved out of stone for all the expression she showed. Altogether, there was something decidedly odd, even eerie, about the girl.

On only one occasion did Sarah display the slightest hint of animation. The coach stopped in the road for a moment, and young Sarah looked out of it, staring intently at something in the distance. When Penelope leaned over, she saw the object of the girl's fascination was nothing more than an ugly old crow seated on a fence post. Then, Sarah put her lips together and began to caw!

"What on Earth are you doing?" Penelope cried out.

"I was trying to speak to him," Sarah replied as the coach began moving again.

"You're too old for such childish fancies," Penelope said sharply. "No more bird calls!"

Sarah simply shrugged and said nothing more for the duration of the trip. The carriage passed hordes of beggars and itinerants on the road, far more so than had been seen in England in previous years. It was to the considerable relief of Penelope when the driver announced their destination.

As the coach entered the town of Weberley, laying right along the southern coast, it passed a row of tidy houses with clapboard shutters, narrow garden spaces, and brass handled doors on either side of the road. On the largest of these houses hung a sign announcing it as the Parsley School for Young Ladies. Sarah's new home.

Inside was a simple but tastefully decorated interior which boasted no pretensions but looked exactly for what it was: an honest old-fashioned boarding school where respectable, if not always wealthy, girls received a suitable education without injuring their health or with any risk of "developing notions." There were a dozen or so boarding students and several day students from within the town itself.

Weberley was considered an especially healthy location thanks to the sea air, which put color in the girls' cheeks. It attracted a considerable number of visitors who enjoyed bathing in and drinking seawater. Wealthy invalids would come to Weberley and hire sedan chairs to carry them around town and help them save their strength. The chairs also proved invaluable on rainy days. These visitors tended to taper off with the advent of autumn, though an occasional brave, or foolhardy, soul was known to go bathing in seawater as far into the year as November.

Weberley also enjoyed the benefits of a sandy beach, perfect for long walks, and a lending library which offered the girls of Parsley school a special rate.

In spring, summer, and early autumn, the girls would assist in the garden as well as attend to their lessons. From the garden came fresh herbs and vegetables to be served up by the household cook, Maisy. In winter, the proprietor, Mrs. Gates, tended to chilblains and runny noses.

Mrs. Gates was a plump middle-aged woman with ruddy cheeks, firm smile lines around her eyes and mouth, and a white bonnet. She was assisted by Miss Leigh, her niece, a woman of washed-out coloring and with a pinched nose. Sometimes, other instructors were brought in to teach languages or, as in the case of the recently hired Miss Currer, embroidery and lace-making. As Miss Leigh gave the day's instruction in geography, Mrs. Gates offered Sarah and Penelope a tour of the house, including the kitchen and schoolroom.

"Yes, yes, it will serve," Penelope said absently. "Shall we discuss payment?"

Mrs. Gates took her aside, out of the child's hearing, and tuition for the first year was begrudgingly dispensed from Penelope's pocketbook. She reminded herself that she would be speaking to Harold later to make sure he compensated her for his share. If he thought he could cheat her, he'd soon know differently! Penelope handed Sarah over as quickly as possible before taking her leave to make her homeward journey. She never returned to Weberley to visit, and neither did Harold Embry. They never wrote to Sarah directly, but only to Mrs. Gates on the matter of fees and how the girl's education was coming along.

When Penelope left, Mrs. Gates felt momentarily at a loss, faced with the silent child in mourning. Sarah was looking in the direction of Mrs. Gates, but her gaze seemed to be focused on something else that only she could see. After a long and awkward pause, during which Sarah did not speak a word, Mrs. Gates interrupted the girl's thought train.

"Well now, you must be tired after your journey. Shall I show you to your quarters?' Sarah nodded, and Mrs. Gates ushered her to a small bedroom she'd be sharing with two other girls. As Mrs. Gates helped Sarah with her trunk, she noticed the girl's bandaged hand.

"What is that?" she grabbed Sarah's arm and pushed back the bandage to get a full view.

Right in the middle of Sarah's palm was a jagged line. The gash was quite fresh and pink, only newly scabbed over. The size and shape of the wound indicated to Mrs. Gates that it had been made by some kind of blade.

"My lord, what happened?'

Sarah appeared to be examining her shoes, contemplating whether or not she should answer.

"It was the day of the funeral. I was cutting myself some cheese and the knife slipped."

"Good lord! Does it hurt?" Mrs. Gates gingerly touched the ugly mark. It didn't bleed fresh again, which was a good sign.

"Oh no, ma'am," Sarah reassured her. "It feels just fine."

"The wound looks angry! In the future, dear, I recommend you stay away from knives."

"Yes, ma'am," Sarah replied. She wordlessly laid down on the little bed, fully dressed, and stared up at the ceiling. There was a second long, awkward pause, and Mrs. Gates spoke again.

"Do you need anything?"

Sarah shook her head, and Mrs. Gates decided perhaps the girl simply needed some time to herself. She left the room and instructed Sarah's future room-mates not to bother the new girl if she didn't approach them first. She dropped similar hints to Miss Leigh. Mrs. Gates, in the days ahead, would wonder many times about the child's stillness, but she had many girls to supervise and Sarah never gave her any mischief.

When the girls first experienced their monthly bleedings, it was Mrs. Gates who explained to them what was happening and who would give them *the facts of life* speech that her own mother had given her. She would also, as delicately as she could, explain to the girls the nature of male appetites and certain expecta-tions they would have to meet once they were married. She never discussed the possibility of female appetites. Indeed, the very idea never occurred to her at all. When the time came that the young girls under Mrs. Gates's care would feel a "tingle down there," they'd learn to touch themselves in the dark, to wrap their legs around poles, or to simply tremble in silence.

Sarah's Journal

And that's how it all began. With a grieving little girl learning she was to be given away, like an unwanted kitten. To hear Aunt Penelope and Uncle Harold talking about mother and father the way they did, I wanted to hit them. I wanted to smash their bones and hurt them as badly as I could. But I couldn't hurt them, so I hurt myself instead.

It was not something I could explain to a doctor or a parson. I could barely explain it to myself. But pain on the outside helped make the pain on the inside easier to bear. Nobody else ever wants to see or hear about someone else's pain. Everyone has troubles enough without dealing with an unhappy, grieving girl. The only thing more disagreeable than a sad girl is an angry one. It doesn't do to scream, or curse, or break things when you're the orphaned charity case, you know. You're expected to be eternally demure and grateful and to know your place. Over time, I found I did not just hurt myself when I was sad but when I was angry, too. On more than one occasion I would quite literally bite my tongue.

And while I kept it secret, I didn't think of it as being a great secret. Not then. It was just something that was, like letting your attention wander when someone dull is speaking to you. Everyone does that, even if they're not supposed to. Not that I thought everyone did what I did. Far from it! But it didn't seem like such a bad thing was all. After all, I wasn't hurting anyone else, now was I?

Two

"The pain of the mind is worse than the pain of the body."
–Pubilius Syrus

A few months after Sarah first arrived, a troubling incident occurred. Mrs. Gates had been returning from an errand in town when Fanny Morris, a day student from the town of Weberley, ran up to her. Fanny was a rather stout child, and the exertion left her red-faced and out of breath.

"Mrs. Gates! Mrs. Gates!" she wheezed in agitation.

"What is it Fanny? What's happened?" The girl's manner had her quite alarmed.

"Sarah Pole stuck herself with a needle!"

"Well that's nothing to fuss about. I can't remember all the times I've pricked mysel–"

"No, no! You don't understand. She stuck herself all the way. The needle's jammed in!"

"But how on Earth could she get a needle jammed all the way through?"

"I don't know, but she has. It's in her leg! Miss Currer was teaching us embroidery, and everyone was looking down at their work when Sally happened to look up. She saw the little pinhead coming out of Sarah's leg and the blood, and she screamed, and then she fainted. Then Miss Currer had a fit, too, and Miss Leigh had to splash water on both of them, and now she's seeing to Sarah!" Fanny finished her tale triumphantly at being the first to break the news. "Is Sarah going to die?"

"People don't die from pinpricks, Fanny," Mrs. Gates replied automatically. Still, it was with her head swimming that she entered the schoolhouse where she was swarmed by all the other pupils, eager to share the morning's excitement, all to be disappointed to learn that Mrs. Gates already knew.

Miss Currer was a local woman who did piecework and lacework while also giving lessons at Weberley. Ordinarily, she was a rosy-cheeked lady of fine figure and with sausage-like brown curls, but in the fright of the incident, she had been reduced to lying down on a sofa in a state. All her apparent robustness had deserted her. By contrast, it was the sickly-looking Miss Leigh who had taken Sarah back into the kitchen area. She had already extracted the pin and had the wound cleaned and dressed by the time Mrs. Gates arrived on the scene. Wordlessly, she handed Mrs. Gates the pin

"Well," said Mrs. Gates, "what happened?"

"The pin got stuck," Sarah replied calmly.

"Yes, I heard that the pin got stuck, but how? It didn't jam itself in. Did one of the other girls do it?" she asked suspiciously.

Mrs. Gates was all too aware of how children can sometimes bully and abuse one another. She had a strict code of never standing for anything of that nature. Not under her watch.

"No," Sarah's big, dark eyes stared at the floor. "I did. I had my embroidery in my lap, and I was, well, I was careless." Sarah gave an apologetic shrug for her clumsiness.

"Careless! Well, you can't be so careless with needles in the future, now can you?"

"No," said Sarah. "I suppose not."

"Lord, look at all the commotion you've caused! The whole school's in an uproar—and look at poor Miss Currer."

"I'm very sorry, Mrs. Gates," Sarah looked up with her queer eyes that seemed too large for her face, "I'll never cause you any uproar or trouble again. You have my word." There was a solemn intensity to her words.

"Well then, it's back to class now for both of us. Time for history."

And the incident was history. The day's business wore on, but that night, when she was alone in her room, Mrs. Gates found her thoughts returning to the pin jammed in the leg and remembered the scar, and she suddenly felt inexplicably cold. It was silly, she told herself. The idea was preposterous. Little girls didn't hurt themselves on purpose. *Did they?* Mrs. Gates remembered a long-forgotten incident in the village of her youth.

A young servant girl, little more than Sarah's age, had been employed by the vicar and his family as a general maid of all work. One day, the vicar's wife discovered her young maid was, as they say, in the family way. She was, of course, immediately dismissed from the household despite her entreaties punctuated with tears and screams. All of this was unpleasant, but in no way unusual. No, what made this sordid little incident a legend in the village was what came after. One Sunday morning, the young girl climbed the bell tower of the church. Just as day broke and people started walking to church, she flung herself from the tower to her death below.

Blood, bone, and brain matter all stained the churchyard that day. One dark splotch on the stone never fully went away, no matter how many times it was scrubbed. Then, there was the matter of the girl's burial. She could not be buried in the consecrated ground of the churchyard, so instead she had been buried at a crossroads head turned downward to prevent her spirit from roaming forth. This did not prevent the usual nonsense of hauntings from circling in town.

Most folks were concerned with questions of whether the girl's ghost would forever haunt the bell tower, or if the vicar's wife would ever recover from the shock of all this. But to a young Mrs. Gates, the chief question that had troubled her then was how despairing and hopeless the wretched girl must have been to do such a thing. What was on her mind as she climbed to the top of the bell tower? How did she manage to bring herself to make that jump? Mrs. Gates couldn't imagine the level of desperation it would take to make the plunge. How distraught would you need to be to go against your own bodily instincts and harm yourself?

This wasn't the same situation, though. Sarah wasn't involved in any illicit love affairs, and the prick of a needle can hardly be compared to tossing oneself from a tower. Still, Mrs. Gates was troubled.

The next day, she took the unusual step of suggesting to Miss Leigh that Sarah no longer be included in embroidery lessons and instead spend the time reading or with her beloved sketchbook. Miss Leigh was astonished.

"But needlework is such an important accomplishment for a young lady," she protested.

"I know, and ordinarily I consider it a crucial skill for our girls to master. But after yesterday's accident, I think it best if, for now at least, Sarah stays away from needles... and scissors... and anything else sharp or pointy."

"Well, clearly, she'll have no future as a dressmaker or milliner," Miss Leigh washed her hands of it.

"Yes, but this way she might still have a future," Mrs. Gates responded cryptically, leaving Miss Leigh quite puzzled.

As a result, Sarah was excluded from embroidery and sewing lessons. Sarah raised no objection to this, but she used the time to draw instead. By the next day, Miss Currer had recovered her usual aplomb. Mrs. Gates privately kept—or tried to keep—a more watchful eye on Sarah, but Mrs. Gates had many responsibilities to attend, and Sarah was generally quiet.

As time passed, and without any further trouble in the future, Mrs. Gates was quite able to put the whole unpleasant incident out of mind. As for Miss Leigh, she'd never suspected anything in the first place. Sarah didn't misbehave, always completed her lessons diligently, did whatever was asked of her uncomplainingly, and, best of all, she didn't talk back. Sometimes, she barely talked at all. Apart from Sarah being somewhat clumsy, Miss Leigh considered her, in many ways, an ideal pupil.

Sarah's Journal

The lesson I took from the day with the pin was the need for discretion. Other people could not, or would not, understand my compulsion. If I were caught, it would only make Mrs. Gates unhappy, and I truly did not want that. She was very good to me, and I appreciated her kindness. As time went on, it occurred to me that behavior like mine might be grounds for commitment to a madhouse, and I could not imagine a worse fate.

I didn't miss embroidery itself. I'd always considered it rather dull, but it did become more difficult to find the proper instrument for my self-treatment regimen. I didn't dare take any of the knifes from the kitchen—Maisey kept careful track of every item in her command, and it would have been missed at once. For a time, I had to content myself with pinching until black and blue marks decorated my skin, or occasionally banging my arms and legs against tables and walls, but it was never quite as satisfactory as the feel of a blade and drawing blood. Though never again would I even dream of cutting my own hand like I had the first time. It was entirely too visible. Moreover, what if I damaged myself in some way so that I could no longer draw?

One day, we were taking a ramble by the seashore. Mrs. Gates often took us on such excursions, citing the healthy effect of sea air, and the beach at Weberley was quite a pleasant place to walk. But what proved most memorable to me about that day was that I spotted half an oyster shell in the sand. To most people, it wouldn't have merited a second glance, but I observed that the edge was quite sharp. I picked it up. Then I covered it with my handkerchief and carefully brought it home with me. I found it a home in a little pouch, which had been discarded by some other girl, and I hid it under my mattress. That pouch became my angel. My savior. Over the years, I was able to add to it: *a piece of flint, a shard of glass, and finally, some years later, a shiny new razor, which I purchased with out of pocket money from Mr. Tewkes at the store. He wrapped it up all nice and neatly in brown paper for me. Thankfully, he did not ask any questions or ever mention my purchase to anyone else.*

When I felt the need come upon me, I would take the pouch and find a way to be alone, usually by pleading the call of nature. Then I would find a place on my body where the marks wouldn't show—the back of my neck where it'd be concealed by hair, my upper thighs, sometimes even the interior of my mouth—and make a quick prick. And of course, the soles of my feet were excellent places to hide little nicks. With the feel of something sharp digging into my flesh always came an inevitable feeling of release and relief. Sometimes, I'd kiss the razor before I cut. Once or twice, I kissed the razor after I had cut. I learned the taste of blood evoked copper on the tongue, or at least my blood did. I had no one else's to compare it with. I also found that, depending on the deepness of the wound, handling the blood was another tricky matter. I had to use old rags sometimes to staunch up wounds, and the scabs itched a lot and were a real nuisance.

The first few years I was at Parsley, I had to make these cuts fairly regularly, but as time went on, I did so less and less. Indeed, my final year at Parsley, I didn't intentionally cut myself even once! I felt quite pleased with my new-found self-control. I'd found ways to occupy myself and even be happy with books, my work at the school, long walks by the sea, and even, to a small extent, friendships with other girls. Clara, with whom I shared a room, while clever with her needlepoint, found it most vexing to conjugate French. I began helping her, and we, in turn, became very close. Sometime later, Clara and I happened to catch Geraldine entering the building one night through the window. Miss Leigh heard the noise and came to check on us while Geraldine hid in the closet. I made up a story of having woken up in the middle of the night and gone looking for water. Miss Leigh believed me, and Geraldine didn't get into trouble.

I asked her later why she snuck out, and she said she wanted to walk on the sand and see the sea. When Clara said she could do that any day, Geraldine insisted that she wanted to do it at night simply because she wasn't supposed to be out then.

"Everything's more fun if you're not supposed to do it," Geraldine proclaimed with the all the wisdom of thirteen years. "Don't either of you saints ever do anything you shouldn't do?"

To this, Clara and I had no response. I doubted, when Geraldine talked about the joy of forbidden actions, she had any notion of my little hobby.

After that encounter, though, all three of us were fast friends. The hours I spent with Geraldine and Clara were among my happiest in those years. I learned to love the seashore and the fresh, briny smell of the sea itself. I came to love the sound of gulls in the distance and the waves chopping on rocks. I appreciated the way light can form over the oceans, casting itself into small radiant pools. Weberley and the sea were very, very different from Walnut Hill, but far from making me hate it, the freshness of the surroundings turned out to be a blessing.

Still, I kept that pouch. I knew I shouldn't have kept it. I knew I should have thrown it away. I did throw it away once, on the dust heap, but I found myself digging it out hours later and clutching it to my chest like a talisman. I wasn't strong enough to throw that pouch away, and my own weakness shamed and frightened me.

Three

"*Perhaps the most delightful friendships are those in which there is much agreement, much disputation, and yet more personal liking.*"
–George Eliot

The matter of the needle was soon forgotten, and Sarah seemed settled in at Parsley School. She was withdrawn, to be sure, and didn't make friends those first months, but she was never ill-behaved, and no complaints could be made about her academic progress. In fact, she seemed, by far, the most studious of the girls and showed a talent and interest in draftsmanship.

In the years to come, she'd not only exhaust the entire school bookshelf but would become something of a fixture at the Weberley lending library as well. Normally, Mrs. Gates might have worried that any girl so thirsty for knowledge could render herself unsuitable for matrimony. Even men enlightened enough to not insist on fools for wives tended to prefer their women at least more ignorant than themselves, but Sarah's situation was different. A pretty girl may find a husband even without a fortune, and a girl with a fortune can wed even if she isn't pretty, but the marital prospects for a girl without beauty or dowry were very bleak indeed. If marriage wasn't in Sarah's future, then she'd need her education and wits to survive.

Once Mrs. Gates had overheard some of the other girls refer to her charge as "Sarah Crow."

"That's very unkind of you," she castigated them.

"But it's what Sarah calls herself," came their retort. She had later confirmed this with Sarah, and while Mrs. Gates informed Sarah that such nomenclature was inappropriate, she could not say it was inaccurate. Sarah's bony frame, beaky nose, and deep-set eyes framed by dark hair did indeed make her look like a crow. And a rather hungry one at that.

Fortunately, the girl was clever at least. She usually headed the class in lessons, and she could draw and paint far better than anyone else at Parsley School, including the instructors.

Sarah showed a fondness for doing sketches of the seaside. She once did a watercolor of the school and gardens that was really quite charming as a personal present for Mrs. Gates.

"You know," said Miss Leigh after Sarah had been at Parsley School for a year or so, "Sarah Pole seems to always be in the company of Geraldine Nesbitt and Clara Tulling."

"It's only to be expected," Mrs. Gates replied. "They're all the same age."

"But they're so different in terms of temperament. Sarah, bless her, is such an odd creature, while Clara's a perfect little lady. And Geraldine is... well, Geraldine's Geraldine." There were a lot of other names Miss Leigh would have liked to use to describe the girl, but none of them were appropriate for a discussion in polite company.

"Girls don't always become friends based on what they have in common," Mrs. Gates noted wisely. "Sometimes it's just the opposite. Life's more interesting when you're not just talking to yourself."

"I'm not sure Geraldine's the best influence on Sarah or Clara," Miss Leigh came to the point. "I doubt Geraldine's a good influence on any of the girls here. Perhaps she shouldn't be here at all."

"She's a little rough around the edges," Mrs. Gates admitted. Miss Leigh raised an eyebrow. "All right, more than a little, but I think the other girls help refine her. Clara's far too well brought up to mimic Geraldine, and Sarah keeps her own counsel. Besides, I think it's good for Sarah to have them. Have you noticed the closest Sarah ever comes to merriment is when she's with them?"

"She does seem to show more life around them. She even gets more color in her cheeks," Miss Leigh grudgingly admitted. "And I suppose the more eyes there are on Geraldine, the better."

Geraldine had dusky skin and flashing black eyes that made some wonder if there wasn't Spanish or gypsy blood in her veins. She loved tales of romance and adventure—usually tales on the high seas or of foreign lands, but a rattling good story of a haunting or vicious skullduggery would satisfy as well. Geraldine was in the habit of loudly proclaiming that she would like nothing more than to be a pirate, though she might settle for being a barbary queen instead. Geraldine was the daughter of a widowed merchant captain who was often away at sea, and she seemed to know every sea shanty ever written, and what she lacked in musical ability, she made up for with sheer exuberance. Her favorites were The Ballad of Captain Kidd and Hanging Johnny. She'd belt them out loudly on the shore, frightening the gulls.

Geraldine had spent a lot of time around sailors and had picked up a rather shocking vocabulary. While she couldn't use certain expressions around Mrs. Gates without getting her mouth scrubbed out with soap, Geraldine felt free to share with her playmates when they strolled along the beach together. This was perhaps their favorite place to walk. Sometimes, if alone, they'd take off their shoes and stockings and delight in feeling the wet sand and seafoam between their toes. This day was somewhat chilly, though, so the girls remained shod.

"Damn it! Got a stone in my shoe," Geraldine spat out. "Give me a moment to get it out."

"You're not supposed to say words like 'damn,'" Clara objected. "It's really quite shocking, it is." Clara had curly hair and was already developing a soft, curvy figure. She did the best needlepoint in the school and could never see a dog without wanting to pet it. Both of Clara's parents were alive and in excellent health, but her father, the son of a Yorkshire blacksmith who had become a banker, sent her to Parsley School to learn gentility. It was his hope that with proper manners and an ample dowry, Clara would marry up. Clara had decided this plan suited her as well, provided her future husband was of an amiable temperament, of course.

"Damn! Bloody! Bollocks! Balls! Tits! Ass! Shit! Buggery!" Geraldine sang out these blasphemies like a cheerful ballad.

"Geraldine!" Clara's mouth was agape. This was a frequent reaction to Geraldine from Clara—so much so that one might be forgiven for wondering if the whole point of Clara's friendship with Geraldine was derived from a secret desire to be shocked. Geraldine, in the meanwhile, made no secret at all of her delight in shocking others. Having extracted the stone, she gave it a hearty toss to the open sea and was gratified to see it skip twice before sinking into the waters.

"She just likes attention, Clara. Don't encourage her." Sarah shook her head in amusement.

"I do not know what that last word – 'buggery' – even means," Clara frowned.

"Neither do I," Sarah admitted

"Buggery? You two don't know what buggery is?" Geraldine hee-hawed with laughter. She gestured to her companions to lean in closer to her while she whispered a clear, concise, and graphic description to them. Clara pulled back her face, red as a cherry, and Sarah remained unperturbed but wondered, "Is that not rather uncomfortable?"

"Suspect it is, but men do it anyway! You'd be amazed at the places they'll put it in!" Geraldine spoke with gusto.

"You'll never get a husband speaking of such things, Geraldine," Clara shook her head.

"Will too! Father's friends like the way I talk. I'll marry one of their lot and spend my days on a ship while you two stay here on land and throw tea parties and die of boredom," Geraldine stuck out her tongue.

"We would not die of boredom," Clara retorted, "and who wants to live on a boat anyway? You get seasickness and scurvy."

"Not everyone, and it's still better than being a dried-up old spinster who's too prudish to say 'damn.'"

"And what man wants to marry a hoyden?" Clara countered.

"No, I'm the one who's never going to marry," Sarah reminded them both before they could really get into it. "I'm the old maid of the group, so neither of you need worry."

"Oh Sarah, why say something so dreadful?" Clara cooed.

Sarah remained unflappable. "Because it is true. I have no money, no beauty, and no connections. No man will ever want me. Don't worry, Clara, it does not upset me the way it would you. I'm not sure I am the marrying sort," Sarah absentmindedly rubbed a scab as she said this.

"What happened to your arm?" Geraldine asked.

"Oh, that? Nothing. Just an accident," Sarah replied hurriedly as she pulled back her sleeve.

"You get into more accidents than anyone. You must be the clumsiest girl that ever lived!' Geraldine rolled her eyes.

"Yes, I suppose I am."

They stopped by a longtime favorite boulder of theirs, which provided enough seating for all three of them to watch the tide come in. They smelled the open sea brine and watched large quantities of kelp get washed ashore.

"Have you ever wondered where it all comes from?" Clara pointed to the seaweed. "Can there really be plants that live within the ocean? You'd think the salt and the waves would make it impossible."

"I think it looks like the hair of mermen and mermaids myself," Sarah said. "Perhaps they shed it constantly, like dogs and cats do with fur, or maybe it's sheared from them, like wool is cut from sheep."

"I've heard a girl was once carried off by seaweed," Geraldine proclaimed. "It wrapped itself around her and carried her under the waves to drown!"

Clara rolled her eyes again, a newly developing habit of hers.

"Some kinds of seaweed are edible you know," Geraldine continued. "In the Orient, they eat it all the time. That and rice."

Meanwhile, Sarah had brought out her sketchbook and begun drawing the ocean with a great boat in the distance.

"There is no boat out there," Clara pointed out.

"This is for Geraldine. It's her ship. A pirate ship, and she's the captain and pirate queen."

"Good!" Geraldine laughed. "I'll sail from South America to China and collect treasure everywhere and wear a big hat!"

"If she gets a picture then I want one, too."

"Agreed," Sarah replied.

"But don't draw any pirate nonsense for me," Clara warned.

"No, I'll draw you a knight on a white horse."

"I don't think I want a knight," Clara mused. "They are always going off into battle and getting killed, and it's no good thing to be a widow."

"What would you like then, Clara?"

"I would like a castle and a prince. But not a gloomy castle full of cobwebs and ghosts. I want a pretty, cheerful one, and I want a happy prince with a happy kingdom full of happy farmers."

"All right, I can draw that," Sarah conceded.

"I want a big garden, too, with lots of room for children and dogs to play around in," Clara added.

"Garden and dogs," Sarah repeated.

"That is so dull," sighed Geraldine.

"I don't mind dull," Clara said wistfully.

"Well, of course, you don't," Geraldine retorted. "You must be the dullest girl I have ever met."

"I'm drawing what you both want, not what's most exciting," Sarah decreed, attempting to head off an argument, "and if Clara wants a castle and a garden then that's what I'll draw for her."

"And what about you Sarah? What will you draw for yourself?" Clara asked.

Sarah sat and thought for a minute. Eventually, she shrugged her shoulders, "Let me surprise you."

They laughed and chatted on the rock until the sun went down and the air turned cold. Soon enough, Geraldine got a sketch of herself decked out as a pirate with a cutlass, tri-cornered hat and a handsome parrot in front of a grand looking ship. It all looked quite bold and dangerous. Clara was drawn among the turrets of a very pretty little castle that stood on a rolling green hill. Sarah, indeed, surprised them with her own picture. Sarah had clearly drawn herself, but in the most peculiar fashion imaginable. First, she had changed her nose, which was understandable, but instead of minimizing it as anyone would expect, she had drawn it as a giant beak. Her long dark hair had been drawn into feathers, and her hands curved as bird's claws. From her shoulders sprouted two massive black wings.

"Here," Sarah said, "Sarah Crow. What do you think of her?"

"Well that is… that is… different," said Geraldine.

"She's spooky," Clara shivered and then frowned. "I am not sure it was a good idea for you to draw that. Why would you want to be a crow?"

"What's wrong with being a crow? They're clever creatures and they fly," Sarah philosophized. "And I certainly have the coloring for one," Sarah absently pulled at a lock of her hair.

"I thought crows meant death," Clara objected

"That's just superstition, Clara," Geraldine rolled her eyes, though privately there was something about the picture she found frightening as well. Both Geraldine and Clara were relieved when Sarah put the picture away, and they each secretly hoped she would destroy it.

Sarah's Journal

"Sarah Crow" was the only self-portrait I dared show the girls. My other sketches weren't really fit to be seen by children. For example, the one where I did half my face as a skeleton might have made poor Clara faint. Even Geraldine, for all her bravado, wouldn't have been pleased by the one where I drew myself naked with all my scars covered in glass and blood. I do not know why I felt the need to draw such things. But I did. And drawing was at least better than cutting. Better to mark paper than skin.

I loved Geraldine and Clara like they were my own sisters, but I could not help but envy them too. Geraldine may have lost her mother but she'd never even known her, so she never mourned her. Clara had all her family. And both of them were wanted. They had families who desired them and doted on them. Clara's parents visited her regularly and even took her home on holidays, while Geraldine's father sent her boxes with the most wonderful gifts from all the places he sailed to. Meanwhile, I never received so much as a letter from Aunt Penelope or either of my uncles. Someday, Geraldine and Clara would marry good, suitable men and have families of their own. For me, that was just out of the question. Neither of them would ever have to work and I would.

And most of all, I envied them their unmarked skin. Or rather, I envied them that they did not feel the need to mark their skin.

Four

"Ordinary fortune-tellers tell you what you want to happen;
witches tell you what's going to happen, whether you want it to or not."
—Terry Pratchett

Every September in Weberley, there was a great fair. The days before the fair always saw a great deal of house-cleaning, painting, wall-washing, and street-clearing. Shopkeepers polished and shined their wares, laying them out to their most dazzling effect. The town confectioner spent the whole week baking treats. Then came the setup of the fairgrounds. Wagons entered town bearing exotic creatures, jugglers, organ players, fiddlers, wooden horses, gaming tables, and, of course, following all this came a trail of beggars. The excitement carried over to Parsley School as well. The pupils were allowed to attend but only under the chaperonage of Miss Leigh or Mrs. Grant, and only during daytime hours when some propriety was still observed. It was well known that the revels became progressively more booze-ridden and bawdier during nighttime hours.

In theory, the local magistrate was supposed to keep order. In practice, the magistrate had made it something of a yearly tradition to end up dancing drunkenly on a barrel at the fairgrounds until he passed out.

Naturally, this presented to Geraldine an irresistible impulse to visit the fair during twilight hours—and to go unaccompanied. Sarah was happy to go as well. Even Clara didn't take very much persuading for once. There was, however, still the question of how to get out.

Eventually, they settled on climbing out a window of the second story using a nice rain spout to make their way to the ground. Clara tripped a little coming down and stubbed her toe, but, eventually, they were all safely aground.

"Let's go," whispered Geraldine.

"Wait a minute," Sarah said as the thought occurred to her, "how will we sneak back inside later?'"

"Oh, don't worry about that," Geraldine reassured her.

"You haven't thought about it all, have you?" asked Clara.

"Honestly Clara, you're hopeless. You can just stay here and be a frightened little field mouse while Sarah and I go have fun. Come on, Sarah."

Geraldine marched off and Sarah followed. For a moment, Clara hesitated. The fairgrounds stretched along Weberley's main wharf, enticing townsfolk and sea voyagers alike with music, laughter, and light. A light breeze carried appetizing smells upon the air.

"I'm coming!" Clara said and hurried after them. On one side of the road were the shop booths allocated to furniture makers, jewelers, silversmiths, drapers, tailors, lace-makers, ironmongers, and toymakers. Occasionally, the girls would stop to admire a particular object.

They passed stalls selling fruit, cheese, and gingerbread. The latter smelled so good Geraldine insisted on buying a large bunch and sharing it with her companions as they rambled on their way. There was a large theatrical booth with a company of comedians whose buffoonery earned guffaws from the audience. Other booths housed jugglers, conjurors, acrobats, and rope dancers. One was home to a giant man, who was easily over seven feet tall, and his companion, a dwarf. The latter would often ride on the back of the former to the roar of the crowd.

Even the crowd itself was something to look at. It seemed the area was swarming with people. Some were people of means, some tradesmen, some servants, and many were beggars. A number of people had clearly been making good use of those stalls, selling cider and wine. In fact, several people had wandered out into a sandy beach area to either vomit, pass out, or both. One group of fellows bobbed clumsily around the square together, arm-in-arm and singing off key. Another group was having a lively game of dice around a campfire.

The girls came upon a tiger in a cage, which batted and growled at the bars most fiercely and everyone *ooh*-ed and *aah*-ed.

"Don't you just wish you could touch it?" Geraldine inched closer to the cage. Clara instinctively grabbed her by the shoulder. Sarah simply looked mesmerized. Almost in a trance, she recited a few words by heart, lending an air of enchantment to the evening.

> *Tyger Tyger, burning bright,*
> *In the forests of the night;*
> *What immortal hand or eye,*
> *Could frame thy fearful symmetry?*

The spell cast by Sarah's recital was broken by an unknown voice in the crowd, "Eye doesn't rhyme with symmetry."

Both Geraldine and Clara booed and groaned, and Sarah sharply remarked, "It doesn't have to rhyme."

At the very end of the line of show booths was a small caravan beside a tent that had been stitched together from many different cuts of cloth, giving it the resemblance of a patchwork quilt. There laid a crudely painted sign depicting a giant palm and announcing, "Let Madame Demelza Tell You Your Future."

"A fortune teller," Geraldine crowed. "Oh, we must go!"

The girls ran up and entered the tent that smelled of incense. Inside was a little wooden table covered in an emerald green cloth with two wooden chairs across either side. There was paper on the table, inkpots, and quills, as if someone were planning to write a letter. There was also, curiously enough, a little brazier on the table, smoldering lightly. More curious still was Madame Demelza herself. Everyone knew gypsy fortunetellers were supposed to be skinny old hags, but to the girls' surprise, the woman was a plump, jolly-looking lady who could not have been more than thirty. Madame Demelza had long red hair that hung down her shoulders. She wore a green and white muslin dress that showed more than a hint of ample bosom.

"Good evening," she called out to them. Her manner of speaking marked her as Cornish. "Come to hear the future, have ye? I have the gift of scrying."

"The gift of what?" Clara was confused.

"The gift of scrying," Madame Demelza repeated. "I see things in the fire."

"How do we know you're not some charlatan?" Geraldine demanded.

Madame Demelza smiled cryptically. She passed her hand over the little brazier, and from the embers, a new bright flame suddenly shot up like a rose in full bloom. All three Parsley students gasped audibly.

"Now, here be the rules," Madame Demelza stated flatly. "It's one at a time for each of ye while the others bide aside. But bide thee this warning: I cannot guarantee you'll like whatever answers I give ye."

"How much?" Clara asked, coming to the essential point.

"Tuppence each."

"Well now, that takes me out of the running then since I haven't a coin on me," Sarah said, "but you can both go on." Predictably, it was Geraldine who entered the tent first.

"Can you write your full name or can you only make a mark?" Demelza asked.

"Of course I can write my name," Geraldine scoffed.

"We can all write. We're in school." Clara spoke up.

"Good, then write down your name."

As Geraldine made a bold signature, Madame Demelza added, "And write something about yourself as well. But don't show it to me or anyone else! Now fold up the paper and kiss it."

Geraldine obeyed all the instructions, her eyes wide with wonder. Madame Demelza put the paper in the brazier and let it burn. She stared deeply as the paper was consumed by flame. The flame was reflected in Demelza's eyes. Then she spoke.

"I see waves," she said. "Somehow, you're tied to the sea. And a ship as well. You'll not be in England all your life. I see a long journey and foreign lands in your future."

"I knew it!" Geraldine's voice was exultant. "I'm going to travel the world and see new things. I'll be an adventuress!" Geraldine gloated.

"I thought you already were," Sarah responded.

"Be patient, though," Madame Demelza cautioned. "It will be years before you do, and you won't be traveling alone."

"With whom then?" Geraldine asked. Demelza held up her hands. "That part, I can't see. Nor do I know where you'll be going either. I can only tell you what the flames show me."

Geraldine would have preferred more specifics, but she left well satisfied with what she did know. Then came Clara's turn. Clara took the time to write with perfect penmanship, and Geraldine rolled her eyes.

"She's only going to burn it anyway," Geraldine pointed out. Clara ignored her as she folded the paper into tight creases and then carefully kissed it and handed it to Demelza. More paper burned while Demelza gazed on. Finally, she spoke.

"I don't see any great voyage for you, my child, but I do see prosperity and fortune. A great fortune, even, and you'll travel in some of the finest circles. You will be much loved, and your life will be a comfortable one—but it will be a tame sort of life. No adventures."

"That's all right with me," Clara replied, a mixture of smugness and relief painting her tone. "I like comfort, and I don't want adventures."

As she left, Clara pressed an extra coin into Madame Demelza's hand. "This is for my friend Sarah's reading," Clara explained. She went out and proudly announced, "I'm to be a great lady!"

"Of course you bloody well are!" Geraldine retorted.

"And now it's Sarah's turn," Clara added, ignoring Geraldine.

"I told you, I don't have any money to spare," Sarah reminded her.

"I already paid for you," Clara informed her, "so now you have to go."

Moments later, Sarah, over her own protestations, was sent in to have her fortune told.

Sarah went through the same procedure as Geraldine and Clara had. When asked to write something about herself, she wrote, "I hurt myself on purpose." It felt good, somehow, to put the words to paper, even if they would never be read—especially, in fact, since they'd never be read. When she passed the paper to Madame Demelza, the woman's finger entangled with hers for a moment as she stared into Sarah's eyes. Finally, she broke the stare to put the paper to the flame.

"Well," she said at last, "nothing smooth about your life. You have talent and could create great things, but there's so much pain in you as well; such torment."

Madame Demelza's voice broke off, and her face froze. Suddenly, she grabbed Sarah by the arm and pushed back the sleeve on her dress.

"What are you doing?" Sarah yelped. "Let go of me."

Madame Demelza carefully examined old lines and scars on Sarah's arm.

"Well," she said finally, "I knew there was something different about you from the others." She gazed at Sarah with interest, "You're not a very safe person, are you? But you already knew that."

Sarah managed to free her arm from Madame Demelza's grasp and began walking out of the tent. As she exited, Sarah heard Demelza's final words, "Remember to come in out of the rain!"

Outside, she found Clara.

"What did the palm reader tell you?" Clara asked eagerly.

"Nothing of any interest," Sarah said. "Where's Geraldine?"

"She said she was thirsty," Clara explained. A minute later, Geraldine, flushed and excited, found them. She carried with her a large mug of spirits, which she offered to share with them. Clara refused entirely. Sarah had a single sip. She found she did not care for the taste, leaving Geraldine to finish the drink herself before they all tottered back to Parsley School. Geraldine sang a particularly off-color sea shanty on the way. Just as they came within a hundred yards of the school, the skies opened and rain began to fall, making them run all the quicker, slipping and sliding all the way.

Then came the matter of finding their way inside. Surprisingly, it was Clara who was inspired to use the coal cellar. They found that, with some maneuvering with a stick, they were able to open the latch and make their way inside. Of course, from the coal cellar, they still had to make their way upstairs. Geraldine sobered up long enough to produce a match, and they used its feeble light to make their way out of the cellar to the main floor. Then they had to make it to their room on the second floor without rousing anyone. It was with considerable diffi-culty that they made their way upstairs. They were all slippery from being outside, and a still-tipsy Geraldine was clumsy on her feet. Worse still, she was noisy.

There were a couple near-misses when they'd been sure the whole house-hold must have woken, but, somehow, they all made it into their room without being detected. They tore off their wet things, and the next morning, Geraldine had a truly awful headache. She was sick in a basin as well.

Mrs. Gates tended to her as best she could, wondering aloud what Geral-dine could have eaten to provoke such symptoms. Miss Leigh was suspicious and made an attempt to question Clara and Sarah about Geraldine's activities the night before, but they both claimed Geraldine had simply gone to bed as normal. Just when they thought they were home-free, Miss Leigh happened to examine the dress Geraldine had been wearing the previous day.

"It's damp," she declared, "and there's coal dust on the skirt!"

Further examination proved that all three girls' dresses were damp. Since the rain had not commenced until after curfew the night before, there was noth-ing for it but to admit they had been outside. Harsh punishment was the lot for all three of them. Geraldine mourned her loss of freedom. Clara mourned the loss of her previously pristine school record and blamed Geraldine. Sarah said nothing at all but seemed almost relieved to spend the next month housebound, far away from the fair and from Madame Demelza's tent.

Sarah's Journal

The encounter with the fortune teller unnerved me. It wasn't because she said my life would be full of upheavals, nor was it even to hear her describe me as tormented or tell me I wasn't a safe person. As she noted, this was nothing I hadn't already known, but because she was the first person to learn my secret, and that upset me greatly. All the more so because it had been a perfect stranger who'd learned the truth, which made me even more fearful that other people closer to me might learn as well. Thankfully, being a perfect stranger and a transient, there was never any risk she'd tell my secret to anyone else at Weberley. Still, I'd had enough of an alarm to avoid using the pouch for a time, and to even try to use it less in the future.

I also took from Geraldine's example a lesson in the dangers of over-indulgence in drink. And a lesson about the dangers in following Geraldine at all, much as I loved her.

Five

"If you have a garden and a library, you have everything you need."
–Marcus Tullius Cicero

Eventually, the girls served enough time under lock and key that Mrs. Gates decreed they'd learned their lesson and could be outside again. Clara wasn't likely to get in any serious trouble, nor was Sarah. Being inside all the time was just making them pale and listless.

Geraldine was more than capable of getting into all kinds of shenanigans, but it was frankly more trouble than it was worth to keep Geraldine inside. She paced back and forth, like a lion in a cage, bridled with unspent energy that seemed to emanate from her body like sparks from a fire. Even Miss Leigh allowed that a cooped-up Geraldine was simply maddening to be around.

So, the girls were allowed once more to take rambles by the sea and go back and forth to certain approved places, like Weberley Library. Sarah and Clara both gave Mrs. Gates their solemn word that there would be no more future shenanigans on their part. As for Geraldine, Miss Leigh alerted her that if she should ever find her way to spirits again, or worse yet, be seen in the unchaperoned company of any young men, she would face a fate far worse than flogging: exile to some horrible sort of convent school. The thought of barred windows and forced prayers was a sobering one. Geraldine agreed to avoid any mischief in the future, or at least she would avoid getting caught in any mischief in the future.

The Weberley town library was run by a Mr. Bauer, who slept in the back room. Anyone meeting Mr. Bauer for the first time might be forgiven for mistaking him for a gnome with his diminutive size, trim little beard, and twinkly eyes. He was a man of education who had tried – and failed – at several professions before taking up the opening at Weberley Library out of sheer desperation. He'd been down to his last square meal. He had not been in office more than a week before deciding that, low pay or not, he liked the trade of librarian better than all his other endeavors combined, and had now been happily ensconced there for more than a decade. He considered it a spiritual, even sacred, duty-vocation on his part, far better than being a clergyman.

Many who join the clergy do so out of a desire for a comfortable income without any particular calling to the church, while Mr. Bauer was truly, sincerely devoted to the Weberley Library. The smell of old books, to him, was holier than incense, and the crinkle of pages being turned a form of prayer. There was a communal aspect as well.

People came to the library to attend evening card games, enjoy musical soirees, and even just to chat amongst themselves. Moreover, as the library received each evening a coach delivery of all the major London newspapers, it could rightly be said the library was the key to maintaining knowledge of greater world events inside Weberley.

Besides the pleasure of being surrounded by books all the time, Mr. Bauer also took enormous satisfaction in finding the exact right volume for each person. The book to provide guidance for a young man seeking his way in the world? *Tom Jones* by Henry Fielding! For any young person in the pangs of first love? Shakespeare's *Sonnets*, of course! When three Parsley schoolgirls, by then aged fifteen, started coming in together to find books to read, he was happy to assist them. To Geraldine - that lively, saucy young sprite who always loved melodramas - he recommended Anne Radcliffe and suggested *The Mysteries of Udolpho*. For prim and proper Clara, he prescribed Maria Edgeworth's *Belinda*. But for the third one, pale, thin, and stony-faced Sarah, he found himself at a bit of a loss. At the library,

Sarah asked for books on famous artists that included biographies and lithographic reproductions of famous paintings. She seemed especially impressed with the work of William Blake—both his drawings and his poems. But Mr. Bauer firmly believed that all young people should have the pleasures of a good novel as well as poetry and nonfiction volumes. He just wasn't sure which novel would appeal to the odd Miss Pole.

In such circumstances, when all else failed, he turned to that most popular volume, *Pride and Prejudice*, published anonymously by 'A Lady.' The girls took turns reading it aloud to one another.

"Well, it's certainly well written, but I don't understand why it takes Elizabeth so long to realize the truth about Darcy and Wickham if she's supposed to be so clever," Clara gave her verdict.

"Well clever people aren't always clever about everything. Sometimes you can be very clever about some things and very stupid about others," Sarah observed. "Miss Currer seems quite clever with the needle, but she doesn't appear to be well read."

"Also, I'm not sure why Elizabeth's father tells her to refuse Mr. Collins," Clara went on. "It would keep her mother and sisters from being thrown out of their own house! Then she turns down Mr. Darcy, too, when she's not getting any younger. And she doesn't have any money of her own. It doesn't seem very wise, does it?"

"I loved it," was Geraldine's verdict. "Elizabeth and I could have been twin souls, and Clara's just like Jane Bennett – or maybe Mary." She added this last detail maliciously, and Clara rolled her eyes. "But I don't know which Bennet sister Sarah is. Maybe she's like Georgianna Darcy?"

"How am I anything like Georgianna Darcy? She's beautiful and rich," Sarah wondered.

"Well, she's described as being quiet and accomplished," Geraldine noted. "And she seems somehow delicate, too. I picture her as a wan and slender wilting flower, just like our Sarah. A girl who looks like a puff of air could knock her down."

"Thank you," Sarah responded very dryly, "but I'm not a wilting flower. I'm a crow, remember?"

"I don't think *Pride and Prejudice* has any girls in it like Sarah," Clara wisely mused. "In fact, I don't think I've ever read a book that does."

After that, the three made it a point to plow through all of the books published by 'A Lady,' which they eventually learned had all been written by the same author: Miss Jane Austen. Miss Austen's relatives only announced the truth of her identity after her death. They would take turns reading aloud from Miss Austen's novels, which sparked many discussions. *Northanger Abbey* was great fun. The girls howled with laughter over Catherine Norland's misadventures.

Geraldine liked *Persuasion* because of all the sailors. Clara liked it because she thought it was romantic, and she liked Anne Elliott. When it came to Emma Wodehouse of *Emma*, Geraldine liked her, but Clara found her insufferable. Sarah thought she'd liked to have read more about Jane Fairfax. Geraldine was adamant about her dislike of *Mansfield Park* and Fanny Price.

"She is completely spineless," Geraldine's verdict came. "Why doesn't she tell the whole lot of them to boil their heads?"

"Actually, I'm rather on Fanny's side," Sarah mused. "When you're completely dependent on rich relations, you can't very well insult them, no matter how much you'd like to."

"And really, who gets ill from walking in a rose garden?" Geraldine continued. "If you came upon a dog or cat so sickly, you'd drown them just to put them out of their misery."

"Well not everyone's as strong and hearty as you are," Sarah observed. "And living near Mrs. Norris would exhaust anyone."

There was one particular discussion they had over *Sense and Sensibility* to which Clara would later give much thought.

"I like Marianne," Geraldine declared. "I feel quite a kinship with her."

"You would," said Clara with emphasis. "Marianne is so selfish and reckless. Elinor's the true heroine of the novel. She's so steadfast in her duty."

"Elinor is dull as dishwater," Geraldine retorted. "So is her lover, Edmund. Willoughby is much more exciting!"

"Willoughby's a scoundrel and a blackguard!" Clara was once again shocked. "He seduces and deserts Eliza, then breaks Marianne's heart, then marries Miss Grey for her money. How could you possibly like him?"

"At least he's interesting, which is more than I can say for old Brandon."

"But Brandon's such a good man…"

"But whoever fell in love with good?"

"Well, it's better than falling in love with someone solely because he's handsome," Sarah noted. "And Marianne does get a happy life with Brandon."

They went on like this for some time, walking along Weberley's main street. A couple young men who sighted the girls whistled in admiration. At fifteen, Geraldine and Clara were starting to develop very nice figures, though Sarah remained angular and flat-chested as ever. Clara's cheeks colored, and Geraldine beamed. Sarah didn't react at all. She knew she wasn't the one at whom they were whistling. She never was.

When outside, or on the very rare occasion any male visitors were invited to Parsley School, Geraldine and Clara were objects of admiration. Sarah was not. In fact, consciously or not, men seemed to treat Sarah as the chaperone among the three girls, despite her being the exact same age as them. While technically still a pupil, Sarah had already acquired the air of a governess, and everyone knew governesses were sexless, dried up, old prunes.

Finally, Geraldine let her attention fall back on their odd duck friend, "Come on, Sarah, who do you think you're more like: Elinor or Marianne?"

Sarah thought for a moment before answering. "I look like an Elinor, but I feel like a Marianne," was the answer she finally gave. "But something confuses me. The Dashwoods keep talking about how poor they are, but they have a nice cottage and three servants. How poor can you be if you have three servants?"

"Well, some might say that depends on the servants," Clara interjected. "Some are cheaper than others, you know."

"Then the truly poor ones would be the servants, and you don't hear them worrying about whether they'll have enough to eat like the Bates women do in *Emma*. The Dashwoods," noted Sarah, "have four or five hundred a year to live on between the four of them. That works out to at least a hundred pounds a year each. That's not exactly the poorhouse, is it?" She didn't wait for an answer but went on, unusually animated by the topic, "If I had a hundred pounds a year to live on, I'd be quite well off. Even fifty pounds a year, and I'd be able to live somewhere cheap without a servant. I could paint and draw full-time." Sarah sighed and looked wistfully as Geraldine and Clara exchanged glances. It was the first time Sarah had ever mentioned any dreams or ambitions of her own other than her inevitable future as an instructress.

"You want to be an artist then, Sarah?" Clara asked carefully.

"I would," Sarah admitted, surprising herself. Her eyes stared off into the distance. "Drawing and painting have always been my greatest pleasures. I feel driven to do them."

"Then you should do them," Geraldine chimed in, eagerly. "There's no reason you can't be an artist, Sarah. You could be like Artemesia!"

"No, I won't. Even if I had the talent, I could never afford to do it."

Sarah spoke no more on the matter.

With spring came Mr. Phillips, a silhouette artist offering his services. He set up his stall in the center of town, offering fully traced shadow profiles for as little as half a crown. Those who patronized him would sit in a chair in front of a candlelit screen to illuminate their profile in shadow. Then, Mr. Phillips would cut out their likeness in black cardboard and mount it on a white background. He immediately caused quite the stir in Weberley, and Mr. Phillips quickly had a long line of patrons. He was finally getting to the end of a work day when he noticed a thin, dark-haired girl with an oversized nose staring at him through piercing eyes.

"Hello, young lady. Would you care to have your likeness drawn?"

She shook her head, then asked, "Is this how you earn your bread? Cutting out likenesses for people?"

"It is," he answered, and she seemed excited.

"Tell me more," she pleaded.

It was a novel experience to be asked about his work, and Mr. Phillips happily gave Sarah an explanation of the trade of shadow tracing. She showed remarkable interest in the technical aspects of the craft.

"And do you go like this from town to town?" she asked finally.

"I do, indeed. That's how I find new customers. I sometimes trail fairs or market days, and sometimes I just pick resorts like Weberley here," he informed her with pride. "I travel by foot, by cart, sometimes by hired carriage, if I can afford it. And I stay in inns and hired rooms. Sometimes people let me stay with them if I do their likenesses for free. It's quite a life."

"And are there many people who pay to have their silhouette traced?"

"Oh yes, lots of people want a likeness of themselves, and it's a lot cheaper than getting a miniature portrait painted. Much quicker, too. Once you've mastered the art, you can do it in a few minutes. Some in the profession do thousands of tracings in their lifetime."

The girl seemed lost in thought. Finally, she asked him, "So, if I could get the right things – like scissors and black and white paper – then I could maybe make my way doing shadow tracings, too!"

"I'm afraid it wouldn't be that simple," he responded as gently as he could through his surprise.

"Why not? I'm sure I could learn to make likenesses as good as yours. You could teach me! Or I could teach myself."

She seemed so eager and excited that it was with genuine reluctance he threw cold water on the whole idea, "Perhaps you could, miss, perhaps you could. But you would need money for your initial travels, and without any kind of references, it'd be hard for you to find work."

"Well, maybe I could borrow some money," she said, "to start with from my friends, and they might write me letters of introduction."

Mr. Phillips shook his head, "No, it's not something young women do. I don't know of any women in the field. You see, it would be neither proper nor safe for any woman, but especially a woman of your sort, to be constantly on the road, going from place to place without an escort. It's best if you put any thoughts of the matter out of your head right now." Her face fell, and she turned around and hurried off without another word.

He hadn't been entirely truthful. There were, in fact, women who'd made a trade from creating silhouette images. Indeed, one of the foremost silhouette artists of London was Isabella Beetham, who had her own shop on Fleet Street, but Mr. Phillips firmly believed he had done right by not allowing the child to kindle any sort of false hope. He felt sorry for the girl, but wasn't it kinder to disabuse her of any foolish dreams now before they could ferment? He knew all too well how difficult it could be to carve out a niche for oneself as an artist, even for a young man. For women, it was even more difficult, and often not a little disreputable as well. Many young people fancied to become artists, but it was a castle in the air for almost all of them.

Sarah's Journal

Speaking with Mr. Phillips made me feel like a fool for even entertaining the idea I could somehow make a trade via drawing.

I liked to think I was born to be an artist, but I knew better. Who ever heard of a girl making her way in this world as an artist? Maybe a few young men did so, but it was different for men. Everyone knew, and everyone said that the only professions open for a girl of respectable birth were as governess, companion, or possibly seamstress, and since I wasn't even taking embroidery or sewing lessons anymore, clearly I was not going to be a seamstress. Of course, you could always marry as well, but no one seemed to think that very likely for me either. So that left companion or governess, and between the two, governess seemed less dull. Besides, it would probably be easier to manage the company of children than that of some querulous adult woman who had to hire herself a companion. No, a governess I would be. Hopefully, I'd still have some time to myself to paint and draw. Those were, after all, some of the few things that could take my mind away from my pouch.

Another was my reading. Some poets write only about pretty things, and sweetness, and light, and I eschewed such poets and their insipid frivolity. Other poets seemed to see the world as nothing but a black abyss filled with tears, and I didn't care much for them either.

But William Blake saw the world as filled with light and dark, and that, as well as his sense of whimsy, were why his poems spoke to me. He wrote of innocence and experience. Of lambs as well as tigers. Tigers, to be sure, are far more exciting than lambs, but the world has both and needs both. Blake knew that man was born to joy and woe because, even though I was often in pain, both the figurative sort and – thanks to the little pouch – the literal sort, I had plenty of happy moments as well in those years at Weberley.

One passage William Blake wrote in particular, though, did worry me.

Every Night and every Morn
Some to Misery are Born.
Every Morn and every Night
Some are Born to sweet delight.
Some are Born to sweet delight,
Some are Born to Endless Night.

Somehow, I didn't think I was born to sweet delight, but perhaps I wasn't born to endless night either, and my years at Parsley School were by no means marked only by grief and misery. With my art, my friends, and the sea, I did come to rely on the pouch less and less over time. In my final year at Parsley School, I scarcely needed to use it all.

Then everything changed. Again.

Six

"*There is no other class of laborers for hire who are thus systematically supplied by the misfortunes of our fellow creatures.*"
–Lady Eastlake on Governesses

Time marched on. A new princess was born at Kensington Palace and christened Victoria. Poor old mad King George III passed on, and the Prince Regent became George IV. However, since the prince had already been ruling England for the last nine years, this didn't seem to change much of anything. At the age of seventeen, more than five years after she'd first come to Parsley School, a host of separations came. First Geraldine and Clara were sent for from their families to be brought home and begin their matrimonial searches. The night before Geraldine and Clara left, they and Sarah snuck out for a long walk by the shore with provisions, including elderberry wine. There was talk, laughter, and tears as they all promised to write to each other forever. The next day, Geraldine and Clara were both taken away in carriages, and Sarah was left at Parsley School, alone.

As it happened, she was not going to remain alone at Parsley school much longer. Mrs. Gates had already privately decided it was time for Sarah to move on.

She'd already learned all that Mrs. Gates and Miss Leigh could teach her. Indeed, for the past year or so, she'd been acting more as an instructor to the younger girls than as a private pupil. More importantly, Harold Embry – whose family by now had grown to six children – and a recently widowed Penelope had grown impatient to rid themselves of their shared burden. Besides the expenses of tuition, there had also been the cost of clothes bought in town to replace the old garments as Sarah grew out of them. Garments which Mrs. Gates had been methodically billing them for all this time. They had more than done their duty. It was up to Sarah now to make her own way in life. Thus began Sarah's long-dreaded search for a situation. It never occurred to good Mrs. Gates that Sarah would ever object, that the girl might not want to leave everything she knew once more for a new environment, and, indeed, might detest the very notion of it. It was of no consequence. Sarah had to go, and that was that. Mrs. Gates sent out advertisements and letters to agencies. About a month later, she received a response.

"The Mandeville family of Bromley Hall. They're offering room and board and a salary of twenty pounds a year. They have two little girls. They're looking for an obedient, hard-working young woman of good breeding and unimpeachable morals. Oh, Sarah, I thought of you at once!"

"I suppose it seems like a good enough position," Sarah haltingly replied. "What do you know of the Mandevilles, though, or of Bromley Hall?"

"Not much," Mrs. Gates confessed, "but they're not only wealthy but of an ancient, reputable line—not some upstart merchant or mill owner family. I'd never dream of sending you to any household like that," Mrs. Gates reassured her.

"Why not?" Sarah asked. Mrs. Gates was momentarily taken aback.

"Well, I've heard such households can be very ill-bred for all their money. Indeed, many of them don't know how to treat governesses and tutors properly at all. Families like the Mandevilles are generally more respectful, my dear."

"Oh," said Sarah.

"And, of course, I let them know all about your background and situation. I wanted to let them know how well you've been brought up and how respectable your antecedents are," Mrs. Gates hastily added.

"Oh, yes. I'm as respectable as they come," Sarah agreed in a flat tone.

One detail Mrs. Gates tactfully omitted was that the letter specified that, while they wanted a younger and more pliable governess, the Mandeville family also preferred a plain one. They did not want a girl who might prove any sort of temptation to Mr. Mandeville's two sons by his first marriage, Hugh and Charles. Both were fine-looking and unmarried young men who spent substantial time at the hall. Mrs. Gates felt quite confident this would not be an issue with Sarah. Many times, a plain child of twelve blossoms into a beautiful maiden at seventeen. That had not been the case here. Rather, Sarah's resemblance to a crow had only grown more distinct over the years. Moreover, she lacked anything like natural coquetry or any apparent interest in acquiring it. Hugh and Charles Mandeville would be quite safe. Mrs. Gates was also able to reassure the Mandevilles that Miss Pole would not put on any airs or take any liberties. In fact, as she'd written back to them, accepting the position on Sarah's behalf, "I doubt you'll see much of her at all outside of the schoolroom. She prefers her own company."

The day of her departure dawned. Sarah and her old trunk bid farewell to Parsley School, Mrs. Gates, and all the younger pupils she'd instructed at sunrise. It was her first time riding a carriage since her trip with her aunt to Parsley School all those years before. It did not begin auspiciously. Sarah found herself squeezed in between two heavyset people on the coach, one of whom reeked of garlic. The ride itself was very bumpy. One of the passengers, a rather green looking young man, called to the coachman to stop, saying all the jolting was making him ill. He got out and vomited in the road moments later, much to the disgust of the coach-man. Sarah stepped out, too, and silently handed him a handkerchief, which he used to clean his face.

"Keep it," she told him when he tried to give it back.

Back on the coach, everyone else squeezed in, even more tightly, to give their ill fellow traveler more space to himself, while watching him intently for signs of further regurgitation. Eventually, they changed horses at an inn, and the sick young man thankfully decided to stop for the night. Sarah had no experience with public taverns, but she was quite famished, and so she decided to take some refreshment. She made her way through a noisy room with many patrons boister-ous on ale despite it not being even teatime yet. Then she stopped in the middle of the room, unsure where to go or what to do.

Sarah was greeted by the innkeeper—a big, beefy-looking man, "You there, lass! Looking for a room or a meal? Or a drink?"

"Just something to eat please," Sarah responded, "and perhaps a cup of tea, if you could manage."

"Right, we go. Here, sit down," he guided her to an empty table with two empty chairs and two empty steins, which he hurriedly took away. Sarah gratefully sat down, enjoying the extra leg room after so many hours of being cramped.

"Not often you see a gentle-lady travelin' alone," the innkeeper said, as he served her cheese, bread, and tea.

"I'm not a gentle-lady. I'm a governess," Sarah explained calmly.

"Ah, I see."

Though, in fact, the innkeeper didn't see at all and wondered privately if the young miss, with her somber face and dark dress, could be having a go at him. She barely had time to finish her meal and pay the bill before the coach drove off again.

Almost ten grueling hours later – and over sixteen hours since her journey began – the stagecoach dropped her in front of Bromley Hall. It was, by then, after midnight, and both Mrs. Brown, the housekeeper, and George Posey, the footman, were put out at having to admit her. Mrs. Brown led the way with a candle while George followed with the trunk.

"We didn't expect you until tomorrow, Miss...?" Mrs. Brown paused.

"Pole. Sarah Pole."

"Well, as you can see, we're not ready for you. You'll be wanting me to send you up some refreshment, I suppose?'

"No, I'll just rest for tonight is all."

"Ah, well then. I'll just have George make you up a fire."

"No need for that."

"Are you sure?" asked Mrs. Brown, suspiciously. "It's starting to get a bit nippy out there."

"I have been living north of here and by the sea, so I am used to far colder. You need not trouble yourself about me at all."

"Well," said Mrs. Brown, slightly mollified by the new governess's attitude, "breakfast will be served at seven o'clock. You'll want to wake up and wash by six in the morning."

"Lord, this trunk is heavy. What are you hauling in here? An ironworks?" George Posey moaned.

"Just my wardrobe, a sketchpad, some watercolors, and some books," Sarah replied.

"Hmmppph. Some books, you must have. Are they engraved in stone?" he grumbled.

"Oh, do be quiet, George. Here, Miss Pole, this will be your room.'"

Sarah's quarters measured seven-by-nine with a narrow bed covered by an embroidered quilt. Beside the bed was a tiny desk, on top of which sat a tea tray to make a table. There was a small wardrobe in one corner and a little wash basin in another. Underneath the bed was the necessary chamber pot. That was all.

"Squeeze the trunk in by the foot of the bed, George," Mrs. Brown ordered, and he complied.

"Thank you," said Sarah. Mrs. Brown and George left.

"I tell you," said George as they walked down the hall, "I don't care much for them governesses. Give themselves such airs all genteel-like, but their wages are no better than us regular servants, is they?"

"Well, someone has to do the job, I suppose," Mrs. Brown philosophized. "The young ladies need to work on their accomplishments, and their mama does not want them sent away from home. At least this one doesn't seem the type to try and give orders or act like one of the masters." Privately, Mrs. Brown sometimes felt there were too many self-proclaimed "masters" in the house, as it were. She could manage household affairs much better if she didn't have them interfering all the time.

"She'd have a devil of a time if she did, ma'am. You and the chambermaids would eat her for breakfast," George snorted.

Sarah's Journal

Of course, I heard the servants talking about me. Perhaps they didn't know how loud their voices were, or perhaps they didn't care. I had no intention of ever acting like one of the masters, and I wasn't sure what "airs," if any, I possessed. But as Mrs. Gates had warned me on many occasions, the downstairs class have a peculiar dislike for governesses for some reason, and it was clear I would not be making any friends in the servants' hall. So be it.

The first thing I did even before taking off my travel clothes was pull out my trusted pouch and...

mark the occasion.

I knew it was wrong. I knew it while I was doing so, but I couldn't help myself... all the goodbyes, the strange new place, the hours of being in that cramped, comfortless stagecoach and feeling like I could vomit... the nerves all on edge about the next day...

I needed some relief. I needed it. And I knew only one sure way to get it. The little razor this time, right on the underside of my upper arm. The moment the blade hit the flesh, I felt a release of tension, like putting down a heavy load you've been carrying a long time. I didn't even have to worry about waking anyone or someone seeing me bathing or dressing, and if any of the maid servants or laundresses noticed an occasional smear of dried blood on the sheets of my bed or on my clothes, they mercifully kept silent. Or maybe they thought it was just my monthly time. Thankfully, I always wore drab colors, so such stains weren't very visible.

This newfound privacy was both a blessing and a curse. I'd soon learn that there was no one in the household, be they downstairs or upstairs, with whom I could converse as equals. No one to play mother, like Mrs. Gates. No Geraldine or Clara to laugh with. No bracing sea air to refresh me, or friendly Mr. Bauer at the lending library to suggest a copy of Austen or Edgeworth to read. It was now just me and my sharp little helpers.

Seven

*"She'd become a governess. It was one of the few jobs a known lady could do.
And she'd taken to it well. She'd sworn that if she did indeed ever find herself dancing
on rooftops with chimney sweeps she'd beat herself to death with her own umbrella."*
–Terry Pratchett, *Hogfather*

The next day, Sarah was introduced to the masters. First, there was the squire himself, Thomas Mandeville, a red-faced, grey-haired, old gentleman of florid disposition whose fondness for good food and drink had given him a gouty foot. Besides the pleasures of the table, he lived for hunting and sports. His wife, Mrs. Mandeville, was significantly younger than him. A very fine looking lady of about thirty years old who made a point of keeping up with London fashions. Thomas and Mrs. Mandeville had two little girls together: Elinor, nine, and Violet, eight.

Mrs. Mandeville had a private meeting with Sarah in the parlor. "I assume Mrs. Gates discussed salary with you?" she asked as delicately as she could.

"Yes, Mrs. Mandeville. She said it would be twenty pounds a year."

"Correct. Though, of course, four pounds a year will have to be deducted to pay for your washing," she added quickly. "Sixteen pounds a year. We'll pay you four pounds every quarter," She paused, but Sarah made no comment, only giving a slight nod. Once they were off such a sordid and disagreeable topic as being compensated for labor, matters could proceed much more easily. Mrs. Mandeville went on to outline her expectations for her children's education.

Sarah was expected to endow a maximum number of accomplishments the girls could show off with a minimum amount of exertion on their part. However, they must not strain themselves in any way that could damage their health or beauty. Sarah's most important function would be to act as an example of decorum and as chaperone, as each, in time, would come out into society.

To this end, what the girls needed to practice most was their French. After all, one could hardly be called a gentlewoman if one was not fluent in French. They should learn music, since music and artistry were marks of refinement. They needed a basic understanding of literature, history, and geography. No need to go too much into depth on any of these topics, but Elinor and Violet needed to be able to carry on dinner party conversation without embarrassing themselves. Beyond that, they didn't require anything else. No need to study mathematics, science, or Latin. Indeed, cultivation of such pursuits would leave them labeled as bluestockings and unfit for marriage.

"Do you want me to instruct them on how to keep household accounts?" Miss Pole asked quietly. "It may be useful to them later in life."

"Heavens, no! Did anyone bother teaching you that?" Mrs. Mandeville felt slightly shocked.

"Yes, actually. The headmistress did. In fact, she even had me assist her with the bookkeeping from time to time," Miss Pole stated calmly.

"Well, I suppose it is all very different for women who must work for their bread," Mrs. Mandeville said, dismissively. "But there is no need of anything of that sort for my girls. I've never bothered with household accounts. I can't even decipher a tradesman's bill," she boasted. "So, no. Just keep to accomplishments and so forth with Elinor and Violet, and supervise their recreation as well. They do love to play outside, and the fresh air and exercise does them such good."

"Can I meet the children now?"

Sarah was quickly introduced to Violet and Elinor Mandeville. Both girls were cheerful, rosy-cheeked creatures, full of vitality, and not over burdened with excessive cleverness. Elinor's hair was straight while Violet was blessed with curls. Otherwise, the girls looked remarkably similar. Indeed, but for a negligible difference in height, they could have been mistaken for twins.

Sarah was also introduced to the Mandeville children from the first marriage. Hugh Mandeville, the future squire, was a divinely attractive young man whose air of natural superiority was as much a part of his intrinsic being as were the color of his eyes. He had been born into a life of importance, owner of a handsome house and excellent income with no need to work for it, and he took justifiable pride in position. Modesty and humility, Hugh reasoned, only become those persons who have something about which to be modest and humble.

Charles Mandeville had a sardonic mouth and a hungry look around the eyes. Unlike many younger sons, Charles did not lack for ambition or industry. He was visiting home from London, where he was studying to join the bar. He had chosen the law over the church, reasoning that the former gave far more room than the latter in which to distinguish himself. And Charles Mandeville very much planned to distinguish himself. He had hopes of running for parliament someday. He had already been making a few extra coins as a special pleader, writing briefs for practicing barristers, and was eager to make a name for himself.

Alicia Mandeville was seventeen years old and the youngest of the children by Thomas Mandeville's first marriage. She possessed an extraordinary beauty—the kind about which ballads are sung. Every young man – and quite a few older ones as well – within twenty miles was besotted by her. Even if, by some chance, one of them suffered some nearsightedness that rendered them immune to her beauty, the sound of her singing and playing the pianoforte would easily win them over instead, for Alicia had a genuine talent for music. Indeed, she might have made her fortune as a stage singer had she not been born a respectable and rich gentlewoman, but birth and fortune had sealed Alicia's fate long ago. It was her destiny to be a great lady. Except for an occasional idle daydream of packed concert halls and traveling through Europe, Alicia embraced her destiny. Indeed, Alicia was quite impatient to make her debut and begin accepting courtship in earnest.

When Sarah was introduced to them, only Charles mumbled a greeting, and Hugh gave a curt and silent nod. Alicia simply flounced her hair and walked away. Afterward, none of the three adult Mandeville children gave Sarah so much as a second glance.

The room in which Sarah had spent the night was actually part of a schoolroom suite. It was in a separate wing from where the adult members of the family stayed. Her chamber adjoined a dayroom, in which to instruct her pupils, and a washing closet. Both girls' rooms were just down the hall from the schoolroom suite.

"All right," Sarah began with Violet and Elinor in the schoolroom. "First, I'd like to see how far you've gone in your lessons. Dites-moi quelque chose sur vous-même en français?"

"Oui," said Elinor. "Je suis Elinor la plus age et la plus jolie."

"Menteur!"

"Assez! Votre dernier professeur vous enseigne des bonnes mannieres francais mais pas tres bonnes!"

"Now, I'd like to see an example of penmanship from each of you," Miss Pole asked of them. "Take your slates and write out the following after me, 'Tyger, Tyger, Burning bright/In the forests of the night.'"

The girls did so, and Miss Pole examined their efforts.

"Elinor's cursive is very good," was Miss Pole's verdict. "Violet's is a little shaky. Don't look so smug, though, Elinor. You are older. Now, let's try you both on sums."

The dayroom was well supplied with a pianoforte, parchment, art supplies, and slate boards. Inquiries soon revealed a well stocked library in another area of the house with good natural lighting as well. It would soon become Sarah's policy to instruct the girls more often in the library than in the suite because there was easy access to books, unless the library was otherwise occupied at the time, of course. The atlas collection was an invaluable resource for geography lessons, and having the girls read aloud from volumes in French was an excellent teaching method. She would also have them write her short essays in French.

Other times, she took them on walks around the grounds to enjoy the benefits of exercise and fresh air. Elinor liked horses and was a favorite among the stable boys—one lad, in particular, was called Joe. But for the state of his clothes, Joe could easily have been mistaken for a classic Greek sculpture brought to life.

He was tall, raven-haired and blue-eyed, had a broad chest, slender waist, and sculpted muscles. Joe's only charms weren't in his appearance either. He showed a profound gift of getting on with horses, dogs, cats, and children. Joe would let Elinor ride on his back and swing her around like she was no more than a bag of flour.

Violet was fond of singing and was known to give impromptu recitals in the halls, whether anyone asked for them or not. Both girls adored rolling down a green hill, even it meant grass stains on their dresses, a habit of which their mother unsuccessfully tried to cure them. They had a music instructor, Mr. Vincetti—a man with a great black mustache and shiny bald head, which he constantly wiped with his handkerchief. Mr. Vincetti appeared at the hall twice a week to instruct the girls on the pianoforte, or at least attempt to instruct them. Elinor and Violet, while not devoid of other merits, showed no signs of having Alicia's natural ear for music. During their lessons with Mr. Vincetti, everyone else in the household tried to stay out of hearing range.

Bromley Hall had originally been a Tudor manor to which additions were made by every passing generation. It had grown into a rambling old pile, which, while it wasn't perhaps the most organized of properties, nevertheless possessed great charm and was quite picturesque. The surrounding park and farmlands were even lovelier still. Sarah arrived in October, when the leaves were at their most colorful, just before they began to fall, and the woods blazed in shades of scarlet and gold. The actual hall was only a mile east from the town of Greenberry.

Greenberry, in Hertfordshire, some twenty miles north of London, was on the opposite side of the town Widebourne, the seat of the Ambrose family. North of Greenberry, bordering on both the Ambrose and Mandeville estates, was Gaskell Park, home of Sir John Tudbury. The Tudburys, Ambroses, and Mandevilles comprised the three great landowners of the community with the Tudburys in the lead, the Mandevilles a close second, and the Ambroses a distant third.

The bulk of the homes in Greenberry itself were cottages of varying degrees of comfort. A little outside the main town area stood a series of hovels—damp, earthen-floored huts with thin, rotting thatch roofs where sickness and poverty invariably lay intertwined. Around town, the fields alternated between green hay, brown soil left fallow, and yellow barley.

All three leading families attended services at St. Mary's Church, presided by the young Reverend Graham, who owed his living to his uncle, Sir John Tudbury. The rectory was a pretty, modern home of red brick and white shutters. The church itself was far older, having been built by a Norman lord in the year 1220. It had originally consisted of a small, plain building with only a nave and chancel built out of local flint and with the flourish of a Romanesque arch over the doorway. Over the centuries, two important additions had been made to St. Mary's.

First, a bell turret had been constructed at the West End, housing three small bells that could be rung for all necessary occasions. Second, the yew tree, which had been present for generations and now spanned a length of twenty feet. The yew was widely considered to be the pride and joy of Greenberry, and was rumored to be over a thousand years old—older even than the church itself.

Time went on and Sarah never gave any of the adults any trouble. She was rather so unobtrusive that it was quite easy for them to forget she was even in the house at all, which they very frequently did. Elinor and Violet both quite liked their new governess, who let them jump in piles of leaves and made them necklaces of acorns. As the nights grew longer, and All Hallow's Eve approached, she entertained her charges with some of the ghost stories she'd heard from Geraldine. They shrieked and shivered in delight just as she and Clara once had. When the leaves gave way to snow drifts, Sarah assisted them in constructing snowmen and snow angels. Come spring and summer, she let them gambol about the grounds and build flower crowns. When they had to stay inside, she read stories to them using such amusing voices. They especially enjoyed her drawings. Since they were pleased, their mother was pleased as well, and even their father, on those few times a month he engaged his younger daughters in prolonged conversation, noticed they were progressing well in their lessons.

The only one who harbored any doubts regarding the new governess was the eldest daughter of the house. Alicia had been prattling about only to turn and find Miss Pole silent and grave behind her. Alicia very nearly screamed. It took her a moment to catch her breath.

"What do you mean by sneaking up on me like that?" Alicia barked out.

"I beg your pardon, Miss Mandeville, but I wasn't sneaking. I was simply walking."

"Well, why don't you make any noise when you walk?" This was something about Miss Pole Alicia had noticed before. The only response Sarah gave to Alicia's query was a noncommittal shrug, and Alicia's irritation at the governess grew, "What do you want anyway?"

"Your stepmother wants you to come to the parlor with her to take tea."

Miss Pole walked out as soundlessly as she had come in, but the incident stayed with Alicia and rankled her. Over tea, Mrs. Mandeville noted that Alicia seemed somehow of sorts. She was, for once, not talking of London or herself. In fact, Alicia appeared to be thinking for a change.

Alicia was thinking. Furthermore, she was thinking of Miss Pole—someone to whom she had never given a moment's thought before. She had barely given any thought at all to her governess when she'd had one as a girl, but she was now in the uncomfortable position of thinking about a governess who wasn't even employed by her. Alicia considered it strange that Miss Pole insisted on wearing long sleeves all the time, even in hot weather. Still, Miss Pole was clever, no doubt, and definitely possessed some skill in draftsmanship. But there was just something so queer about her.

She seemed remote and uncanny. You never quite knew what she was thinking. Sometimes, Alicia felt rather frightened of her without being able to explain how or why, so much so that she took the unprecedented step of consulting with her stepmother.

"We need to talk about the governess you've hired," Alicia announced to Mrs. Mandeville after the tea things had been cleared away. Mrs. Mandeville was working on a piece of embroidery.

"Uh huh... what about Miss Pole?" Mrs. Mandeville was intent on the piece and resented the interruption.

"I think you should get rid of her," Alicia proclaimed. Mrs. Mandeville dropped a stitch and looked up with irritation.

"Dismiss Miss Pole? What on Earth for?" It was a simple question, but one Alicia found rather flustering.

"Well, you asked her to tell me it was time for tea..."

"And she failed to convey the message?" Mrs. Mandeville, interrupted, as she put her embroidery aside for the moment.

"No, she delivered it just fine. She snuck up on me and gave me a fright!"

"She gave you a fright?" Mrs. Mandeville repeated. "What did she do? Clap her hands or yell 'boo?'"

"No, but I didn't hear her when she came in. Have you noticed she never makes any noise when she walks?" Alicia paused, and when her stepmother didn't answer but rather gaped, she desperately went on, "And it's not just her walk. I never hear her laughing or coughing or anything."

"Let me see if I understand you properly. You want me to dismiss Miss Pole, whom Elinor and Violet both adore and who's been doing such a good job in the schoolroom, and then go through all the trouble and expense of hiring a new governess, because Miss Pole is too quiet?" Mrs. Mandeville was incredulous.

"Have you noticed she never talks to us?" Alicia demanded.

"She's not supposed to talk to the adult members of the family. She's the governess," Mrs. Mandeville reminded her stepdaughter with an eyeroll. "I, for one, appreciate that she knows her place and doesn't take any liberties."

"And why does she always wear such long sleeves all the time? And dress so solemnly?" Alicia went on.

"Again, she's a governess. Would you rather see her in ribbons and bows? I wouldn't."

"But she's such a witchy looking thing, too!" Alicia considered this a particularly grievous sin. If every woman's ordained purpose is to be admired, then a woman who fails to do so – and worse yet, seems indifferent to the matter entirely – can only be judged a sinner. Still, her stepmother remained unmoved.

"We specifically asked them not to send us a pretty girl. I would think you'd be pleased not to have a possible competitor under the same roof."

"Competitor?" Alicia was incensed. "How could she? How could a governess possibly be a competitor?" The whole idea was almost as preposterous as the notion that she would ever have reason to envy Miss Pole.

"Well, that's the point, isn't it? She's not a competitor."

"No, but she's…" Alicia stumbled. "She's peculiar."

Mrs. Mandeville gave a wearied sigh, "Honestly, Alicia, if you have nothing useful to contribute, I'd like to get back to this piece."

Alicia flounced out. Mrs. Mandeville took no heed of her opinion. Sad to say, if anything, Alicia's antipathy toward Miss Pole was rather accounted as a point in her favor by Mrs. Mandeville, who found it not a little irksome that her stepdaughter had the advantages of a great inheritance from her grandmother of some twenty-thousand pounds and musical talent and such dazzling beauty when her own darling daughters did not. No, Alicia could jolly well let her half-sisters have their beloved governess whether she liked said governess or not.

Alicia did not like Miss Pole, and time did not ameliorate her views on the matter. Fortunately, at a great estate like Bromley Hall, it was very easy for the two young women to avoid each other. Particularly since Alicia had never been one to play nursemaid to her half-sisters, nor did Elinor and Violet seek out Alicia's company. Furthermore, Alicia spent at least a month every year at her aunt's townhouse in London. While enjoying the city's delights, especially its music, Miss Pole was the last thing on her mind.

Sarah's Journal

I was often hungry at Bromley Hall. Partly, it was a physical hunger. Dacres, the maid, often forgot to fetch me supper, and there were too many nights when I went to bed with an empty stomach. But there was a greater inner hunger, too. I was starved for company, and that was one thing I hadn't quite counted on. I'd accepted that I'd be losing all my former friends and that I couldn't expect to be treated as a person of any status, but I didn't realize that, except for the children, I wouldn't be acknowledged as a person at all. The older Mandevilles, other than Alicia and her curious antipathy, paid no attention to me, and neither did the servants or the townsfolk. Not a single person ever addressed me in church or even made eye contact. For all intents and purposes, I spent my first year at Bromley Hall as an invisible woman.

Even though I was in the town of Greenberry quite regularly, I felt quite as much ignored by them as I was by Mr. Mandeville and his adult children. Mrs. Mandeville would often send me on certain household errands or to negotiate with tradesmen, knowing I knew how to keep accounts and tabulate bills. The poorer cottagers I was asked to call upon were cordial at least, but my visits to them were few and far between.

Without the sea, the town library, Mrs. Gates, or the other girls, I was more reliant than ever on both my sketchpad and my pouch to fill those long, lonely nights in the s choolroom. So many stories about governesses revolve around the governess having a scandalous love affair with one of the men of the house. There was no danger of that in this instance. Neither Sir Thomas nor his sons had any designs on my virtue. Perhaps it was all for the best really, that I'm not a beauty. As Miss Austen and other authors have so carefully documented, grand passion never ends well, and young masters don't marry the hired help.

Still, to have no one address me at all, I can't help but feel snubbed. It doesn't help when one's in a home with dozens of rooms, and you frequently find yourself getting lost. By the time I did learn my way, Alicia Mandeville had taken a particular dislike to me. I had no idea why. Not only had I never done anything to her, I could be of no consequence to her at all from my lowly position. You would think I'd be beneath her notice altogether, but something about me got her back up. If it wasn't so preposterous, I'd have said Miss Alicia feared me. More likely, Alicia's disliking of me stemmed from the fact that I didn't like her either.

Eight

"A decent provision for the poor is the true test of a civilization."
—Samuel Johnson

Though Sarah had been employed as a governess, she soon came to learn that her duties at Bromley Hall were not always limited to the children. Neither Mrs. Brown nor Mrs. Mandeville ever hesitated to use Sarah for any other tasks they needed doing, whether it was delivering messages or dealing with a tradesman bill, Sarah could be sent. She could be sent into town to run errands as well—the sort of errands that simply couldn't be trusted to a common illiterate servant. Moreover, Sarah proved to be the ideal solution to what had been a vexing problem at Bromley Hall.

It had long been a custom of the Mandeville family that the ladies of the household play benefactress to the poor cottagers who worked the estate. This was all very well and good, according to the theories of Ben Jonson and Edmund Burke. The difficulty was that, in practice, the mistresses of Bromley Hall often didn't much care for playing benefactress. For that matter, it wasn't always clear the tenants cared for it either, but no one ever asked them. Mrs. Mandeville may have enjoyed knitting things for the poor, but she didn't actually enjoy spending time with them, and neither did Alicia. It was one issue in which Mrs. Mandeville and Alicia were in perfect agreement. Such people were rude, uncouth, frequently ill smelling, and it was not as if you had any common interests to discuss with them anyway. Really, what was the point then in making conversation or paying visits to such people? But the tradition of distributing bounty to tenants and townsfolk had to be honored, whether anyone wanted to do it or not.

Shortly after Miss Pole's arrival, Mrs. Mandeville had the clever idea of appointing the new governess to serve as Bromley Hall's official representative and gift-giver to all the hovels on the estate. Though no one had asked the residents of the hovels themselves about the matter, they, too, preferred this arrangement. Mrs. Mandeville and Alicia were always so uncomfortable whenever they had visited. They'd hold their hands over their faces to protect themselves from smoke and the scent of the unwashed, and were fearful of staining their patterns on dirt floors. In contrast, Miss Pole didn't seem to care – her clothes never showed dirt easily anyway – and she'd even sit for a cup of tea if invited and look you in the eye over conversation.

So, it developed that Sarah became acquainted with a great number of the Mandeville's tenants. There was old Nellie Bloom, who let her prized goose, Gertie, sleep in bed with her. She sometimes asked Sarah to read aloud to her from the family bible. Eventually, Sarah started bringing copies of old newspapers to Nellie's to have something other than the Bible to read aloud. She also took the liberty of doing a sketch of Gertie that become one of Nellie's most favored possessions. Then there was Jem Howe, the local carpenter. Jem was known for both his great proficiency in woodwork and his even greater proficiency in alcohol consumption. He liked to boast that he could drink anyone under the table. So far, he'd yet to meet a challenger who could prove otherwise. Jem had been banned from church since he'd attended service one day dressed only in his nightshirt. Jem loudly proclaimed to one and all that this was no loss since Reverend Graham was a fool anyway. Secretly, though, Jem missed the music, even if he did not miss the sermons. At least Miss Pole was willing to listen to him sing a ditty or two.

Then there was the Riggs family. The Riggs were the worst off of all, living piled on top of one another in a leaky old thatched dwelling that scarcely seemed large enough for one person, let alone five. Last fall, Mr. Riggs had gone out one night for a walk and never came home, leaving thirteen-year-old Adam as the man of the household to care for his mother and sisters. Somehow, the family had managed to survive through their garden, straw plaiting, charity, and by taking whatever menial work, however ill paid, came their way. That went for all family members, except Rosie, the baby. Even if there'd been a country school in Greenberry, the Riggs children would never have had the time to take advantage of it.

One day, Sarah was visiting the Riggs family with a basket full of apples, a giant loaf of bread, and a handmade shawl for Mrs. Riggs to keep her warm in the coming months. Extra coal might have answered that purpose better, but Mrs. Mandeville enjoyed knitting, not mining, so a shawl it was. Even from twenty yards away, you could hear endless wailing from the baby of the family. Sarah knocked on the rickety door to hear Mrs. Riggs perpetually tired voice bidding her to come in. Sarah did so.

Mrs. Riggs's arms were filled with little Rosie. Mrs. Riggs was only about thirty, but looked at least ten years older. Her two eldest girls, Polly and Meg, stood off to the side with dirty, pinched faces.

"She's teethin'," Mrs. Riggs explained. "There, there, dear. It's all right," she tried rocking Rosie, who continued to bawl.

"I'll take her for a minute," Sarah suggested, exchanging the basket for Rosie. Mrs. Riggs's eyes showed her gratitude. Sarah began rubbing the baby's back, and Rosie, perhaps exhausted, began to quiet down. Mrs. Riggs and the girls gathered at the table and began pulling out the contents of the basket.

"Thanks, ma'am," Meg said, immediately grabbing an apple to bite into it. "But," she said between bites, "meat pies be more fillin'."

"Meg!" Mrs. Riggs gave her daughter a sharp look. "Don't sound ungrateful. My apologies, Miss Pole."

"There's no need. Next time, I'll ask them in the kitchen to include some meat pies," Sarah answered. "Perhaps some cheese as well?"

"Thank you, ma'am," Meg gave a wide smile, revealing two missing front teeth.

Mrs. Riggs deemed the offer overwhelming in its generosity. It emboldened her to try the family's luck further. "Do they need any servants at the hall?"

Mrs. Riggs asked hopefully. "Meg's old enough to work in the kitchens or scullery, and Polly soon will be, too."

Polly and Meg nodded their heads eagerly, and the latter tried her best to smooth the wrinkles down on her ragged frock.

"I'm strong, Miss," Meg informed her, "and a good worker!"

"So am I!" Polly interjected.

"I don't think they need any new maids right now," Sarah said gently, and the faces of both girls fell, "but Mr. Sayres might need an extra pair of hands to help out on the estate. I can ask if he has any work for Adam."

"Bless you!" Mrs. Riggs beamed beneath her worry lines and grey hairs.

"Where is Adam anyway?"

"Huntin'," said Polly. Mrs. Riggs and Meg both looked at Polly sharply.

"Adam," Mrs. Riggs explained to Miss Pole, "sets traps around here and the town for rabbits."

"Yes, rabbits be awfully fillin'," Meg hastily added. "We'll be sure and tell him Mr. Sayres needs him. He'll be happy to have the work."

"Yes," said Sarah in a completely even, neutral tone. "Also let Adam know that hunting, even rabbit hunting, has its risks. Tell him to please be careful."

Conversation soon turned to other matters, like the yearly crops and Greenberry's perpetual lack of a physician. It was nearly an hour later when Adam arrived. He'd have been a handsome lad if not for the dirt on this face and hunger in his eyes. He was, indeed, pleased to hear of a chance to work with Mr. Sayres.

"Look at the time!" Miss Pole exclaimed. "I should go back."

"I'll lead you there!" Adam offered. "It'll be dark soon, and you shouldn't be out there on your own."

"Thank you, Adam, that's very kind," Sarah replied, and Adam's chest seemed to swell. He made a grand show of safely escorting Miss Pole back to Bromley Hall.

"Quite a house, isn't it?" Adam noted. "Are all great houses like it? And are all great families like the Mandevilles?"

"I wouldn't know," Sarah confided in him. "This is my first situation. Before I came here, I was at school myself—at Weberley, by the sea."

"The sea," Adam repeated, excitement glinting in his eyes. "I've never seen the sea. Is it as big and wild as they say?"

"It is," Sarah told him. "It's grey and green and blue all at once, and the air smells of salt."

They arrived near the front entrance, and Adam took his leave.

Sarah's Journal

I rather enjoyed my visits with the needy. Not only for the satisfaction in helping others but also for the company, and, if I'm to be honest with myself, to be someplace where I wasn't automatically categorized as a social inferior. In fact, to families like the Riggs, I was considered quite the proper young gentlewoman. I admit, I found it pleasant to be treated with such regard. The cottagers would at least talk to me, which was something I didn't get from either the adult Mandevilles or their servants, and from the spiritual side, it's good to gain periodic reminders that however daunting one's own sorrows may seem, you can always find someone else whose problems are much worse. It helps put things in perspective. Besides, I must confess, I took no small amount of amusement from figures like Nellie Bloom and Jem Howe. I sympathized with the Riggs family and found both Polly and Meg to be nice enough girls. But my favorite of them all was young Adam, in whom I sensed a maturity and intelligence beyond his years.

Nine

"The crow wished everything was black, the Owl, that everything was white."
–William Blake

One morning, Miss Pole and the girls observed the land agent, John Sayres, dragging a large sack over to the heavily wooded area where wild game was abundant. It was evidently quite heavy, judging from the sweat on his brow and the grunts escaping his lips.

"What's that?" Violet ran up to him as Sarah and Elinor followed quickly behind. Mr. Sayres obligingly opened the sack and first drew out several rifles with elaborate firing mechanisms.

"Oh, can you teach us how to shoot?" Elinor asked.

"Can I have my own gun?" Violet chimed in.

"No," responded Mr. Sayres and Sarah at once, much to the girls' disappointment.

"First of all, you might shoot yourself or your sister. Secondly, your mama would never forgive me if I even let you touch a long arm," Sarah intoned. "She'd consider it completely inappropriate for any girl, much less her daughters."

"Besides, these are spring guns anyway," Mr. Sayres added. "They're not meant for regular sport shooting."

Next, he withdrew from his sack a number of flat, rectangular objects armed with metal teeth.

"These are man traps, they are. Don't touch them, girls," Mr. Sayres warned.

"We won't," said Elinor. "They look horrible!" Violet nodded her agreement. Unlike the tempting firearms, these things didn't look like they'd offer any chance for fun playtime at all. Rather they looked like something that would tear away arms and legs.

"Aye, that's the idea. Your father's orders to help against the poachers. We're putting up traps all over the woods now to catch the bastards," Mr, Sayres paused, "excuse me, forgot what company I was in... catch the rascals. Anyone comes sneaking around for your father's deer and partridge is in for a nasty surprise, I can tell you!" Mr. Sayres wore an expression of deep satisfaction as he said all this.

"It looks like the mouth of an iron dragon. Like something out of the Spanish Inquisition. And guns, too. It seems rather a lot for the sake of partridge and deer," Sarah said, slowly fingering the outline of one of the traps. The metal had the same coolness to the touch as her beloved razor. For one mad moment, Sarah imagined what it might feel like to be caught in such a trap. She could almost feel the sensation of iron teeth biting into flesh. It was a vision both beautiful and terrible at the same time, and she shuddered.

"Poachers are getting more brazen every day. So many folks being kicked off their land or losing their jobs to mills. There's lawlessness everywhere now. Whole country's going to the dogs! Someday, I wager we may have marauders in the night, coming to steal the silver and slit our throats," Sayres brooded.

Violet gave a small cry of alarm, and Sarah loudly cleared her throat.

"Or we would have marauders," he quickly amended, "if we didn't have such strong doors and fine locks, not to mention me and my men on watch." He made a bold, confident smile, but then added darkly, "But I don't know how safe the neighbors are." Sayres continued on his way as Sarah shuffled the girls off in the opposite direction.

"Well, let this be a lesson, girls, as to why you should never ever go running in the woods." She told them, and they solemnly promised not to.

Later, Sarah drew a black and white sketch of a terrible dragon made of iron and steel, hiding amidst dark trees, to hang in the schoolroom and further illustrate the point. It had to be taken down, though, when Violet reported the sketch had given her nightmares.

Sometime after Sarah arrived, Mrs. Brown learned she'd been keeping a secret supply in the schoolroom of jam, breads, cheese, and tea things.

"Why you've got nearly a whole pantry here," Mrs. Brown exclaimed. "What on Earth for?"

"Well the girls often like to take tea after their walks. It's easier to have everything ready and on-hand rather than having to send for it."

"I suppose that makes sense," Mrs. Brown admitted.

"Also, some nights, I get hungry," Sarah added.

"Hungry? I'd think supper would be good enough," *especially for a bony thing like you,* was what Mrs. Brown wanted to add.

"It is when I get it. Dacres, though, is sometimes rather late in bringing it."

"How late?" Mrs. Brown asked shrewdly.

"Nine or ten... and sometimes she forgets entirely. So, you see, it makes sense for me to keep food up here," there was no reproach in Sarah's voice, no complaint. She might as well have been reporting on the daily weather, yet Mrs. Brown still felt flustered, even somehow embarrassed, though it was not really her place to see to Sarah's welfare. She made a point of giving Dacres a scolding, punctuated by boxing her ears. After that, Sarah's suppers always arrived promptly.

Not long afterward, Sarah produced a watercolor painting depicting Elinor and Violet as flower fairies. Violet was, of course, dressed as a violet, and Elinor was patterned after a waterlily. Besides their petal dresses, both girls had the gossamer wings of butterflies. Mrs. Mandeville was so charmed by the picture, she had it framed and hung up in the hall. Sarah did a number of sketches of household members, including Thomas and Susan and Mrs. Brown. This garnered her much more respectful treatment from the servant's quarters. She did a portrait of Hugh Mandeville looking proud on a horse. On Hugh's suggestion, she did a sketch of Joe to recognize the exceptional service he'd been providing with the horses. Joe posed for her with his shirt open, his sculpted muscles made for an excellent anatomical study. Finally, Miss Pole produced a sketch of Alicia's lovely visage.

Everyone proclaimed it an excellent likeness, but Mrs. Brown thought there was something rather glass and artificial in the expression. Wisely, Mrs. Brown kept such thoughts to herself. Alicia herself was pleased enough with the likeness, but it did not make her feel any warmer toward Sarah.

One day, on one of their rambles, as Violet bounded ahead, Elinor took it upon herself to inform Sarah of the family's personal matters.

"I heard Papa tell Mama it was time for Hugh to marry. In fact, they were saying it's his duty to wed and further the family line so Bromley Hall stays in the family. They were talking about who he should wed, Venetia Ambrose or Miss Tudbury."

Both Venetia and Miss Tudbury were regular visitors at Bromley Hall, and while Sarah had never spoken to either one of them, she had ample time to observe them both, and noted they were at a disadvantage in the local marital market. Neither girl was a gargoyle, but neither girl could hold a candle to Alicia.

"Venetia's prettier, but Miss Tudbury's father's a baronet. Mama says either one would do nicely if Hugh would only make up his mind. Who do you think he'll wed?"

"I don't know," said Sarah. "I've never spoken with either of them. For that matter, I've never even spoken with your brother, but Hugh's not your parent's only chance at a grandchild. Charles may find himself a wife in London, after all."

"Mama says it'll be much harder for Charles to find someone suitable because he is a younger son, and no one wants a younger son. Mama says that, when we go out into society, we shouldn't even talk to younger sons. She says he can't even think of marrying until he's been established. What's it mean to be established?"

"I believe it means attaining a sufficient degree of success in one's profession. Primarily financial success, but reputation is of value as well."

"Are you established, Miss Pole?"

"No, I don't think governesses can be established."

"So, you're a lady."

"No, governesses aren't ladies either."

"So, you're a servant."

"No, because I'm not allowed in the Servant's Hall."

"You're not?"

"No. I walked in once by accident, and Mrs. Brown chased me away. She said the Servant's Hall was no place for the likes of me."

At the time this had happened, the servants had been engaged in their favorite pastime of gossiping about the masters, and Sarah's arrival had put a damper on this. Who was to say that a governess might not repeat some of their words to the masters? There was no telling whose side she might be on. It had been to everyone's relief to have Sarah leave so that lively conversation and colorful storytelling could recommence.

"But if you're not a servant and you're not a lady, what are you then?" Elinor asked in the same moment as Violet ran back to them, curious to know what they were talking about.

"I'm a crow."

"You can't be a crow."

"Why not?"

"You have no beak."

"I do." Sarah tapped her nose.

"You have no claws!"

"Oh, but I do," Miss Pole stretched out her thin, bony hands and clawed them at the air as if they were great talons.

"You have no wings."

"Really? What do you call these?" Sarah spread her arms out wide and flapped them like wings. "Caw! Caw!" Sarah cried as both girls shrieked with delight.

Sarah's Journal

It was a lonely first winter I spent with the Mandevilles, but there was a certain liberation as well I would find later. For, as I would soon learn, when you're invisible, you can learn so many interesting things about people, and there was much at Bromley Hall to learn. I learned that Thomas Mandeville secretly imbibed port behind his wife's back, which did his gout no favors. I learned that Tom, the footman, paid courtship to both Annie in the kitchens and Bessie, the milkmaid, and was quite the Romeo of the Servant's Hall. I learned that Mrs. Mandeville had been daughter of an attorney and niece to a tradesman when she'd been lucky enough to captivate Thomas Mandeville after his first wife died in childbirth. As stepmother, she did not get along particularly well with her stepdaughter, though Mrs. Mandeville was by no means evil or even mean, and Alicia Mandeville was certainly no Cinderella. Neither Alicia nor Mrs. Mandeville really ran Bromley Hall, though. That honor belonged to Mrs. Brown, just as it was Mr. Sayres, the land agent, who actually ran the estate. That was one of the first things I learned at Bromley Hall: the masters weren't really running anything because they didn't actually do anything. It was often difficult to make out how they spent their days.

Strangely, no one other than me seemed to see the way Hugh Mandeville looked at Joe, the stable lad, or some of the other better looking young men from the village. Or maybe they wouldn't allow themselves to wonder why he took frequent visits to London for days and weeks at a time, or wonder exactly what he did and whose company he kept. After all, acts of sodomy in England are punishable by death. The adult Mandevilles would scarcely want to entertain the thought of anything so scandalous in their family, but that reticence should hardly have applied to the servants as well. Or maybe it didn't. Maybe the servants gossiped about it all the time in their hall, where I wasn't allowed to visit.

I still had the pleasure of reading and availing myself of the household library. And the joys of a nearly unlimited supply of tallow candles for late evenings to read by, draw by, and cut by with no one to raise a hint of protest. I indulged heavily in all three. Perhaps too much with the last one.

Ten

"For the life of every creature is its blood: its blood is its life."
−Leviticus 17:14

Given how much experience she had in the matter, Sarah never quite understood how she could have slipped so badly.

But slip, she had.

One cold evening in February, following eating supper alone in the schoolroom, Sarah had felt the need come upon her again. Since there was a letter opener within the schoolroom, she had turned to that rather than going back to her own quarters and using the pouch. Later, she wondered if it was the use of a different instrument than she was used to that caused her mistake, for this time things went very wrong. Perhaps she cut too deeply. Perhaps she cut in the wrong spot. Whatever the cause, instead of the usual few drops of crimson to accompany the sweet sensation of pain, she found herself spurting blood at an alarming rate. She tried stifling it with the black skirt of her sleeve, but the blood kept coming. It dripped onto the floor and seemed to go everywhere as she stumbled about the schoolroom. She felt her heart racing and panic coming on. She grabbed a rag from the sewing pile and kept pressing and pressing against the wood until the bleeding stopped. Finally, she bound her wrist as tightly as possible under a pile of bandages. That still left two other problems, though.

Firstly, there was the matter of cleaning up all the blood itself. It seemed as if the blood had taken on a life of its own and devilishly contrived to launch itself everywhere in an effort to cause as much trouble as possible. That which had spilled on the floor or on the school desks, Sarah carefully sponged off with a damp rag. She also sponged off the sides of the sewing basket. Unfortunately, some blood had spilled onto the area rug, and she did not know how to get it out. *Perhaps lemon water would do?* But to get lemon water, she'd have to ask one of the servants for help, and they'd want to know how the blood got there. *Perhaps she could explain away the cut? Tell everyone she'd been using the letter opener and simply tripped?* No, saying it aloud, it was a thin excuse, indeed. Better not to let anyone know of the cut at all.

Eventually, Sarah came upon a solution. First, with great effort, she moved the schoolroom furniture out of the way. She then readjusted the area rug so the stained part was underneath the bookcase, hidden from view. It solved that problem, but the exertion left her panting with exhaustion, and her wrist throbbing quite painfully.

The throbbing was not unpleasant, but Sarah feared the wound might start to bleed again. *Did she detect some dampness beneath the bandages?* She rebound her wrist again, more tightly than ever. At that point, a wave of dizziness overcame her, and she had to lie down on the schoolroom floor for a while. Her breathing was rapid and shallow, and her heart seemed to race. She forced herself to inhale and exhale slowly multiple times and was eventually able to sit up and shakily rise to her feet. She somehow staggered back to her own room, even if she had to steady herself by her hand against the wall at least once. She hid the blood-soaked rags beneath her bed and later burned them. During her years at Parsley School, Sarah had assiduously avoided any examinations by a physician, surgeon, or apothecary, and she was determined to maintain that streak here.

The next morning, her wrist was still sore, but the wound had at least scabbed over. Now she'd have to explain the bandaging on her wrist, though. By breakfast, she'd devised a strategy.

"Silly me," she told Violet and Eleanor loudly and gaily while Mrs. Brown was in the room. "I tripped last night and sprained my wrist, so now I've got it all wrapped up." She showed them her tightly bound wrist and smiled—or rather, she attempted to smile, but it came out looking more like a grimace.

"Does it hurt?" asked Violet.

"Oh no, dear. It's quite all right," Sarah gave another unsuccessful attempt at a smile.

"But you look so pale," Elinor noted.

"I'm always pale," Sarah replied.

"Paler, even, than usual," said Elinor. Violet nodded. They also saw that Miss Pole's eyes seemed ringed with shadows, as if she hadn't rested well the night before. She also seemed somewhat unsteady on her feet.

"You really don't look well," Mrs. Brown interjected. "Perhaps we should send for someone to come and see you?"

"Nonsense!" Sarah gave a loud false laugh. "It's just a little sprain is all. I'll be fine. Besides, for whom would we even be able to send? Greenberry hasn't any proper doctor."

"We could call for someone from a neighboring town or village," Mrs. Brown pointed out. She felt herself curiously concerned for the governess. Mrs. Brown didn't know why, but something felt strangely off about Miss Pole. More so than usual.

"It's very kind of you, but there's no need to trouble yourself!" Miss Pole hastened to say. "I assure you, I'll be fine, especially if I could get some of that good medicinal tonic you've told me about."

This was a good tactic. Mrs. Brown bought a certain tonic from an apothecary in London which she had always sworn by, and she was more than happy to share. Mrs. Brown administered two doses of the foul tasting potion to Sarah, who just barely managed not to spit it out. Mrs. Brown then suggested that Sarah get some rest, and to this suggestion, she heartily agreed.

Sarah spent the rest of the day in her own quarters. She constantly checked her wound, worrying it would become infected or would need stitches, either of which might necessitate a visit to a surgeon. She started to consider what sort of cover story she could give. *She could perhaps explain away one wrist cut, but how would she account for the older scars? Could she convince a medical man to keep silent perhaps by offering him a bribe?* But no, the risks of exposure and being committed to a madhouse were too great. Sarah had heard stories of what took place in lunatic asylums and decided she'd rather risk death than end up in such a hellhole.

By some miracle, though, the wound healed on its own, without any complications. Within a few days, the bandaging came off Miss Pole's wrist. She did appear to be completely healed from her mishap. Indeed, she proclaimed herself better than ever. The matter was quickly forgotten, and when some weeks later a scrub maid found a mysterious reddish-brown stain on the schoolroom carpet underneath the bookshelf, no one made any connection between the events. Mrs. Brown groused about the expense, but the carpet was simply replaced, and life at Bromley Hall went on as usual.

Sarah's Journal

I should have stopped after that. I know I should have stopped, but I didn't. Curiously enough, I remember, at the time, being less worried about bleeding out than about being discovered. I also noted, with interest, my physical symptoms the day after that particular cut. I was, indeed, a little light headed, but I was surprised by how thirsty I was as well. I'd heard somewhere that patients having experienced blood loss need to eat red meat, so I put in a particular request with Dacres for some kidney pie, and I did feel stronger after eating it.

Thank heavens I wasn't at Parsley School when it happened. I remember thinking to myself that Mrs. Gates would have had her suspicions for sure. I was also perversely enough rather pleased at how well I'd managed after my little slip with the knife. I had not only taken care of myself well enough to make a full recovery, but I had done so without activating any sort of suspicion. It was something of a triumph on my part, was it not? Still, I clearly couldn't risk having it happen again. The risk of inciting suspicion would be too grave.

That I may have been at grave personal risk either never occurred to me or I never cared. All I took from the whole incident was to be a little more careful in the future, to confine myself to cutting within my own room – although I would have had just as much trouble explaining a big blood pool there – and, of course, to avoid new, untrustworthy instruments of harm and instead stick more closely than ever to my beloved pouch.

Eleven

"Everybody allows that the talent of writing agreeable letters is peculiarly female."
–Jane Austen, *Northanger Abbey*

Let it not be said that Sarah's friends Geraldine and Clara had abandoned her once she took up her post. They, instead, kept up a vigorous correspondence once Sarah had written to them of her new address. Soon, Sarah found herself contemplating the following messages. There was one particular letter of note from Clara.

To Miss Sarah Pole,

Firstly, I'm sure you will wonder at this letter being posted to you from Bath when I went home to live with my parents in Bristol. Well, I am staying here as a guest of the Gargerys. Mr. Gargery has done business with Father and has recently been in poor health. His doctor recommended he "take the waters" for the winter season, and Mrs. Gargery and Mother agreed that I should spend the season with them! They thought it would be good for me not only to see the sights in Bath but also to expand my circle of acquaintances.

We are currently lodged on Milson Street, which Mrs. Gargery assures me is a very fashionable address. The first thing we did on our arrival was go shopping. I'd brought my best dress and a couple of others I thought were quite pretty as well, bur Mrs. Gargery insisted that we both needed to freshen our wardrobe with the latest fashions so as not to be laughed out of Bath. So, I have two new dresses, a new pelisse, and a new jeweled fan! Mrs. Gargery assures me that I look quite the elegant young lady.

I believe that Bath may be the most beautiful city in all of England. We are surrounded by hills that form a sort of amphitheater, and the river Avon runs directly through the valley. The buildings are all made of fine, light-colored stone, so they seem very modern and elegant. The Royal Crescent is simply magnificent. We've also visited Blaize Castle. The whole structure feels like a giant playhouse, or rather a play fort made of stone. You almost expect to see giant toy soldiers marching around the turrets. Father and Mr. Gargery happen to have as a mutual acquaintance, a Mr. Thewlis, who owns a silk spinning factory in a nearby village in Somerset. I have not seen it, but Mr. Gargery tells me the factory employs over fifty children, some of them not even six years old! He says the pay is good for these times, but the children work twelve hours a day!

Every day, we go to the Pump Room at certain hours to take the waters. I must confess, the waters do not taste all that good even if they are drawn from a marble urn, but the real point is not to drink but to be seen. As you may have heard, the Lower Rooms were destroyed in a fire, but Mrs. Gargery assures me that was no great loss since they had quite fallen out of fashion anyway. Instead, we attend dances at the Upper Rooms. Obviously, there are a great many invalids here, and they're often drawn about in little hand carriages and not so many young people as one might wish. But fortunately, on my first dance at Bath, the Master of Ceremonies was kind enough to introduce me to one Mr. Paul Stamford, the younger son of Lord Lomberdale. Mr. Stamford took orders last year and was given the living on his father's estate in Wiltshire, and I have seen him numerous times since – in Sydney Gardens, at the Lending Library, and at concerts and the theatre. He has even called upon us once or twice. I overheard Mrs. Gargery telling her husband, "It would be a good match for he's got a family name, and she's got a fortune."

Such communications make me very uncomfortable and seem quite vulgar, but I confess that personally I find Paul Stamford to be, if not handsome, then all other things worthy and amiable, and I like him. I like him very much, and while I haven't seen his future parsonage yet, Paul describes it as a most charming and pretty place to live. I wonder how he can stand to be away from it so long, but there's a curate Mr. Wooten who takes on the work when Paul is away, which he is a lot. If – and I say if – Paul and I do wed,

then you could come and visit us in the parsonage and think how pleasant that would be!

Affectionately,
Clara

P.S. Oddly enoughm, Paul's been to Greenberry himself! It came up in conversation when he saw I had a letter from there. It seems his mother's sister married a gentleman named Ambrose, and Paul has visited them once or twice. What a coincidence! I don't know if you've had any contact with the Ambrose family, but if you have, I confess I'm curious as to your general observations for they may soon be my relations as well.

Then there was Geraldine.

My dear, queer, darling Sarah!
I'm staying with the Johnsons now in Portsmouth. Mr. Johnson is a shipbuilder and old friend of Father's, and because Father is now sailing around the Cape of Good Hope, he's bid me to stay with them. Mrs. Johnson's decreed herself my chaperone. As if I needed one! Honestly, she's worse than Mrs. Gates ever was, but at least Mr. Johnson keeps a lively table and has all sorts of jolly old salts over all the time, including one in particular, but I'll save that for later!
Let me tell you a little about Portsmouth. The city is filthy, noisy, and chaos and confusion are everywhere. It's a hotbed of vice, full of brawling, drunkenness and prostitution. Everyone's always yelling and usually cursing, too. So, of course, I love it! There's always something happening here.
We are surrounded by walls and gates with hundreds of cannons and mortars within the walls. Naval men, marines, and army officers, too, are everywhere. You can't throw a stone without hitting someone in uniform. Indeed, the city would die without them, as would the British Empire, I should think. I've visited the Royal Naval Academy and seen boys as young as twelve. Some of them get billeted on their first ship by the time they're fourteen! No offense to old Mrs. Gates and Parsley School, but sometimes I wish I'd been born a lad. I might have had my own fleet.
Of course, so many of them are on half-pay now that Bonaparte's dead and gone. I heard a couple of them the other day bemoaning that England's so bloody peaceful now,

a man could starve! But perhaps we'll have another war with France or Spain. That would cheer many folks around here right up!

Even with the navy in contraction, Portsmouth keeps growing and growing and swallowing up every country village in its path. Southsea Castle once fired its guns on Portsmouth, and now it's part of the town! Isn't that funny? I went to visit it once. It's been completely renovated for more guns and a bigger garrison. They've just installed gaslights in Portsea, too, can you believe it? They're a marvel, they are, and I've heard it said that soon they'll have those lights in Old Portsmouth and everywhere in England, not just London. Think of it!

There are a lot of prostitutes here in Portsmouth—it comes with having all the sailors. You can spot them a mile off. They dress like parrots and laugh like monkeys! I think they have more fun than proper ladies do, though, I dare say Clara would think otherwise. Of course, Mrs. Johnson won't let me talk to any of the prostitutes, but maybe someday I'll get a chance to slip away from the old prude and chat with them. I bet they have all kinds of stories!

Now, the main reason I'm writing to you: I'm in love! Not with a pirate but a captain... or he will be a captain soon enough. His name is Joel Harris, and he's wonderful! So handsome and a born sailor, and he likes the fact that I'm not some proper and boring girl like Clara. He's first mate, for now, on The Antonia for The East India Company, and he expects to get his captain's papers within the year, and then we can marry! I feel rather sad for Clara, since I'll probably marry before she does. Won't she be mad!

I've no doubt Father will approve, and he's sure his family will be fine with me being that I'm of sea blood as well, and when I do wed you must come and visit me and Joel here in Portsmouth. There's so much to paint here!

With love,
Geraldine Nesbitt (soon to be Geraldine Harris!)

Sarah's Journal

I was happy for Geraldine and Clara. I truly was. Their letters gave me tantalizing hints of a world far beyond Bromley Hall, a world full of beautiful views to draw and paint. How I longed to sketch the ships at Portsmouth or the streets of Bath! But reading about how promising their futures looked made me dig the pin particularly hard into my thigh that night. Both of them would soon be well settled, happily married, and in all likelihood, starting their own families. I could look forward to none of that. Just spending the next twenty years or so trudging from schoolroom to schoolroom, educating other people's children, and eating my dinners alone. Even if I were to ever meet a man, which seemed unlikely, why would he even give me a second glance much less want to court me? And once I am over forty... everyone wants younger women for governesses, not sad-eyed, middle-aged spinsters with wrinkles and grey hairs. What will happen to me then?

I came across a newspaper article that haunted me. It described the case of a former governess between forty and fifty years of age. She had clearly been of respectable origins once, but had been reduced to living in a tiny room while scouring the streets of London every day, trying to find work. She searched for weeks and weeks to no avail, until finally, one afternoon, she took a final cup of tea with her landlady before locking herself in her room from which she would never emerge alive. The paper was careful not to explain the exact cause and circumstances of her death, which I could only imagine.

And I did. I spent many hours in the dead of night, imagining.

Twelve

"First loves are not necessarily more foolish than others;
but chances are certainly against them."
–Maria Edgeworth, *Belinda*

The Mandeville family had their own pew in church. Reverend Graham made a point of paying them obsequious attention each week after delivering his sermons that outlined obscure liturgy and stressed the need for the poor to show humility and deference to their betters. As governess, Sarah did not sit in the family pew but would attend service in the back of the church.

It was late March, just after the spring thaw had commenced, that Robert Healey made his entrance. Everyone had already pulled out their hymnals and begun to sing when the back door swung open, and in darted a lanky young man with freckles strewn across his nose, cheeks, and forehead. Reverend Graham momentarily halted, and everyone stared. The young man turned red-faced and murmured an apology for his tardiness. Everyone turned back to the hymnals and tried to proceed as if there had been no disturbance while the young man took a place beside Sarah and began studying the hymnal quite intently, holding it upside down. Sarah quietly grabbed the hymnal in his hands and turned it over, directing him to the right page.

"Oh, thank you," he whispered. A couple of other churchgoers turned around again. Sarah put a finger to her lips, and he quieted down. It was only after the service, when they were outside in the shadow of the legendary yew, that he spoke.

"So sorry about all that! I'm afraid I overslept this morning," he spoke with an Irish lilt. "I was up late with anatomy journals, and I was in such a rush to get here. I think my pants are on backwards. And my socks don't match either. Oh, dear. Wait, where are my manners? We haven't been properly introduced yet... but, who is to introduce us?" he looked around as if hoping to find a Master of Ceremonies or at least a helpful curate, but neither appeared.

"I don't know," Sarah answered him. "You're the first person in this church to ever speak to me. Perhaps we can introduce ourselves?"

"Dr. Robert Healey, at your service," he gave a half bow. Something about his height and thin build gave the impression of a heron. His sand-colored hair was unruly and stuck up in patches.

"Oh, yes. I've heard the town's been without a doctor now for more than a year since the last one passed away. I'm Sarah Pole. I'm governess at Bromley Hall for the Mandeville family."

"The Mandeville family! I've heard a lot about them," Robert exclaimed.

"Where are you staying?" Sarah asked.

"I've rented the old White Cottage on Durden Lane," Robert told her. "It's been vacant for a while, so they gave me quite a bargain."

"Miss Pole!" Susan's voice called out.

"I have to be going," Sarah said, apologetically.

"Shall I'll see you at service next week?"

"Yes, I suppose you shall."

Sarah hurried off to find the Mandevilles, who were waiting by the coach.

"Finally! You've certainly kept us waiting long enough! Where on Earth were you?" Mrs. Mandeville harangued her, then before Sarah could answer, she added, "We're having guests tonight for dinner." Then, much to Sarah's surprise, she continued again, "You'll be attending as well."

"Me?" Sarah questioned, as if her ears had betrayed her.

"Yes, you. And don't stand there with your mouth wide open like that.

You look like a frog. Really, what's extraordinary about attending dinner?"

What was so extraordinary, Sarah thought, was that she had never been asked to attend dinner with the family before, much less with the family while they were entertaining guests.

"This way, we will have an even ten people to dine. Four women to six men," Mrs. Mandeville explained. *Ah, so that was the reason for the invitation.*

Her employer's next words were a shock as well. "So do find something decent to wear," Mrs. Mandeville pursed her lips and gazed dubiously at Sarah's frock made of stuff.

"All my dresses are the same," Sarah admitted.

"Well, surely you have one that's better!"

"No, actually I don't, ma'am," Sarah's voice was dry as paper. "Back at school, there was never a need for me to wear anything better." She didn't add there had never been a need for her to wear anything better at Bromley Hall either. Not until now.

"Hmm... well, you're nearly the same height as Alicia. Perhaps she can lend you something."

Alicia was not at all pleased to learn she'd be supplying Sarah anything from her wardrobe. Her ill humor was mollified by remembering that one gown she'd gotten that had been made by some accident in a hideous shade of olive green rather than the emerald fabric she'd chosen. The olive color washed her out, making her appear sallow. In one of their rare moments of perfect accord, Mrs. Mandeville and Alicia had both detested the dress and agreed to make a point of not paying the milliner for the abomination. The gown had sat in the back of Alicia's closet ever since, unwanted even by her maid. She happily and generously bestowed this garment on Sarah as well as some old beads of which she was sick of the sight.

They were walking through the hall when Elinor and Violet stopped them to see how they were dressed.

"You look pretty tonight," said Violet.

"Thank y–" Alicia began.

"Not you. Sarah."

"Miss Pole looks pretty?" Alicia was flabbergasted.

"Thank you for being polite, Violet," Sarah answered, and Alicia remembered that, of course, that's what Violet was doing—being polite

"Alicia always looks beautiful," Elinor noted wisely, "so there's no need to point it out, but Miss Pole doesn't."

"Run along now, both of you," Sarah instructed, and they did so, leaving the two older women to make their way to the main dining room.

Sarah was seated silently at the table where she had never eaten before, and that evening she was introduced to each of the guests one-by-one. Sir John Tudbury was there, along with his very eligible daughter, Miss Maria Tudbury, and even more eligible son and heir, George Tudbury. The latter possessed a rather brutish, simian appearance. Sir John had just decided that Gaskell Park needed a conservatory and was happy to lecture anyone within listening distance on his plans to grow exotic flowers and fruits all year round.

"Think of it. I'll be able to serve guests fresh oranges every year during Christmas!"

Reverend Graham was in attendance as well, and more surprisingly, so was the lanky Dr. Healey. Ordinarily, a country doctor, even a proper licentiate physician like Dr. Healey, would not have been eating with landed gentry. As it happened, though, Thomas Mandeville's gouty foot had been particularly painful as of late, and he was eager to make the acquaintance of – and take the measure of – the new town doctor.

Dr. Healey had been most pleased by the invitation. For a man in his position, it was vital that he start making connections within the Greenberry community. The only reason he'd bothered to attend church service at all was for precisely that reason. He wasn't given to religious ceremony at all, and when he'd first met Reverend Graham, he'd privately judged him a pompous, pious ass. The Reverend Graham had his doubts about Dr. Healey as well. Greenberry needed a doctor, of course, but an Irishman in the community? Their political loyalties were always suspect, and the Celtic race in general was so thoroughly unreliable and a backwards group. He'd been relieved to learn the doctor was at least Irish Protestant. An Irish Catholic would have been beyond the pale.

All of Dr. Healey's thoughts on Reverend Graham, or even Thomas Mandeville, however, were swept aside by a far greater object of interest. Dr. Healey had never, in Ireland or in England, beheld a young woman as lovely as Alicia Mandeville. He had been too preoccupied and embarrassed at church to properly observe her, and that only added to the strength of the impression she made that evening when she came forth, resplendent in pearly satin. Robert drank in her perfect rose and cream complexion, her golden hair, her bright blue eyes, her heart shaped face, her swanlike neck, and the subtle curve of her breasts. To all of this was added a most singular delicacy of feature. Alicia's features were extraordinary to the point of luminescence. No one beholding a face like Alicia's could come to any other conclusion but that its wearer must be someone of exceptional sensitivity and angelic virtue. To suggest otherwise would be akin to thinking Aphrodite, the goddess of love herself, a common pickpocket! Robert Healey would ride home that night, his head awhirl, like those unfortunate mortals who've been kissed by goddesses in dreams. Still, he managed to collect his wits enough to answer coherently when his host inquired about his education.

"I attended Trinity University in Dublin," he explained. "Then I came down for further study at Guy's Hospital in London."

"Is it true," Alicia asked, "they carve up bodies right on display with hundreds of people watching? And that the bodies often are stolen from cemeteries?" She gave an exaggerated shiver. At this point, there had been a lull in the conversation. Sir John having finally exhausted the topic of the planned conservatory and oranges, which was why everyone happened to be listening.

"They are. I recognize how gruesome it must seem to a young lady such as yourself, but it is the best way to way to learn about anatomy and the human body."

"Michelangelo did that," Sarah spoke up. These were the first words she'd said all evening. Until now, she'd been silent as the grave, barely touching her meal, observed by no one. Now, however, all eyes had turned to her, some in surprise and some in irritation. It didn't take a genius to figure out which gazes belonged to whom.

"He began dissecting bodies at eighteen years old," she went on, "to make sure his artistic renderings of anatomy were thoroughly accurate. That is why he could do such realistic renderings of musculature and bone."

Mrs. Mandeville looked up sharply during this speech, and for the first time, fully took in Miss Pole's appearance, noting to her surprise that she wasn't all that bad looking a girl after all, not by candlelight at least. The olive dress that had been so detestable on Alicia looked rather well on Miss Pole against her dark hair and intense eyes. Of course, it was all wasted on such a queer, quiet creature as the governess, especially when she was inevitably outshined by Alicia.

"He did," Healey agreed. "In fact, his sketches were so good we physicians still study them."

"Then couldn't such drawings be enough?" Alicia asked. "With no need to practice on bodies at all?"

"I'm afraid even the best illustrations are no substitute for hands-on experience."

"And have you had such experience?" Sarah spoke again.

"Oh yes, I've had to set my fair share of bones and have done enough dissections. Gets messy, especially with the stomach. The entrails are so slippery and slimy to the touch, but at least they're easy to get to! The heart is so much harder to reach. You have to saw through the ribs, you see, and they make such a cracking sound," as Dr. Healey spoke and gesticulated, Sarah stared with undisguised interest.

Others at the table did not seem so enraptured. Sir John Tudbury, in particular, was starting to feel downright queasy.

"But there's something about holding a human heart in one's own hands. It's almost like touching God," Dr. Healey continued on, oblivious. "Why, one time we had a patient come in with an open chest wound that exposed part of his heart to the open eye, and to actually see it pumping..." Dr. Healey could have waxed quite poetically on the matter, but Mrs. Mandeville saved the situation with a change of subject. This was done quite in the nick of time, too, since poor Sir John had feared he might see his dinner again.

"Did you enjoy living in London, Dr. Healey?"

"Well, I was mostly busy with my studies and my work, but it's certainly an exciting place. Lots to be seen there."

"I find London to be so delightful! We visit every year," Alicia chimed in. Soon, they were all discussing the various merits of Vauxhall, Hyde Park, and the theatre.

"What made you come to Greenberry?" Alicia later asked with genuine curiosity. As someone who hated the country and had always found the delights of London irresistible, it seemed quite inexplicable to her that anyone would voluntarily choose the former over the latter.

"Well, I'd once hoped to establish a practice in London," Dr. Healey admitted, "but competition there among physicians is strong, and the costs of renting rooms was quite high. Just as I was finishing my studies, one of my professors told me how he'd heard word of a town that needed a medical man and suggested I might be able to set up a good practice here much more economically than in the city. He was right. I was able to find rooms twice as large for half the cost as I could in the city, and already I've been seeing clients. I think I'll be able to make my way here quite nicely."

"Well, we all must make our way somehow or other," said Sarah, who'd been completely silent on the topic of London.

Thomas Mandeville was displeased that night. Both he and Sir John Tudbury were of the opinion that, given the closeness of their estates, it would be very desirable their children married one another – which children didn't really matter. Hugh Mandeville to Miss Tudbury or Alicia to George or, perhaps best of all, a double wedding with Bromley Hall and Gaskell Park doing a fair exchange of daughters. Even Mrs. Mandeville could see the desirability of such matchmaking. Having titled in-laws would enhance Elinor and Violet's own social circles in years to come and help bring them into the proximity of wealthy young suitors. So, it was that parents and stepparents alike did everything within their power to encourage conversation among their children. Alicia, it couldn't be denied, rose to the occasion admirably, even managing to laugh at George Tudbury's attempts at wit. George couldn't keep his eyes off her. All quite satisfying. Hugh, however, had scarcely looked at Miss Tudbury and not once spoken to her except to ask her to pass the salt. Instead, he had kept on with how he couldn't wait for hunting season and to be out again among the horses and dogs.

"Blazes, what is wrong with that boy?" Thomas thundered to Mrs. Mandeville later on, when they'd retired to their chamber.

"Well, there are plenty of other girls besides Miss Tudbury," Mrs. Mandeville soothed.

"Yes, but he's not looking at them either, damn it! Spends all his time riding or at the bloody stables these days. Do you think if I threatened to take his horse away he might finally engage in courtship?"

Wisely, Mrs. Mandeville did not reply to this but instead asked, "How do you feel about Dr. Healey?"

"He seems all right, as doctors go. I spoke to him after dinner about my foot and he suggested a regimen of Epsom salts and bleeding."

Alicia Mandeville was much more satisfied than her father about how things had gone. She had looked beautiful, spoke prettily, and every man at the table had been quite transfixed by her. George Tudbury was, of course, the best prize—ugly as he may be, he was going to be a baronet someday, and Gaskell Park was a fine seat. But she could take pleasure in her other conquests as well. It was amusing to have a clergyman like Reverend Graham dancing attendance on her. She was not at all inclined to discourage him just yet. Rather, she planned to bat him around like a cat with a ball of yarn. And then there was Dr. Healey, a clever young man. Very clever. And not unattractive. Of course, as a mere country doctor, he was a pointless prospect, but there could be no harm in enjoying his conversation. Nor, she decided, would there be any harm in a little casual flirtation. It was, after all, the sworn duty of every pretty young girl to make as many conquests as she can, and Alicia was nothing if not dutiful.

Sarah's Journal

Ironic, wasn't it? I'd been so careful for years to avoid an examination with any sort of doctor, and then here one came along whose company and friendship I found myself craving. The night after Dr. Healey dined at Bromley Hall, I began searching the family library for books on human anatomy. I finally found one in the science section that I began to faithfully peruse on my own time. The studies of human muscles and bones were quite engrossing. I was immediately flooded with ideas for improving the likeness and veracity of my sketches of human figures in the future. I learned there were over two-hundred bones in the human body, which seemed so... rickety, somehow. So many delicate pieces that could break. I'd pinch my arms and try to feel the bones and joints under my skin, but muscle and flesh impeded a thorough examination. My ribs and hipbones were far easier to trace.

I had never considered the sciences, much less medicine, of much interest before, but I was pleasantly surprised to realize I had been entirely wrong. Far from finding the material dry, I read with real fascination. William Harvey's discoveries on circulation of the blood was riveting, but what fascinated me most, by far, was an illustration of the human heart. It was not at all like the classic heart shape painted on cupid's bow, but rather a most convoluted pumping contraption. Strange to think that such an awkward looking object, so baggy and protruded with all those valves, ventricles, and arteries, could be so central to human life. This allowed me to see how much worse that one deep cut could have been. How close I could have come to accidentally nicking an artery and bleeding uncontrollably. It certainly wouldn't have been fair to the girls to hear their governess was dead by her own hand, now would it? The shock might have given them nightmares. Still, there was something about the thought of exsanguination that was compelling and horrific, like seeing a terrible street accident. You wanted to look and not look all at once.

I also read of miasma theory that disease is caused by poisonous vapors in the air characterized by their foul smell. Such vapors were particularly common in filthy slums. At this, I had to shut the book. My father's parsonage had not been in any slum. Everything had been quite clean, and if there'd been any foul odors, I'd missed them. Yet fever had come and taken three of us away while I survived, and there lay a question for which I doubted any book or person could have an answer. Why had the fever taken Papa, Mama, and William, but left me?

Thereafter, I took a considerable interest in medicine and human anatomy, not so much for the knowledge gained but rather because I took an interest in Dr. Healey. How could I help it? He was the first person I'd met since I'd come to Bromley Hall to engage me in adult conversation as equals. To be engaged on an intellectual level! It was intoxicating. In the future, I'd be constantly looking out for opportunities to be in the doctor's presence, to find excuses to talk to him and hear that wonderful Irish accent. It wasn't, I knew, particularly appropriate behavior given my position, but there was nothing for it. When a starving man sees a loaf of bread, he can't help but devour it. Dr. Healey was my bread.

Of course, I knew I wasn't his. I knew I couldn't be as important to him in any respect as he was to me. He was, after all, a busy country doctor. His life was far more filled than mine could ever be. I did not deceive myself into thinking he was ever going to conceive a grand passion for me.

Nor could I deceive myself about the way he looked at Alicia. Jealousy is such an ugly emotion. Whenever I found the green-eyed monster rearing its head, I'd slap myself in the face and give mental rebukes. I had no claim whatsoever on Dr. Healey, and even if I had, it would have been far more appropriate to pity him for his affection for Alicia. For it was, after all, as a hopeless a case for him to covet such a wealthy young woman of breeding as it was for me to want him.

Thirteen

"Incidentally, it's easy to write prescriptions,
but difficult to come to an understanding with people."
–Franz Kafka, *A Country Doctor*

Robert Healey did not personally consider bloodletting a particularly valuable medical tool in most cases. Quite the contrary, he believed it often did more harm than good, but Thomas Mandeville, like so many other patients, believed in bloodletting and expected it. Robert knew better than to try to talk them out of it completely but rather to limit the practice to a manageable level. Thomas would get the mental reassurance of regular bleedings but without doing so to an extent to do any serious damage to his health. In the meantime, he would put Thomas Mandeville on a change of diet and regular Epsom soaks that could actually help the man. Besides, regular bleedings would be a chance to visit Bromley Hall and see more of the bewitching Alicia Mandeville. After studying anatomy for so long, he could not help but take an aesthetic appreciation of such a superb example of female pulchritude.

Something peculiar happened the first time Mr. Healey bled Mr. Mandeville. He had finished the process, properly bandaged the wound, and was about to call for a servant to attend to the dish of blood when he noticed Sarah lurking outside the door, like a bird sitting on a branch. She had started guiltily when she saw that he had noticed her.

"Can you summon a maid for me?" he asked. She nodded and immediately called to someone named Molly to come along. Molly, about fourteen years old with a snub nose and spots, no sooner saw the dish then she let out a yelp.

"Oh, lawds, sir! I can't touch that. Just the sight of blood makes me sick!"

"For God's sake, girl," Mr. Mandeville had recovered enough to chime in, "you carry chamber pots!"

"That's different, that is! I can't even look at this…" Molly was green around the gills already, and she swayed slightly, as if she were about to swoon.

"Molly take a seat in the hall. Dr. Healey, I'll dispose of this," Sarah briskly whisked away the dish herself, blood sloshing against the sides but fortunately not spilling. She returned a few minutes later to show Healey the way out of the house.

"I'm dreadfully sorry about the inconvenience, doctor. Perhaps in the future I should just be the one to assist you? I don't know who else among the servants might share Molly's squeamishness."

"You don't share her squeamishness," he observed.

She was quiet a moment before answering, "I'm rather more used to the sight of blood than most." He wondered at that, and she asked, "Do you always use a knife, or do you ever use leeches?"

"The knife," he replied. "Leeches are disgusting creatures, and I prefer not to keep them, even if my colleagues do."

Sarah nodded and added, "I've heard that some people become almost addicted to regular bleedings and feel they need it."

"It's been known to happen," he replied gingerly. "I haven't come across such a case yet myself, but a number of colleagues have described them to me. Patients who've been bled so frequently that their bodies become so accustomed to the process that, when deprived of bleeding, they feel ill."

"But why do they want the bleedings in the first place?" Sarah's face was expectant and intent.

"Too many think it's a cure-all, especially for the lazy and indolent who live lives that are too soft and luxurious." At that, he feared for a moment he'd come dangerously close to criticizing Thomas Mandeville in the presence of another member of the household, but Sarah's expression was distant and far away.

"Is that the only reason people become addicted to bloodletting?" she asked with a strange and dark intensity, and without knowing why, Dr. Healey began to feel uneasy.

"Whatever do you mean?" he asked.

"Could it be that some people ask for bloodlettings because they simply want to bleed? Because they want to feel pain?" she asked, her face intent with concentration.

"I don't know. I can't say I ever thought of the question like that before," Dr. Healey's unease grew, "but Miss Pole, this is rather a morbid subject for a young woman, isn't it? And what about your pupils?"

"They have their music lesson now with Signor Vincetti. Though perhaps it is time I give the poor man a reprieve. Thank you for reminding me," she hurried off, and Robert found himself quite perplexed by the whole encounter.

As he emerged from the house, he spotted Alicia Mandeville on the grounds up ahead. Her golden hair and peaches and cream complexion were even more becoming in broad daylight. Naturally, he stopped to pay his respects. He chatted with Alicia so long that he ran late to his next appointment. It was only much later that his mind returned to that strange conversation with Sarah Pole. What an odd sort of girl she was.

In church, Healey was confined to admiring Alicia Mandeville from afar while sharing Sarah's hymnal, but it was a different story when he went to Bromley Hall. Whenever Robert Healey came to attend Thomas Mandeville, his daughter, Alicia, had a way of appearing on the grounds wherever he was present. She would walk with him to stretch her legs and quite naturally engage in pleasant discourse. As time went on, it was only natural that their conversation should become more intimate. Robert couldn't help but enjoy the company of such an attractive and personable young lady. What man wouldn't? She was so full of life and vivacity, and so lovely to look upon. To hear her sing was to be transported to Heaven.

"Tell me about Ireland," Alicia would ask, and he'd find himself telling her all about his childhood as the younger son of a member of the landed gentry, of a boyhood spent running on emerald fields and fishing in lively streams before his schooling in Dublin. She was a good listener with a gratifying habit of opening her eyes wide at times to show what extraordinary interest she took in what he said. The only fly in the ointment was Alicia's lack of curiosity regarding Dr. Healey's work. She made no pretense of the fact that she considered anatomical studies at best dull and at worst revolting. Of course, an aversion to anatomical studies that was only to be expected for any properly brought up young woman. Nevertheless, it was a disappointment.

As for what Alicia herself said to Robert, well Robert was hardly aware of it. What actual words she used were of less interest to him than the way her exquisite lips formed them and how they parted over her teeth. While women may desire men to engage in deep intellectual conversation with, particularly women who are starved for intelligent adult company, the reverse is rarely true. A man who has plenty of others to turn to for mental stimulation seldom seeks it in a potential wife and rather focuses on more vital matters, such as the curve of a lady's neck.

Robert was no fool, and he knew matters with Alicia couldn't go anywhere. A simple country doctor, particularly an Irish one, was not a proper match for a squire's daughter. He continuingly resolved to break the whole thing off and keep Alicia at a distance, and he was continuingly breaking those resolutions. Despite his own best efforts, he found himself entertaining dreams and fancies he knew would never come true.

Here is perhaps a time to address Dr. Healey's experience in the realm of women, or rather lack thereof. He was certainly familiar with the basic anatomical principles of the fairer sex. He'd conducted official explorations on the autopsy tables at Trinity and Guy's Hospital, and he'd conducted explorations of another sort in the brothels of Dublin and London. All of which conspired to give him the impression he was a worldly man on the topic of women, but for all his knowledge of the workings of the female body, Dr. Healey was not well informed about the workings of the female mind. He was all too familiar with the various forms of physical trauma that could bring a person to the autopsy table, but quite unaware of the quieter dramas that can take place in a drawing room. He was in the peculiar position of being thoroughly educated on medical matters and dangerously ignorant on matters of the heart.

In the weeks ahead, Dr. Healey's regimen for his patient yielded mixed results. Thomas Mandeville didn't mind bleeding, Epsom salts, or a host of other treatment interventions, but he proved quite incorrigible on the matter of diet. The old man insisted there was no harm in him enjoying an occasional joint of beef or glass of port. Robert correctly suspected "occasional," in this case, meant almost daily. For that matter, he suspected it was more than one glass of port, and he was again quite correct. The man couldn't be bothered to abstain from the pleasure of the table, yet he had no problem with and, indeed, insisted on the damned bleedings!

At least Sarah, as promised, assisted him on these occasions. Indeed, she displayed quite an interest in medical matters. She constantly asked him questions about his work. Far from being repelled by more graphic descriptions of surgery, she was keen to know all the details. Robert found he enjoyed satisfying her curiosity, peculiar though it was.

"I've noticed doctors keep referring to patients with an excess of bile," Sarah mentioned to him once as Elinor and Violet were chasing each other around the grounds. "They seem to blame it for their patient's irritability."

"Ah, yes, the four humors. Goes back to the days of ancient Greece, when Hippocrates hypothesized that all the body's ailments were a result of an imbalance between the various humors: black bile, yellow bile, phlegm, and, of course, blood. A lot of my colleagues swear by it, but, frankly, I think Hippocrates was talking out of his hat. Egads, the man thought that blood was pumped by the liver!" Dr. Healey rolled his eyes at the folly. "He also started categorizing people as belonging to four different temperaments based on their dominant 'humor.' Though, to be fair, while he was certainly wrong about the body's humors, he might not have been so far off in how he sorted people."

"How did he sort them?"

"You haven't heard of the four temperaments before?" he seemed as amazed as if she'd claimed to have no knowledge of Adam and Eve.

"No one ever lectured on it at Parsley, my old school," Sarah answered. "Indeed, we never had any lessons in anatomy at all. Astounding, but matters related to medicine are generally not part of the curriculum for a girl's education."

She added the latter part almost playfully.

"I suppose not," Robert chuckled. "But do you really want to learn now?"

"I do!" Sarah was adamant.

"Well," Robert began ticking off with his fingers, "first there's choleric, a.k.a., yellow bile. Those are people who are passionate, ambitious, and often very difficult. Quick to temper, you understand. Abrupt, and they don't try to spare anyone's feelings. They're often quite hot-headed."

"I had a friend like that," Sarah mused. Violet gave a wild screech of laughter, throwing a pile of leaves on her sister only to have Elinor retaliate with exactly the same maneuver. It soon devolved into the girls directly pushing each other into the leaves and happily rolling about in a frenzy while the adults failed to pay any attention to them.

"Then there's sanguine, also referred to as blood. They tend to be charming, giddy, impulsive, and lighthearted people—the life of the party, but they're not necessarily cut out for anything too onerous."

"Like Alicia?"

"Yes," he said with a start, "rather like Alicia. Then comes phlegmatic. They tend to be quiet, sensible, calm, and rational individuals who value peace most of all. Very orderly persons, but they rarely take the initiative."

"I had another friend like that," Sarah observed, more for herself than for Dr. Healey.

"Then, finally, melancholic. They're a troubled lot. They're often clever and even talented, especially in the arts, but they're withdrawn and well prone to melancholy. Phlegmatics and sanguine are stable. Cholerics and melancholics are not." There was suddenly an awkward silence as it dawned on Robert which humor Sarah likely came under.

She said nothing to him, but rather called out, "Elinor! Violet!" Her charges were giggling in the leaf piles. "Come here. It's time to go back inside for lessons."

The girls approached her, panting and with leaves embedded in their hair.

Sarah turned to Robert, "Forgive me, Dr. Healey, but it's time for us to take our leave."

"Yes, I have other appointments anyway," he stammered at the abruptness

of it all. It was only later, much later, that Robert stopped to think and wonder what temperament category he came under, or if that was something he even wanted to know. If he cared to take a guess, he'd always considered himself a sensible phlegmatic sort of fellow who went through life peacefully getting his work done. He did not look for trouble or drama. Indeed, he'd always looked with disbelief and a certain disdain on persons who let themselves be swept away in the grip of violent emotion. He instinctively recoiled from such displays himself and felt they could never end well. He also later reflected on how curious it was that Miss Pole seemed to take such an interest in matters of anatomy and medicine. He had never heard of any young woman doing so before. Alicia certainly didn't. But, of course, Alicia was the very model of femininity. Miss Pole sometimes scarcely seemed a woman at all.

Sarah's Journal

So, medically speaking, I was considered of an "unstable temperament." Obviously, it wasn't much of a surprise. I had plenty of scar tissue to tell me I wasn't normal. Still, to hear it stated so boldly aloud was unpleasant—particularly to hear it said by Dr. Healey. The way his mouth had twisted as he talked about people with melancholia, I realized then that, whatever happened, I could never let him see my scars. I couldn't bear see his eyes fill up with horror and disgust at me.

Further reading made clear that melancholics were considered especially unhealthy individuals in body and mind. Apparently, at one point in Greece, it would have been standard practice for doctors to prescribe someone like me a lot of lavender and rosemary. Many doctors probably still would try such remedies. I had nothing against the herbs in question. Quite the contrary, they smelled very nice, and I heard they made for a very good tea as well. Somehow, I didn't think there was any tonic or spice sufficient to allow me to throw my pouch away, though.

Fourteen

"MAY! queen of blossoms,
And fulfilling flowers,
With what pretty music
Shall we charm the hours?
Wilt thou have pipe and reed,
Blown in the open mead?
Or to the lute give heed
In the green bowers?"
–Lord Edward Thurlow, *May*

Every year, it was the custom in Greenberry to celebrate the first of May with the traditional maypole, decorated with sprigs of green shrubs and tassels of green larch, followed by dancing. It seemed that every door in Greenberry had been anointed with leaves and flower garlands. A May Queen was chosen among the village girls, and she would wear a crown of flowers upon her head and lead them all in song and dance.

In theory, it was a merry occasion among the local farmers, for the month of May meant not only the arrival of spring and final departure of gloomy winter and rainy April, but also something of a slack period before the heavy summer labor began. Crops had already been sown, and now it was a simple matter of weeding and gathering cowslips to make into wine while watching the apple trees come into bloom. The smell of fresh green hay was in the air. Common laborers got the day off. However, one thing which regularly – and literally – put a damper on past May Days was that it always seemed to be a time the clouds were determined to gather and rain down upon the festivities. As Jem Howe would dourly note, "There's no surer cure for a drought than to hold an event outside."

But this year, Greenberry was in luck. The day dawned bright and clear with nary a cloud in the sky. Indeed, the weather was so lovely it made Jem suspicious. He kept scanning the sky for sudden signs of a storm and grimly wondered whether they might be about to experience the first earthquake in the recorded history of the country. The safest course of action, he proclaimed loudly, would be for everyone to stay in bed. Finding himself out-voted on the matter, he settled on the next best course of action, namely fortifying himself with copious amounts of ale.

Sarah and her two charges were in attendance. The girls had risen early and even made a point of washing their faces in the dew of the early morning, having heard from Molly the old superstition that this would make them very beautiful for the following year. They had urged Sarah to do the same, but she'd refused, saying, "I'm afraid it would take stronger magic than that to make a beauty of me. You both have the advantage that you're still growing."

Sarah had been more than happy, though, to help both girls make themselves bouquets and flower crowns for the occasion. They looked quite pretty in their little white dresses. They spotted Nellie Bloom wearing her good bonnet with Gertie honking beside her. Gertie, too, wore a tiny bonnet which Nellie had made from the scraps of her own so the two of them might match. They were, indeed, quite the pair and attracted a throng of admiring children.

"Why don't you wear a bonnet, Miss Pole?" Violet asked. "Even Gertie's wearing a bonnet and ribbons."

"Because I'm a crow, not a goose," Sarah replied, as if this explained everything.

"Oh," said Violet.

Elinor nodded, "Crows only wear black, don't they?"

"Precisely!"

Around the maypole, the dancers sang, "Come lasses and lads, take leave of your dads, and away to the maypole high." Sarah and both girls chimed in as well.

"Miss Pole!" Dr. Healey came up to them wearing a green coat with a daisy in his buttonhole rather than his usual somber black attire.

"Hello, doctor," the girls both sing-songed and curtsied.

"I see you're all enjoying the fine weather. Can we expect any other family members?" he added that last bit casually, but Sarah immediately understood his true intent from the way his eyes seemed to search right through her.

"Alicia Mandeville will not be attending, I'm afraid," Sarah told him coolly. "She considers it somewhat beneath the dignity of her station to mingle among the townsfolk and her father's tenants."

"Oh," said Robert, but he was in such a good humor that he quickly recovered from his disappointment. "Well would you and the girls care to be my company for today?" He bent down to address Elinor and Violet directly, "I'm afraid I'm new here, so I'm not familiar with the customs. Could you show me?"

The girls graciously agreed to be the good doctor's instructors on the matter of Greenberry's May Day ceremonies. They even took it upon themselves to make him a flower crown of his own. They took to their task eagerly.

"I'm overwhelmed by your generosity," he proclaimed.

"Try it on!" Elinor ordered him. He obeyed and both girls giggled wildly. One daisy poked out and covered his eyebrow, and even Sarah seemed to be holding back a grin as well.

"O thou with dewy locks, who lookest down, through the clear windows of the morning," Sarah recited from memory.

"That's William Blake, isn't it?" Dr. Healey asked.

"Why yes, it is."

"Be quiet," Elinor commanded. "They're about to choose the May Queen."

To the applause of all, Lucy Warner, the blacksmith's daughter and village beauty, was crowned May Queen. Lucy took her place on her flower bedecked throne to gaze upon her subjects. Then came the Morris dancers in their bright costumes, shaking their bells.

"All this brings me back," Sarah mused. "Some might have thought it was inappropriate for a vicar to celebrate a pagan holiday, but neither of my parents agreed. My father loved giving out the prizes every year on May Day, and mother would leave the fields bare of flowers in order to decorate the rectory," her lips curved into the tips of a smile at the memory.

"You have a father and mother, Miss Pole?" Violet was incredulous to think that Sarah had any family—or had ever been a child at all. She'd always pictured her governess as having hatched from an egg, fully formed in drab clothes and with a sketchpad in her hand. Elinor was also surprised, having assumed governesses were manufactured in some sort of mill or factory.

Even Robert was a bit taken aback by this intimate information she'd just shared. He, of course, knew fully that Sarah had to have been a child once. He was also aware she had to have had a mother and a father, but this had always been more of an intellectual understanding than something registered on the conscious level. Sarah had never once, he realized, spoken of her life before Parsley School, and even that she'd only mentioned briefly and in passing. Nor, for that matter, had he ever thought to ask her about anything else, he realized rather ruefully.

"Had," Sarah gently corrected. "It was a long time ago." Her face and voice reverted back to their usual stance, "Isn't that Henry Ambrose over there? Let's go greet him."

Henry Ambrose was large and strong for his years, with a gap tooth that was visible whenever he grinned, which was quite often. He would soon be going to Eton, but his doting mama was determined to enjoy him as much as she could before that sad day arrived. Soon, Henry was galloping around the village, green with Elinor and Violet taking turns trying to catch him. Dr. Healey stood by Sarah's side and watched the children frolic.

"So, you grew up in the country yourself," he noted. And waited.

"I did."

She was then silent, and he feared she'd speak no more.

"Walnut Hill," she finally continued. "It wasn't as large as Greenberry, or as wealthy. The closest gentry lived some distance away, and we never saw

them. My father's vicarage was probably the most 'genteel' house around, though to Bromley Hall it would have scarce done for a carriage house," she gave a small smile. "We did have a decent little library, though, even if it was nothing to Weberley's."

"Weberley's?" he repeated, quizzically.

"Where I attended school before coming here." And soon Sarah began telling Dr. Healey all about the town of Weberley and Parsley School. Far from having to feign interest, Dr. Healey found he was fascinated by her tale. Their conversation, though, was cut shorter than he would have liked by the children. Somehow, in the midst of play, Henry and Elinor had stumbled on each other's legs and fallen into a heap on the ground that Violet had happily joined. Sarah and Mrs. Ambrose ran over to disentangle the children, after which Sara decreed it was high time the girls returned home, to everyone's disappointment.

Later, Dr. Healey found himself dwelling on their talk and wishing it had gone on longer. It felt strange somehow to think of pale, melancholic Miss Pole as ever having been a child. And a parson's daughter, too! What had she been like in those days, he wondered. Had she always been so severe? Who would she have been had she not met with misfortune? He wasn't sure why he found the questions so vexing, but somehow couldn't help but feel that Miss Pole was a puzzle for which he had yet to find the key.

Sarah's Journal

I hadn't spoken of Walnut Hill in years. It had been a pretty home. A happy home. But it wasn't a home I'd been allowed to stay in. That would have been true no matter what happened. No clergyman's child ever really got to stay home forever. Sooner or later, the father must die and then the vicarage or rectory is given away to someone else. A vicar's daughter is always just a temporary tenant, just as I'd later been a temporary tenant at Parsley School and was now a temporary tenant at Bromley Hall. Admittedly, as a vicar's daughter, and even as a pupil or an instructor, I'd enjoyed more status in both prior positions. But at least for a few hours that day I'd spent with Robert and the children, I had a sense of what could have been if things had been different—of who I could have been. It was enough to make me want to smash my fist through a window, but that would have necessitated awkward explanations, so instead I pummeled my clenched hands against my legs until they were black and blue.

Fifteen

"The love that dare not speak its name."
–Lord Alfred Douglas, *Two Loves*

The calamity began in the schoolroom one day. It was by then July, and time to cut the hay. Every scythe and every cart in the county were being used to bring the hay in. Meanwhile, Sarah and the girls were examining a thick, leather-bound world atlas the size of a breadbasket intricately illustrated with all the strange exotic corners of the world that were not England.

"The Nile River is where?" Sarah asked.

"In Egypt," the girls replied in union, and Elinor pointed.

"Good. And where is the Amazon?"

"Australia!" Violet chirped, and Elinor rolled her eyes.

"I'm afraid that's wrong. Elinor, do you know?"

"The Amazon's in Brazil," Elinor replied with more than a trace of smugness, "where there are jungles, and people go about naked."

"And Elinor, where's the Volga?"

"In Russia. Where it's very cold, and there are a lot of bears."

"Very good, Elinor."

Elinor beamed and Violet stuck out her tongue at her sister. Elinor was outraged and turned to Miss Pole for intermediation, "Did you see what she just did?"

"See what?" asked Sarah, who then gave Violet a quick glance. "Violet, where are your gloves?" she asked sharply. The pair of gloves in question had come from London and were of very fine quality.

"I don't know," Violet confessed, and a search was instigated. Furniture was moved to look over and under. Items were overturned. It yielded no results.

"When did you last see your gloves? Violet, think," Sarah demanded.

Violet's forehead furrowed with concentration. "I took them off to go riding this morning," she exclaimed at the memory. "I'll go get them."

"No, I'll go," Sarah said, halting the girl who had just sprung up from her seat. "You two stay here and keep studying that atlas. I expect you to know where the Alps and the Himalayas are when I get back."

It was nearly dusk, and the heat of the summer day had yet to lift. Sarah felt sweat pooling from her underarms and lower back. It made her dress feel uncomfortably, sticky, and itchy. The air smelled heavily of manure and grass. Almost every cart in the country was now in use, getting in the hay, which had been cut and stacked in fields to dry. Getting it was of great importance. Without sufficient hay, there would be no way to keep the livestock fed during the winter months. Once cut, the hay would be stored up in giant ricks to keep it safe from rats and the damp. All this work to be done had resulted in the gainful employment of Adam and Polly Riggs in the fields. Both Riggs children had been well pleased to make extra pennies while enjoying the sun and fresh air, but the day laborers had all gone home hours ago.

As she approached the stables, Sarah spotted Joe leaving them. Sarah was struck once more with how the stable boy epitomized the very model of masculine beauty. Joe's hair was unruly and yet glossy at the same time, as if someone had run their fingers through it over and over again. Joe's shirt was unbuttoned, offering a glimpse of a chest so well sculpted to put Michelangelo's *David* to shame. Sarah was about to call out to him but was deterred from doing so by something furtive in his movements. While Sarah was still in search of the gloves, it was her curiosity – rather than the gloves – which drove Sarah to enter the stables—the same dreadful mix of curiosity and anticipation that makes readers' hearts race and makes them turn the pages eagerly when they're about to enter the secret lair of the masked fiend.

There were no masked fiends in this tale, but there was still drama. Sarah entered the stables to find Hugh Mandeville. He was still buttoning his breeches as he turned around and gave a start. His shirt was off to the side, and there was a tendril of hay in his hair. Sweat glistened along his defined muscles in the fading light. The stable, as usual, smelled of horses, manure, leather, and hay, but today there was a whiff of a new scent in the air. A musky scent. While others had considered Hugh Mandeville quite handsome, Sarah had never fully understood his appeal. Not until that moment, at any rate. What an excellent artist's model Hugh would make, assuming he'd have the patience for a long sitting. Hugh wore an expression of satisfaction, like a cat licking its whiskers in the sun after enjoying a pot of cream. This contentment was completely shattered when he looked up and saw Sarah staring at him.

"Jesus, Mary, and Joseph!" he cried out. "Where the bloody hell did you come from? What are you doing here?"

"Violet believes she left her gloves here, and I came to fetch them for her," Sarah's face was completely blank and her tone perfectly neutral. "Wait, I see them right over there."

Sure enough, a pair of small, delicate white gloves lay on a shelf by the riding gear.

"I'll be on my way now." And just as quickly and silently as she'd arrived, Sarah was gone.

Hugh fell to his knees, though. *How long had she been out there? Had she seen Joe leaving the stables right before she'd walked in on him half-dressed? Good God! Had she been out there the whole time and maybe seen Hugh come to the stables in the first place? Could she have heard anything? What did she know?* Hugh got no sleep that night as he imagined a thousand different terrors. If Sarah did know something and said anything to anyone, it would be catastrophic. The scandal alone would be ruinous, but the law could also become involved. Sodomy was illegal in England. Men were hanged for it. And even if the law didn't kill him, his father would.

Sometimes Hugh felt ready to shoot himself. More often, he felt he could have shot Sarah. *Goddamned little spy, snooping around on people.* For once, Alicia had been right about something. The governess was a problem, but if he were to ask his father or stepmother to send her away or dismiss her, they'd wonder why. Worse, if Miss Pole were dismissed, it might motivate her to spread her story to any and all who would listen, which left him in quite a fix. The person he now had most reason to fear and dislike was also the person he could least afford to offend. It was a problem that kept him awake at night.

When Sarah arrived back at the library, she found that Elinor and Violet had abandoned the atlas in favor of throwing pillows and cushions at one another. It was to their great disappointment that Sarah immediately ended the battle. They let out a flurry of groans.

"I seem to be spoiling everyone's fun today, aren't I?" Miss Pole muttered to herself. "Now, pick up these cushions and put them back where you found them."

"Can't we just let the servants take care of it?" pled Elinor.

"Not for this, we won't," Sarah commanded, sternly.

Grumbling all the while, Elinor and Violet tidied up.

"In the future, Violet," Sarah instructed, "be more mindful of where you leave your gloves. That goes for you, too, Elinor. Oh, and from now on, girls, whenever you're at the stables, you'd better knock first before you go inside."

This final commandment puzzled both children, but they didn't question their governess.

Sarah's Journal

I confess, I hadn't been surprised or shocked at the state I found Hugh in, but it was still all very awkward. He looked at me oddly after that. He both resented me and feared me. He feared that I would tell. I wasn't going to tell, of course. To whom could I possibly tattle to anyway? It was hardly like I was hosting any tea parties for the local gossips. But when I once tried to tell Hugh not to worry, his face turned red, and he seemed angrier than ever. Not only because I'd confirmed his worst fears, but perhaps because I'd had the effrontery to address him altogether. He had now been placed in the position of familiarity, and even vulnerability, to someone who was, in every possible way, his social inferior. I think he found it as infuriating as he did frightening. So it was without ever intending it that I had managed to make enemies of two out of three of the adult Mandeville children. I might well have found a way to alienate Charles, too, if he'd actually lived at home. Perhaps it was all for the best that I worked with children instead.

Sixteen

"The examination of the bodies of animals has always been my delight; and I have thought that we might hence not only obtain an insight into the mysteries of Nature, but there perceive a kind of image or reflex of the omnipotent Creator himself."
—William Harvey

One morning in August, much to his surprise, Dr. Healey was greeted at the door by Tom, a footman at Bromley Hall. The man was quite out of breath, and it took a few minutes for him to wheeze out that they needed the doctor at the house right away for Molly, who was in "horrible pain, sir. She's been wailin' for hours!"

He rode to the house as quickly as possible to be escorted by Mrs. Brown up a series of narrow staircases into the attic area where servants were housed. Molly, the red-haired young housemaid who had quailed at the sight of blood, was now in a wretched condition, huddled under a blanket and moaning.

"What is it, child? Where does it hurt?"

She didn't answer but rather pointed to her left leg. Robert moved the blanket as gently as he could. She wore only a thin, ragged shift but was far beyond any embarrassment or modesty. It was immediately apparent the source of her malady. Her left knee had swollen up with a reddish bulge roughly the size of an apple.

"It's prepatellar bursitis," Robert announced, though no one shared a knowing look with him at this diagnosis.

"What?" this came from Mrs. Brown.

George, who hadn't wanted to miss the show, furrowed his brow.

"Housemaid's knee," Robert clarified with the less technical, more colloquial term. "It's gotten beyond the point of just treating her with bedrest. I'll have to aspirate." From his medical bag, he pulled out a long silver needle. At the sight of it, Molly yelped like a struck puppy.

"Don't let him stick me with that! Don't! I can't bear the sight of blood!"

After much cajoling and coaxing, Robert managed to give Molly a dose of laudanum, which sent her straight to sleep.

"Do you need any assistance, Dr. Healey?" Sarah had arrived out of nowhere. She was standing in the doorway, framed by light.

"Why, yes, actually," he said, surprised but grateful. "First of all, we'll need something to drain the liquid into."

Sarah went out and came back momentarily with a large bowl and stayed to help. Mrs. Brown and George did not help, but stayed anyway.

"Now, hold that here and try to keep her knee nice and steady for me. That's it." Robert carefully punctured the bulging mass with the needle and then let the liquid and pus drain into the bowl. He then carefully cleaned the affected area and bandaged it before declaring himself satisfied with the procedure.

"It's all done now, Molly, you can open your eyes."

Molly had only started to stir a few moments ago, and now she slowly peeked at her leg. Seeing no visible signs of gore or amputation, she let out a deep sigh of relief.

"Keep her off her feet for a while," he instructed Mrs. Brown. "She should be fine."

"Quite an interesting instrument you used there, Dr. Healey," Sarah noted as she cleaned off the needle with a rag. She fondled it a bit before handing it back to him. "Where on Earth did you find it?"

"Oh, the needle? I got that in London along with everything else in my medical kit," Healey said, not paying much mind to the conversation as he sorted through his instruments.

"Of course. Would you like some tea, Dr. Healey?" Sarah asked.

"Why, yes, thank you. I'm parched."

They took tea in the little schoolroom while Elinor practiced on the pianoforte, and Violet was nose-deep in a book.

"You see this kind of bursitis all the time in maids," Robert explained to Sarah between sips while quietly wincing at the sounds of Elinor's playing. "It's all the kneeling to scrub floors. It's why they call it 'housemaid's knee.' So many diseases and conditions coincide with certain professions. Cotton mill workers get 'brown lung.' Chimney sweeps are susceptible to 'sooty warts.'"

"Sooty warts?" Sarah repeated.

"It is," he cleared his throat, "a cancer of the scrotum." He whispered this last word, lest it be heard by the children, and only after he spoke did it occur to him it wasn't necessarily appropriate to talk about with Sarah either. Fortunately, she seemed neither shocked nor offended at the word, and he continued.

"It's quite fascinating how much of medicine is related directly to a patient's status in society. Mr. Mandeville's affliction of gout is almost never seen among the lower classes since their diets aren't as rich, and green sickness among young women is almost always found among gentlewomen, though no one quite knows why. Laborers, though, are at far greater risk of hernias, and, of course, infections spread much more easily in city slums. Sailors get scurvy. Even diseases of the mind have biases towards certain classes."

"Really?" Sarah paused at that last bit of information.

"Oh yes," Robert nodded. "An old professor of mine who'd worked in a madhouse declared that the most common set of women there were former governesses." It was only after the words left his mouth that Robert remembered his audience and felt much abashed.

"Well," Sarah said, cool and smooth as butter, "that doesn't surprise me one bit."

Fortunately, at that moment, Elinor and Violet called for Sarah, thereby rescuing Dr. Healey in the process. But it wouldn't be the last time he'd find himself out of his depth with Bromley Hall's governess.

Another time, when Robert came to Bromley Hall to bleed Sir Thomas, he found himself outside afterward, walking with Sarah. It was by then the height of the harvest season, and all of Greenberry was working to get the precious corn in. Carpenters and tradesmen labored alongside farmers threshing fields, loading wagons, and driving the loaded wagons to the farmyard. Women and children worked alongside men. There was much competition among the children for who would get the honor of riding the harvest wagon. Indeed, it seemed the only people not in the Mandeville's fields at that particular moment were the Mandevilles themselves. Copious amounts of liquor were drunk directly in the fields, and workers sang of John Barleycorn and Jim, the carter lad.

"You know, Dr. Healey," Sarah began out of nowhere, "I can draw rather well."

"More than rather," he observed, knowingly. "I've seen your work. It is quite superior."

"Thank you," she gave an unexpected smile, which dramatically changed the entire countenance of her face, "but I was wondering if, by any chance, you might need some drawing done."

"Well, I'm flattered, but I don't know if I'd have the time to sit for a portrait."

"Oh no, I meant anatomical drawings. Related to procedures or surgeries of yours."

"You want to draw a surgery?" The suggestion was so shocking he felt sure he must have misunderstood her.

"Yes... or maybe the results of one. It seems such drawings are most useful in medical textbooks and to illustrate papers, and while I'm no Michelangelo, I feel I could be of service."

"Well, they are, but Miss Pole, you certainly can't mean to do so yourself?"

"Why ever not? I'm sure the Mandeville's might be willing to lend me to you on occasion if need be. In the name of science, of course, and I'm quite up to the task. You said yourself, I draw well, and you know I'm not squeamish." Her face was uncharacteristically animated and her tone so excited, Robert felt genuinely sorry to disappoint her.

"First of all, it's one thing to examine minor precise cuts and blood in a bowl, and another thing entirely to deal with the sight of human organs and mangled bodies. Secondly, Miss Pole, unlike you, I'm quite sure your employers would not agree to such a notion, but consider it completely inappropriate. Lastly, I'm not doing any autopsies or interesting vivisections here in Greenberry for which graphic illustrations would even be needed. I've been stitching up minor wounds, setting bones, pulling teeth, and doing a host of other things quite mundane, I assure you. If you really want to be an anatomical illustrator, you'd have to go to London or another big city with medical schools and anatomical theatres."

Sarah listened to all this very intently, then turned on her heel and stomped off, leaving Robert Healey to puzzle over the inscrutable nature of women, which has baffled many philosophers since the dawn of time. Male philosophers at least. Fortunately, at that moment, Alicia Mandeville happened to come along. In the delight of her company Miss Pole's odd behavior was quickly forgotten.

Sarah's Journal

Reflecting later on my conversation with Robert, I realize my anger at that time was completely irrational. Everything he said made perfect sense, and my idea had clearly been foolish. Nevertheless, the incident had irritated me beyond all reason. I had to find a solitary place behind the stables for a time to cry and rage and throw stones. Only by sticking my leg with a pin was I able to calm myself.

Later, I wondered at my reaction. Was it that grievous a loss not to be able to draw and paint severed limbs? I decided it wasn't. Oh, I was genuinely disappointed by losing the opportunity. I had wondered if the sight of other people's injuries might not act as a substitute for having to create any of my own, but that wasn't the foremost cause of my distress. I had been hoping to spend more time with Dr. Healey, and that was the even more grievous loss. But the greatest disappointment, I realized, much to my consternation, was that Dr. Healey had evinced no enthusiasm for a chance to spend more time with me! He had made it apparent that my particular company, while not objectionable and maybe even enjoyable, was hardly something he sought out, the way he so evidently did with Alicia. Despite the fact I'd known all along this was the case and known not to get my hopes up, the realization proved a bitter blow.

Seventeen

"It may be possible to do without dancing entirely. Instances have been known of young people passing many, many months successively without being at any ball of any description, and no material injury accrue either to body or mind."
–Jane Austen, *Emma*

It is an indisputable fact that any eligible young lady hoping to make a proper match must be presented into society. Alicia Mandeville was understandably very impatient to make her debut. She eagerly asked her father and stepmother if she could take the season in London.

"There's even a new academy for music, founded by the Earl of Westmoreland and Nicholas Boscha the harpist!" Alicia enthused. "Imagine!"

"But what does that have to do with you? You can't attend," Mrs. Mandeville reminded her.

Alicia flinched but recovered her aplomb, "But a new music academy means new musicians in London, and wonderful concerts! Besides, I'd like to be presented at court."

"At court? I don't know, my dear," said Thomas rubbing his chin. "Awful lot of trouble and expense to wear oneself out at balls, if you ask me."

"But that's what one does. Balls are how you meet people," Alicia whee-dled. "That is how a girl gets started in life. I never meet anyone here in the coun-try. I'm like Rapunzel."

"No one's locking you in a tower," Mrs. Mandeville pointed out.

"Might as well be! The country's just as bad," she shot back. "Father, please!"

"Yes, well... uh... I leave the matter in the hands of your stepmother," Thomas Mandeville beat a hasty retreat as Mrs. Mandeville addressed Alicia.

"Neither your father nor I have any wish to leave the country for London. So, who would be there to present you in any event?"

"Aunt Margaret! I always stay with her in London, anyway," Alicia pro-nounced.

"Hmmm," Mrs. Mandeville managed without words to give an eloquent speech of exactly what she thought of Margaret as a chaperone for a young heiress.

"It's not fair!" Alicia stamped her foot, losing her patience. "I'm shut away in the middle of nowhere! I'll never meet anyone this way!"

"Really? You've already made the acquaintance of quite a few people around Greenberry, I thought. The Ambroses, the Tudburys, Reverend Graham from church, even that clever young doctor," Mrs. Mandeville's tone was as dry as the desert.

Alicia went on as if she hadn't heard, "I'll never marry! I'll be an old maid!' She made an attempt at weeping that completely failed to move Mrs. Mandeville. She then turned angry once more.

"Oh, you old witch! You'd deny me even the joys of dancing?"

"Actually, you shall have a great many opportunities to dance at the ball."

"Ball? What ball?"

"Your father and I have discussed the matter and we feel it would be opportune to hold a ball in your honor here at Bromley Hall where we would, of course, invite every family of quality for twenty miles. We feel that would give you sufficient opportunity to shine in your natural element." *And where we can keep an eye on you,* Mrs. Mandeville mentally added.

"Well, why didn't you just say so from the beginning?" Alicia's entire mood and countenance had underwent a complete change.

"You didn't give me the chance," Mrs. Mandeville pointed out with nar-

rowed eyes.

"When will the ball be held?"

"We've planned it for the middle of October."

October was always a socially prominent month in the country, that being when pheasant shooting and fox hunting seasons began and just before the advent for the darker days of the year and winter season.

"But's that so soon! I must go into town to shop. I need a brand new gown, and shoes, and a fan, and jewelry... and I must practice my dancing," Alicia was aflutter with plans and preparations.

Soon, the entire house was in an uproar. Hugh Mandeville graciously took his sister to London for a day or two of shopping, not only for her wardrobe but to augment his. While there, musicians were hired as well. The entire servant staff worked day and night to make the whole house shine. Mrs. Brown, the chief administrator for the grand event, planned things out with the same thoroughness and attention to detail of the Duke of Wellington in his command tent the night before Waterloo. Unexpectedly, Charles Mandeville sent word that he planned to attend as well. Even Elinor and Violet, who were of course far too young to attend, were nevertheless excited. Their mama and Sarah agreed to let them see the rooms made up for the ball, and they could watch from the stairs as the guests arrived.

"What dress will you wear?" Violet asked Sarah.

"Probably the same sort of dress I'm wearing now. Maybe it will even be the same dress," Sarah answered.

"How do you mean to go dancing dressed like that?" Elinor was quite affronted.

"I won't be dancing."

"You won't be dancing at the ball?" Elinor was stunned.

"No, I won't," Sarah confirmed. "I won't even meet the guests at all. Governesses don't attend balls, girls. Neither do crows, and you know I'm one of both," Sarah cawed and flapped her arms. Violet laughed, but Elinor's face was grave.

"But everyone else will be going, and if you don't... oh, that's so sad!"

"No, it's not. I'll still see the rooms and watch the guests arrive with you, and I'll still be able to hear the music," Sarah reassured them.

"But you won't be able to dance!" Elinor plainly considered this a grave injustice.

"Dancing's not for everyone, my dear."

"But how will you ever find a husband?" Elinor blurted out. "A girl has to go to balls so she can find a good husband. Everybody knows that."

"Yes, well, I don't think I will ever have a husband," Sarah told her gently. Both girls gasped.

"You'll be an old maid?" Violet whispered.

"No, I'll be an old governess."

Both girls looked puzzled.

"Don't worry, it's not the same for me as it is for you. The thing about being a crow, children, is that no one expects you to marry."

Elinor and Violet took in these facts with pensive expressions. "Does that mean we might be old maids someday?" Elinor finally asked with a tremor in her voice.

"No," Sarah answered plainly. "For one thing, you're not crows. Furthermore, your mama would never allow it to happen. No, she'll find husbands for you both, if she has to scour the whole of England for them."

At that, the girls smiled in relief.

Finally, the evening of the ball arrived. Excitement had spread beyond Bromley Hall, throughout the county, where it was confidently expected that the Mandeville ball would be the social event of the season. Thanks to Mrs. Brown's tireless efforts, the rooms looked fit for a palace. It seemed as if every candle in England had been commandeered to provide illumination for the evening. Carpets and drapes were all freshly cleaned, and the floors had been scrubbed so hard they shone. Vases were filled with late-blooming aster flowers. Elinor, Violet, and Sarah took their seats on a dark corner of the stairs where they found themselves joined by Mrs. Brown and Molly. When the music played, each woman's foot unconsciously tapped out a tune of its own along the wood and carpet on the floor.

Among the first to arrive were Mrs. Ambrose and her daughter, Venetia. The latter looking quite charming in a true Indian muslin with blue embroidery. They were joined by Reverend Graham who evidently did not consider it unbecoming for a clergyman to attend. The Tudbury's arrived soon afterward. Alas, neither the expense of Maria Tudbury's dress nor the weight or shine of her jewels could hide the jaundiced coloring of her skin or improve the state of her chin. Nor could any tailor disguise George Tudbury's ape-like visage, though, admittedly, beauty is of much less consequence for men. More guests followed, including a pack of redcoats from the local garrison. Charles Mandeville paid attention to Venetia Ambrose while Hugh was nowhere in sight.

Finally, after the stage had been properly set, Alicia Mandeville made her entrance wearing a silver silk gown whose pattern swept the floor and shined like the moon. She was as beautiful as the evening star and effortlessly outshined every other girl in the room. There was much teeth-grinding among the young women that night, and among their mothers as well. Alicia had no difficulty filling her dance card and was very nearly the cause of a violent quarrel among two of the officers.

Several of the male guests were ungracious and ungenerous enough to decline dancing altogether, and instead adjourned to a nearby smoking room for a game of Whist. Thomas Mandeville was part of this group and was enjoying brandy and a cigar only to be irritated when Hugh joined their numbers. Despite his father's not-so-veiled hints, and even near orders, Hugh stubbornly refused to go to the ballroom to dance. Instead, he became embroiled in a lively discussion with some of the officers about the old boxing club at Eton.

"Alicia looks like Cinderella, doesn't she?" Violet sighed.

Alicia, having completed one dance with Reverend Graham, was immediately snatched up by his cousin, George Tudbury.

"It is not the best of comparisons. I doubt your sister has ever slept in the attic or swept a floor in her life," Sarah noted dryly as music filled the air.

"Isn't that Dr. Healey?" Elinor pointed.

"It is. Why, I didn't know he'd be attending," Sarah said slowly. Robert had not, in fact, been sure himself he'd be coming. Yes, he had been invited, but, as a dancer, he had always felt awkward. His elbows and feet seemed to fly everywhere. Eventually, he had concluded that, just as with attendance at church, it was important that he be seen at what promised to be the social event of the season in Greenberry. Alicia's presence would just be an added bonus. At least that was what he told himself, as he gazed upon her that night. When she saw him, she seemed to smile, though he could not be sure. Perhaps it was his imagination, *but did her eyes light up for an instant before looking away coyly?* When she finished her dance with George Tudbury, Healey nearly knocked over Mrs. Ambrose to reach Alicia. He wasn't sure he was even speaking properly or that he'd gotten the words out right. But no, Alicia curtsied and gave him her hand to let him lead her to the floor. Robert Healey felt like he'd been carried off to Heaven itself. Elbows be damned!

"Well now, girls," Sarah said, watching from the stairs, "it's high time you went to bed."

"Awww," groaned Elinor, Violet, and Molly in unison.

"I didn't mean you, Molly," Sarah clarified with a smile.

"Actually, she and I should be off ourselves. We have to work tomorrow," Mrs. Brown proclaimed, and they all retired for the evening.

Meanwhile, Alicia Mandeville was only getting started. All too soon, the music finally stopped. Robert asked Alicia to take the next dance with him. She refused, coyly shaking her head.

"I'm sorry, but I promised Captain Fields a turn, and I dare not put him off any longer. And there are others from the garrison as well who will expect a turn," Alicia gave an apologetic smile, and Robert found himself wanting to thrash every redcoat in the room.

"Besides, Dr. Healey," she added, "you know as well as I that it's inappropriate for a girl to dance twice in a row with the same partner." She lowered her voice to a whisper, "No matter how charming that particular partner may be."

Robert felt like his chest might burst. "By the way," he asked suddenly, looking around for a slight, dark-haired figure when he was struck with the sudden lack of her presence, "where's Miss Pole?"

"Miss Pole?" Alicia could not have been more surprised if he had asked about the attendance of a horse at the ball. "Miss Pole is not attending," she said slowly and patiently, as if addressing a simple child.

"Oh, yes," Robert felt an inexplicable pang of disappointment, "I suppose

Miss Pole doesn't dance, does she?"

"I'm sure I wouldn't know," Alicia countered before joining the handsome Captain Fields. Alicia was then monopolized by other partners for the rest of the evening, and while Robert did his duty by dancing with other girls for a time, he left early, feeling vaguely dissatisfied with the whole proceeding.

Sarah's Journal

I still heard the music that night, even in my room so far away. It really was quite lovely. You read so much of balls in books. Indeed, Miss Austen seemed positively obsessed with them. Truth be told, balls had always sounded rather dull to me. I'd never even bothered to learn dancing since I almost certainly would never have any opportunities, but that night, hearing the music and seeing the other young ladies arrive in their gowns, I found myself regretting. I couldn't help but wonder if it wouldn't have been rather pleasant to have at least had the chance to be bored by it all. Or maybe not bored at all? To be led onto the floor, especially if Robert had asked me... what would it be like to be, well, Alicia?

I slapped myself in the face several times for my own stupidity. Had I had a fire in my room, I might have stuck a hand or foot in it. As it was, I once again turned to my beloved pouch. It was only after jabbing myself hard in the foot with one of Mrs. Mandeville's embroidery needles that I was able to calm myself to sleep.

Eighteen

*"The man who reads nothing at all is better educated
than the man who reads nothing but newspapers."*
–Thomas Jefferson

"Dr. Healey certainly comes over a lot, doesn't he?" Violet observed one rainy day in the schoolroom as they practiced sums.

"Well, your father needs him," said Sarah. "Gout is a most painful condition, and then he came to treat poor Molly, too.'

"Maybe he comes here for Alicia, too," Elinor said slyly.

"Maybe he does," Sarah said, her lips suddenly tightening.

"He certainly was quick to ask her to dance. And I heard Mrs. Brown telling the other servants that every man who sees Alicia falls in love with her. That when she marries, she'll break a thousand hearts. If she ever marries. Mama thinks she likes flirting too much," Elinor went on.

"But she has to marry!" Violet replied incredulously. "All girls have to marry, or they become old maids!" She whispered the last two words as if they were some naughty curse term. "And old maids are always poor and wretched, you know."

"Are they now?' Sarah asked so quietly neither girl heard her.

"Alicia wouldn't be poor. She has twenty-thousand pounds," Elinor pointed out.

"That gives her an income of what? A thousand pounds a year? Well! No wonder she's in no hurry to marry if she's so rich anyway. Your sister could stay single and live very comfortably," Sarah could not entirely keep a note of envy out of her voice.

"But of course Alicia will marry. Mama thinks she'll marry very well. She says it's rather unfair that Alicia is so beautiful and rich when other girls have nothing at all going for them," Elinor repeated.

"You know, the rain's let up now. I think we should go out and walk," Sarah announced suddenly, putting down the slate she'd been holding.

"But won't it still be wet out?" Elinor asked.

"Oh, we don't mind getting wet, do we?" Sarah teased cheerfully.

"I do," said Elinor.

"Me too," added Violet.

"Oh, fuss and bother. You'll love it once you're out there! Come on, let's go. If I spend another minute inside, I think I'll suffocate," Sarah said that last part with curious vehemence.

Soon, they were trudging outdoors. It was wet, after all. And muddy. And cold. And grey. What else could you expect in November? Yet, Sarah insisted on walking and kept up a very brisk pace that was tantamount to an army on the march.

"I'm tired," Violet announced after a while. "I want to go home."

"Just a little farther," Sarah said, energetically. "We're just starting to get the blood moving."

"I want to go home now!" Violet's lips were pouty, and her eyes narrowed.

"I want to, too!" Elinor poked her chin out and glared. Sarah realized she was outnumbered two-to-one and was about to concede defeat when they heard hooves. Up ahead, along the main road to Greenberry, was a stage coach. Driven by a damp, miserable, and irritable-looking driver, yelling at wet, tired-looking horses, with one lone passenger hunched up on top. Usually, the top of a coach would be crowded with passengers hoping to save money, but thanks to the wretched weather, this particular traveler had the entirety of the top to himself. His figure and features were obscured by a large black coat and large black hat. He kept peering around in all directions, like an owl on a treetop, scanning for mice, or perhaps even like a crow.

"They should look out," a wide-eyed Elinor began. "They're about to run into that big–"

Suddenly, the coach made an abrupt descent and rocky lurch that sent the sole rider on top careening headfirst into a puddle of mud.

"–hole," she finished. Sarah and both girls ran to the scene. The coach driver was cursing up a storm while the other passengers, who had come out to see why they'd stopped, gaped at the scene before them. Sarah reached the man covered in mud and tried pulling him up. He groaned loudly.

"Elinor! Violet! Run back to the house right now and tell them to call Dr. Healey and bring a stretcher right away! This man needs help."

The next hour was spent waiting in the muddy road for help to arrive. The coach driver cursed the interruption to his schedule and worried about lawsuits while waiting for help to arrive. The other passengers gawked and did nothing helpful while loudly decrying the inconvenience and delay. Finally, several of the stable boys, led by Joe, came along with a broken-down old door, which they used to carry the muddy man and what was identified as his bag back to Bromley Hall. Robert Healey soon arrived and did a thorough examination.

"He's got a minor concussion," Dr. Healey declared. "He'll live, but he has to stay on bed rest for now, and on no account can he be moved."

This proclamation was not received with universal joy by Mrs. Mandeville. Unexpected houseguests are an inconvenience, even under the best of circumstances, but invalids who rode on the tops of a public coach to save money were not the sort of people the Mandevilles would ever normally associate with. As long as the stranger in question didn't turn out to be a brigand or a highwayman, little harm could come from his convalescence. Nevertheless, Mrs. Mandeville couldn't restrain herself from the un-Christian thought that the man could just as easily have taken his tumble in the middle of Greenberry itself, preferably in front of The Spotted Cow. He'd probably have been happier at the tavern anyway.

"I'll come by daily to check on his progress," Dr. Healey told Mrs. Mandeville. "In the meantime, may I suggest having Miss Pole take on the charge of nursemaid? She's been very helpful with Mr. Mandeville's bleedings and assisted in my operation with Molly."

This idea, Mrs. Mandeville agreed to more cheerfully. She knew that neither she nor Alicia were up to the job, and the regular servants were a bit shorthanded at the moment. Just the day before, Mrs. Brown had to dismiss that one girl, Annie, for being with child. Mrs. Brown was already making inquiries for a replacement, but that would take time. Violet and Elinor could spare their instructress for a few days. No doubt they would find ways of amusing themselves, possibly at the expense or inconvenience of the servants, but they'd survive.

So when the muddy man – by now bathed and cleaned with help from Mrs. Brown – woke up, it was Sarah who he addressed first.

"What in the blazes–" he began, eyes frantically flitting around the strange room. The brocade curtains instilled in him an instinctive distrust. "How the devil did I get in here?"

Sarah guessed his age to be about thirty. He was a swarthy man with the sort of short, stocky build that runs to portliness in middle age. His most prominent characteristic were wild, wide, protruding green eyes. He seemed to look in all directions at once before finally settling on Sarah.

"Who the devil are you?" he demanded. His voice and manner marked him as a Yorkshireman. Sarah explained the situation calmly before finally enquiring as politely as possible who she was.

Rufus Clarkson claimed he had important business waiting back in London and needed to leave immediately.

"Dr. Healey said you needed your rest and that you were not to be moved," Sarah told him, somewhat apologetically.

"Oh, I'll be bloody fine," he replied crossly as he tried to sit up. "Just let me get my beari.. ng... sss..." he suddenly swayed, and his head hit the pillow. There was no damage done, so Sarah let him sleep.

A few hours later, he woke up once more. This time, he stayed conscious long enough to consume some tea and broth before returning to sleep. By the next day, he could sit up on his own, and by the third, he was impatiently demanding to be let out rather than "kept captive here like a prisoner in a tower."

"I'll be damned," he started. "My flask? Where the devil's my flask? What have you done with it?" He glared at Sarah suspiciously.

"There was no flask found with you," Sarah replied coolly. "You probably left it on the coach or dropped it in the road when you had your tumble."

"Hmmphh! Likely story. I'll bet the coach driver nicked it. Or one of the servants."

"They haven't even been in the room. You've had no contact with the servants since they took the trouble of carrying you in here," Sarah pointed out.

"I'll bet one of them grabbed it then," he muttered. "Dark days we're living in when folks use a man's injuries to help themselves to his goods!"

"Well, Dr. Healey said you could have a little brandy once you got up. You can stay right here, and I'll fetch it," Sarah quickly returned with a decanter.

After helping himself to a generous dose, Mr. Clarkson became more amiable and pronounced Sarah to be "a good one." He wasn't as approving of his actual hosts. After being briefly introduced to the whole family, he later pronounced Thomas Mandeville to be "a gouty old crab," Hugh Mandeville an "utter coxcomb," and Mrs. Mandeville a "social-climbing parvenu." As for Alicia, he granted she was "quite an armful," but "watch out for the claws."

"First of all, you've hardly had enough time to get acquainted with them," Sarah pointed out.

"Don't need more time to judge them. Benefits of my profession. You learn to take the measure of people right away."

"Then perhaps you should consider the type of first impression you make on people as well."

Mr. Clarkson snorted at that, and Sarah continued, "It's impolite and ungrateful to speak so disrespectfully of people who are putting you up like this. Unwise, as well, since they could throw you out at any time."

"Doesn't make it any less true, though, does it?" he retorted. "Come on, now. You're no fool. Are you really telling me you've never thought the same?"

Sarah chose her words carefully, "They're my employers. I depend on them for everything, and all things considered, they've been very good to me."

"That wasn't a no," Clarkson noted. "Besides, how good can they can be?

I've seen both the young man and the girl giving you the evil eye. What's all that about?"

"I'm not entirely sure myself," Sarah confessed, "but I think it distresses them that I don't make more noise when I walk."

"You're joking!" Clarkson guffawed.

"Oh no, I'm quite serious. It has been a cause of frustration for both Alicia and Hugh that I walk silently," Sarah gave a half laugh. "Which is strange because, generally, I'm not supposed to be noticed at all."

Mr. Clarkson gave another hearty snort before asking, "When's that bloody Irish doctor coming back?"

"It's all looking good," Robert Healey pronounced after his visit when his patient had suspiciously demanded a full accounting of his credentials before begrudgingly deciding Robert "would do." He still insisted on questioning his doctor's advice on everything. Robert reflected, not for the first time, how much easier patients were to get on with when they were insensible.

After leaving the patient, Dr. Healey turned to Sarah, "He doesn't seem to have suffered any permanent damage, and he's healing nicely. I'd say it'd be safe to let him go by the end of the week. By the way, Miss Pole, you've been an absolute marvel through all this. Mr. Clarkson is, uh, not exactly the easiest of individuals to treat. In fact, I would say he's definitely of the choleric temperament, to an alarming degree, but you've borne him quite patiently." Dr. Healey gave a genuine admiration.

Sarah blushed, and Dr. Healey thought it became her. She murmured a "Thank you," before wryly adding, "though he's not so bad really. His conversation's been quite entertaining. He's a reporter in London for The Charing Cross Courier."

"A newspaperman, really?" Robert was surprised and not a little bemused. Judging from the tips of a smile at her lips, so was Sarah.

"Yes, indeed. It seems he was attending the assizes circuit in a nearby Cathedral town, to 'make copy.' He was quite annoyed to learn that by the time he gets home it'll all be old news, and so he has to find something new. He's been asking a lot of questions about Greenberry in hopes there might be some noteworthy items he could cover here."

"Well, I'm afraid he's bound to be disappointed on that score. We're a distressingly dull little town here. The only bloodshed to cover is that all the farmers are now slaughtering their pigs and sheep."

"I don't know. He seems quite determined that there must be some scandal or tale of public interest to be found if one only knows how to look. He claims great country houses are hotbeds of vice and secrecy."

"He's looking for a news story here? In Bromley Hall itself? The man's read far too many gothic novels," Robert snorted. Sarah didn't mind the sound.

"Well, one never knows where a buried skeleton might turn up. Unfortunately for Mr. Clarkson's aspirations, he won't have a chance to mount any sort of excavation here. The Mandevilles want him gone the moment he's well enough to travel. I think they consider having a London reporter on the premises worse than hosting a pickpocket," Sarah mused.

"Well, at least pickpockets have the decency not to slander you in print," Robert noted.

"In any event, he definitely plans on writing a sharply-worded editorial about the dire and dangerous state of England's country roads as a matter to which parliament should attend," Sarah's tone was serious, though a keen observer might have noticed a slight twitch in her mouth as she relayed all this.

"Well, he's the one who chose to ride on top the coach," Robert pointed out, "and the price of that economizing is a greater risk."

"He says that was motivated less by cost and more because riding inside made him feel ill, which is certainly understandable," Sarah remembered the green-looking man who'd been in the coach with her on the ride to Bromley Hall, and her own nausea as well.

"Even in the rain?"

"The rain had ended by the time he chose to ride on top," Sarah explained. "Besides, according to Mr. Clarkson, everyone should travel about and see some of the country! Just without breaking their crowns, of course."

"You two have certainly been conversing quite a bit," Robert felt rather put-out by the apparent familiarity between Sarah and Mr. Clarkson without exactly knowing why. Sarah shrugged.

"He has no one else with whom to talk, and he's loquacious by nature. I confess, it's rather refreshing. He's been a good subject to draw at any rate. His face is filled with character."

When Sarah presented Mr. Clarkson with his likeness in her sketchpad, he seemed quite pleased.

"Well," he began, "you could have made me better looking, but it's accurate at least. Don't know if I'm naturally such a fierce looking fellow, though."

"You are," Sarah stated flatly, and he gave her a keen look as he continued to flip through the drawings. "Did you do all these?"

"Yes."

"Well, for a young girl such as yourself, they're not bad."

Sarah marveled a bit at being called a "young girl." Since she'd arrived at Bromley Hall, everyone seemed to consider her somehow prematurely aged, and possibly sexless as well.

"Not bad at all. Pity you're not in London, lass. We could use an illustrator like you at the Courier. Don't suppose you know how to do wood etchings or lithography by any chance?"

"Sadly, I've never learned either trade."

"Too bad. Still, look me up in London anyway."

"If I ever go to London, I most certainly will. Though I doubt it will ever happen, unless the Mandevilles should take up residence there."

Mr. Clarkson gave her a curious look, "Do you ever think you might not be with the Mandevilles forever?"

"Of course, I do. When Elinor and Violet are grown, they won't need me, and who knows who my next employer will be?"

"What I mean to say is, do you never think of being something other than a governess?"

"What else could I be?"

"Plenty of work to be found in London, young lady, for a girl with your skillsets."

"What skillsets?"

"Your drawings! Awful lot of folks who want their portraits done. People want little landscapes to hang on the wall. Painted miniatures are especially popular right now."

"But I'm a woman!"

"So what? Plenty of women artists in London. Don't see why you couldn't be one, too."

Sarah stayed silent for a time, and then finally spoke. "It's very flattering, sir, that you think I could make a living from my pad, but I'm afraid I'm penniless, and to give up a paid position and comfortable home to try and earn my keep as an artist, of all things, in London, of all places, well... it would be madness," Sarah concluded as she mostly succeeded in keeping the regret from her voice. Mostly.

Clarkson gave a shrewd nod, "The world is changing, Miss Pole. You've heard about the HMS Comet, haven't you?"

"A steamboat, I believe."

"Not just a steamboat. The first steamboat ever to be commissioned by the Royal Navy, and now it sits in Deptford Dockyard by the Thames, and it's just the beginning. Mark my words, someday steam-powered boats will be everywhere. And who knows what other things as well? Soon, it might be possible to travel the length and breadth of England with steam-powered engines in a fraction of the time it takes to ride by carriage."

"Really?" Sarah managed to pack a great deal of skepticism into one word.

"It's true!" Clarkson maintained. "Technology's advancing rapidly, and the world is about to change with it. You don't want to be left behind, out in the bloody country, when it does. Just keep what I said in mind, girl. And remember, the Courier, Miss Pole, for all your news."

Mr. Clarkson departed on another stagecoach the following day – this time, seated inside – much to the satisfaction of the Mandevilles and the Servant's Hall, which had resented having to care for a "guest" unlikely to reward them for their service. This departure was also somewhat to the relief of Dr. Healey as well, although he didn't precisely know why.

The staffing problem was solved too—and oddly enough, it was Sarah who'd managed the task. It was on her recommendation that the older Riggs girl, Meg, was brought in to help in the kitchens and given Annie's old quarters.

Sarah's Journal

I was probably the only person in the house to miss Mr. Clarkson after he'd gone. It wasn't that he made much of an effort to be amiable, but he was the only adult living in the house who spoke to me with any familiarity. And while Mr. Clarkson wasn't the most genteel of company, he certainly made for lively and amusing conversation. Indeed, he rather reminded me of Geraldine. Bromley Hall, with his presence, felt as if windows in musty rooms had suddenly been opened up to let in fresh air.

He had an interesting life story as well. His father had been a butcher in Sheffield, and he'd attended a charity school before being apprenticed to a printer. Upon completing his apprenticeship, he'd made his way to London to work as a print boy at the *Courier*. One day, he'd been asked to fill in for an absent reporter in covering events at Chancery, and as Mr. Clarkson put it, "That was the day I found my true calling." It seemed rather a grandiose statement to me, but I suppose that's only to be expected from a newspaperman.

Something curious happened, too, while Mr. Clarkson had been with us. Dr. Healey seemed to show signs of being jealous of Mr. Clarkson on my account! It was, I knew, an absolutely preposterous idea, but it thrilled me nonetheless.

After all, as they say, where there's jealousy, there's hope.

Nineteen

"Blow, blow, thou winter wind,
Thou art not so unkind
As man's ingratitude;"
−William Shakespeare, *As You Like It*

"What are you reading, Miss Pole?"

It was the first week of December. Signor Vincetti had finished another lesson of letting the girl's pound the keys. Sarah had now put them to work writing out letters to their mama in French. She had her beak thoroughly lodged in a paper.

"The Charing Cross Courier. It's the paper for which Mr. Clarkson writes. I had George fetch me a copy while he was in town."

"We can see you're reading the paper, Miss Pole," Violet rolled her eyes, "but what are you reading in the paper? Any good stories?"

"I heard Father call the paper a blasted, bloody rag," Elinor chimed in.

"Your father has a point," Sarah proclaimed. "It's a lot of political grandstanding over the state of parliament."

"Oh," said Elinor, disappointed. Neither she nor Violet could imagine why anyone would want to read about something so dull as parliament.

"It also offers a lot of very lurid sensationalism. Admittedly, sensationalism written with a certain wit and panache, but sensationalism nonetheless."

"What's sensationalism?" asked Violet.

"Detailed, gossipy stories about scandals and crimes. Some very nasty crimes, in fact."

"Like what?" said both girls, who looked on eagerly.

"Were there any murders, at least?" Elinor pleaded.

"Horrid ones?" Violet was practically panting with excitement. "Like beheadings?"

"Like the sort of things your mama would not approve of me telling you about," Sarah closed the paper as her charges looked on with pained expressions. Surely she could have indulged them with at least one little bludgeoning or shooting, but no, Sarah was utterly heartless and even burned the paper in the fireplace, thereby depriving the girls of any opportunity to inspect its contents.

"Look, it's snowing!" Elinor pointed to the window.

They all crowded in by the glass to see the first few white flakes lazily begin to fall. By the next morning, the grounds lay covered in white powder. Icicles transformed Bromley Hall into an ice palace. Trees that had seemed so bare and dead before without their leaves now took on glorious coats of white. The great yew in front of the church looked as if it had been powdered with copious amounts of sugar. The church itself was soon adorned with bay leaves and holly.

As is often the case, the approach of Christmas meant an increase in the number of parties and dinners thrown around Greenberry. It also meant Sarah, trundled up in a wool scarf and gloves, was sent on another round of "charitable visits" to cottagers. Jem Howe cordially greeted Sarah with a jug in hand, insisting she take a swig and then join him in singing "The Boar's Head." While Jem did not have perhaps the most refined of voices or any sense of melody or pitch, he certainly could not be faulted for lack of enthusiasm. As he sang out "Reddens Laudens Domino," his voice seemed to carry for miles. Indeed, one of the neighbors responded with a shout of, "Quiet down, you old drunk, or it'll be my fist down your throat!"

"Boil your head!" was Jem's retort. "Do you want me to come over and

put my boot up your arse?"

Sarah bid farewell as politely as she could before a feud broke out.

Nellie Bloom still kept Gertie the goose in her cabin and had even extended her hospitality to Wilbur, a handsome mallard duck as well. "Wilbur was hurt, you see. Busted wing. So, he never flew south with the rest of the flock. I just couldn't leave him to freeze, now could I?" Nellie implored.

"Of course not," Sarah agreed and patted Wilbur gently on his soft feathered head. "Is that pile of rags in the corner for him?"

"Aye, ma'am. I'd let him sleep him in bed, but Gertie gets a bit jealous and pecks at him, so I had to make him his own nest."

"I'm sure with time they'll learn to get along," Sarah stated, keeping her voice perfectly serious and neutral. Privately, she wondered if Wilbur might not be a guest at the next May Day celebration and wear a handmade suit as well.

The Riggs household was not so amusing. While Adam and his sisters had been able to find plenty of work during the summer and early months of autumn with the harvest season, winter had brought an end to their labor. Having Meg now working in the kitchens at Bromley Hall had relieved the burdens somewhat, but it still promised to be a hard winter. Everyone in the cottage seemed to have a hungry glint in their eye. Mrs. Riggs's abject gratitude at the sight of Sarah's basket was pitiful.

"How are you doing on fuel for the fire?" Sarah quietly pulled Polly aside to ask her.

"We're all right. Ma and I go out nearly every day to gather wood, except when it's too cold or the snow's too high, of course."

"I can have Thomas bring you a few extra loads of firewood. But wait, you and your mother gather firewood. What about your brother, Adam?"

"He's busy getting food, ma'am."

"Food? How? There's nothing growing now, and little work to be had," Sarah spoke sharply.

"Polly!" Mrs. Riggs called. "Don't talk Miss Pole's ear off."

"I'm not supposed to talk about it," Polly whispered before running to her mother's side. Sarah walked back to Bromley Hall feeling troubled, despite the holiday cheer. The great house was now decorated with strands of holly, gold and silver paper. Charles Mandeville came home for the holidays in an excellent humor. He'd been lucky so far on the district circle and had already picked up a few cases. Even better, he had collected some fees.

A massive yule log cut from an oak tree was brought in by a team of farmhands. It was anointed with wine, salt, and oil by Thomas Mandeville with great solemnity on Christmas Eve. Fueled by splinters from the past yule log, it blazed splendidly through the next afternoon as the whole hall filled with the smells of goose, minced pies, and plum pudding. But to the horror of Mrs. Brown, at one point, the fire in the hearth temporarily died out. She immediately called for George to restart the flame.

"That's bad luck, that is, having the yule fire go out. Heard it means you can expect a death in the house or on the grounds in the next year," George opined.

"Oh quiet, you, and don't go spreading that nonsense around," Mrs. Brown scolded him. Privately, though, she felt uneasy.

Fortunately, none of the Mandevilles themselves heard about the incident and were free from any foolish superstitious fears. They had other things on their mind. The day after Christmas, known as St. Stephen's Day, was one of foxhunting by the household gentlemen for which they had big plans. Twelfth Night would see the traditional fancy dress at Gaskell Park for which Mrs. Mandeville and Alicia had big plans. Indeed, Alicia had already decided she should have George Tudbury's proposal and be married no later than Easter.

The Mandeville women handed out Christmas boxes of old, used clothes to the servants and staff. Mrs. Brown was pleased to get a shawl from Mrs. Mandeville. Molly was over the moon at being bequeathed some of Alicia's old ribbons and a bonnet. George got an old pipe of Thomas Mandeville's. Since Sarah was not titled a servant, she did not get a Christmas box of her own, though she did present Elinor and Violet with a portrait of Father Christmas, complete with a snowy white beard and wearing a crown of holly.

"Miss Pole?" Molly approached her quietly. "Miss Pole? There's a gentleman here to see you."

"What?"

"Dr. Healey, ma'am. He's waiting outside in the hall. He came to call upon all the house, but he wants to talk to you in particular." Molly was quite pleased to relay this information and had the satisfaction of seeing Sarah's cheeks suddenly flush. This would be something new to discuss at the Servant's Hall.

"Merry Christmas, Miss Pole." Dr. Healey's nose may have been a tad red, but his smile couldn't have been broader, and he held out a lumpy package wrapped in brown paper.

"Is that that for me?" Sarah asked dumbfounded.

"Yes, it is," Dr. Healey laughed. "It's not really so surprising to get a present on Christmas Day, is it?"

She took the package gently from his hands, as if afraid she might damage it.

"But, I haven't anything to give you," she protested, quite dismayed.

Dr. Healey shrugged, "You've done enough already, helping me all this time with bleedings, and particularly with Mr. Clarkson. I just wanted to show my gratitude."

"Oh," said Sarah. She hugged the package to her chest.

"Aren't you going to open it?"

She did so and found, to her wonderment, a set of paint brushes clearly designed for fine and delicate strokes.

"Do you like them?" Robert asked anxiously before she'd even been able to get a good look at them. "I picked them out in London when I went down to replenish my kit. The man at the shop assured me they were the best quality, but I wouldn't know the difference."

When in London, Robert had entered a store with thought of getting a present for Alicia, but then realized to his vexation there was nothing in his means to buy her that she wouldn't already have only better. Then, somehow, his thoughts had turned to the peculiar Miss Pole. Miss Pole, who had almost nothing and who might not receive any presents at all. She had been most helpful with Mr. Clarkson and with Mr. Mandeville's bleedings, had she not? It would not, perhaps, be untoward to give her a gift simply to show his appreciation in the spirit of friendship, would it? And quite on impulse, he had purchased the brushes.

"Dr. Healey." Robert was shocked to see Sarah looked almost on the verge of tears. "Dr. Healey, this is the most wonderful, most generous gift anyone has ever me given me."

"Oh, well," Robert felt awkward. "It really isn't that much."

"You must let me do your portrait sometime. That will be my gift to you. A miniature perhaps. These brushes were made for that purpose. Watercolor won't take too long, I promise."

"All right. We'll find a time, and I'll model for you," he conceded. The smile Sarah gave in return was, Robert felt, all the Christmas present he'd ever need.

Sarah's Journal

It wasn't that the gift of the brushes won my heart. For I think, in all truthfulness, my heart had already been won long before. It was more that it fully revealed to me the own state of my feelings, which even as I'd grappled with, I'd never dared to say the words out loud to myself. I had admitted to a partiality to his company, to wanting to spend more time with him, even to hating Alicia for having his attention, but I'd never actually dared to speak the words to myself…

I love Robert Healey.

I love Robert. It was such a simple and yet such an Earth-shattering revelation that I didn't know what to make of it. Before him, I hadn't even considered the possibility I could fall in love.

But I had. I had, indeed, and while on the surface nothing had changed, on another level, everything had. Candles seemed to flicker more brightly, colors become more vibrant, music sweeter, and air fresher. Then, in the dead of winter, it seemed like there was now new life.

And then, of course, it all went to hell.

Twenty

"In the stars is written the death of every man."
–Geoffrey Chaucer

There was nothing remarkable about that day. Nothing inauspicious, like the sight of a black cat or spilled salt; nothing that gave any indication of coming doom. In fact, if anything, it promised to be a day of good winter cheer. The air was cold but not bitter. There was no wind. The sun was shining, which is why Miss Pole took Elinor and Violet out for a nice long morning stroll. Their boots tramped in the snow, making nice crunchy noises. The girls were rosy-cheeked and giggling as they clambered along one of their favorite hills right outside the winds. A snowball hit Sarah on the back of her shoulder, and she turned around.

"All right, which of you threw that?"

Elinor promptly pointed to Violet, and Violet to Elinor, but suddenly a sound came to them on the air—a low, wailing sound.

"What is that?" Sarah asked.

"The wind?" Elinor answered.

"No. Be quiet for a moment."

They were silent, and then the wailing was there again. A phantom carried on the wind. Sarah shivered, and it wasn't from the cold.

"It's coming from the woods. Maybe an animal that's hurt?" Violet suggested.

"Maybe... I'll go and see. Both of you wait here."

"Can't we come with you?" Elinor implored.

"No," Sarah's voice was like a sharp knife. "Both of you stay right where you are. Do you understand me?"

The girls, alarmed by her tone, silently nodded. Sarah walked as briskly as she could through the snow without worrying the girls further. Fir branches slapped at her head, throwing snow all over her. Some of it crept under her pelisse and into her gown, but she didn't care. It wasn't long before she came to a clearing and found the source of the wailing.

Adam Riggs laid in a drift of snow, his face contorted with pain. His eyes were red from tears that were now frozen on his face. His left leg was devoured by the metal teeth of a trap, and there was a dark, red pool oozing underneath him. To the side was an overturned knapsack with the head of a dead pheasant poking out. Sarah ran to him.

"Adam. Adam, it's me, Miss Pole."

He showed no signs of recognition or of hearing her at all. She put her hand to his forehead, and his skin was cold and clammy. Amidst the bloody, gory pile of flesh and sinew that had once been Adam's leg, there was a flash of ivory poking out as well. Not snow. Even if he somehow survived the loss of blood, such an injury would almost surely cripple him for life.

"Adam, it's going to be all right. We're going to get you help." Sarah stood up and called out, trying to project her voice as far as she could, "Elinor! Violet! Can you hear me?"

A chorus of "yes" rang back.

"I need you both to run back to the house as fast as you can and tell them I need help out here. We need the doctor! There's been... there's been an accident."

"Like with Mr. Clarkson on the coach?"

"Something like that," Sarah found herself choking. "Run, run, run!" She returned to Adam. She pulled her chest against his back and unbuttoned her pelisse wrapping it around them both, pulling him tighter against her to try to keep him warm. Her chin brushed the hair on the top of his head, and she kept murmuring promises of reassurance to him. The wailing subsided and Adam leaned against her.

"Miss Pole," he finally spoke, his teeth chattering. "Is it really you?"

"Yes, Adam. It's really me. I'm here."

"What are you doing in the woods?"

"The girls and I were out for a walk. They are getting the doctor right now. Adam, you need to stay still and conserve your strength."

He didn't appear to be listening. "I'm sorry, Miss Pole."

"Sorry for what?"

"Sorry you had to see this. Sorry for everything. I've been poaching. I knew it wasn't allowed, but we needed the meat."

"Shh. I know, it's all right. Everything's going to be all right."

"Tell me mum... tell her I'm sorry."

"You'll tell her yourself. Help is on its way."

"My mum and sisters. I don't know what they'll do without me. They could starve or go to the poorhouse! Help them, will you?" Adam turned his head, and his eyes bored into hers, frantic with fear, "Don't let them go hungry. Promise me!"

"Shh, shh… I promise. I promise I'll help them. I promise."

"It hurts, Miss Pole. It hurts so bad."

"I know, Adam, I know."

Sarah kept rubbing his head, and Adam fell silent. Merciful, really, that he should rest. She hummed and crooned to him a lullaby from her youth.

"They're coming!" Sarah perked up in her relief. "Help's coming, Adam. Everything's going to be fine. Adam?" She turned his face toward her. His eyes had rolled back in his head, now empty and blank. You could no longer see any breath from his mouth. She put her head against his chest and heard no heartbeat. She gave an inhuman cry and began to choke and sob. The only sound to be heard was that coming from her, until she had no tears left. And then came the single, solitary caw of a crow in a tree above.

Sarah's Journal

Death is not an abstract concept for me. It hadn't been since I was a child. I came face-to-face with sudden mortality at a young age, and it's fair to say it shaped and distorted my life every step of the way since. I've become quite used to bleeding and to pain. I've done it to myself for so many years now. Perhaps it was my way of preparing myself for future calamities. And to some extent, perhaps it did. I don't faint at the sight of blood. I don't flinch at the thought of pain—at least not my own pain.

And I needed all that. By God, I needed it. Once more, I found myself staring face-to-face with death as I knelt down, covered in blood. I felt colder than I've ever felt before. I'd seen death before. I'd seen plenty of blood. Yet it hadn't prepared me after all for the sight of Adam's lifeless eyes. It hadn't prepared me at all. Without thinking, I closed his eyes. It was better that way. One might he think he was sleeping. But then there was the smell of pennies, and I became more aware of the blood pooled in the snow. Red on white.

It was so visually dramatic, the contrast, and I suddenly had a new appreciation for the tale of Snow White with her lips as red as blood and skin as white as snow and hair black as night. Or as black as the crow's feather. For there was crow, right there, peering at me through its black little eyes in its black feathered face across the snow on the branch. A trio of red, white, and black, and for all of it, I almost felt the urge to laugh.

Of course, it would be a crow! Of course, it would.

Twenty-One

"The great art of life is sensation, to feel that we exist, even in pain."
—Lord Byron

When Mr. Sayres and his men arrived in the clearing, they found Sarah still cradling Adam Riggs's body against her, staring blankly off into the distance. The tears were unmoving, frozen on her face. They tried talking to her, but she didn't answer. When the men tried to take the boy away, she hugged him even harder and tried to bite at them. Mr. Sayres eventually had to resort to giving her a good, hard blow to the face with the back of his hand to get her to release the corpse. Then came the unpleasant task of extricating Adam from the man trap, and this required the efforts of two strong men. Sarah remained silent during the walk back to the house. While Adam Riggs was now far beyond the help of any doctor or priest, Robert Healey's arrival was still necessary to deal with the blood-covered, stone-faced young woman who had yet to speak a word.

"She's in shock," he immediately pronounced, and then noted the blueness of her lips, "and she shows signs of exposure and hypothermia. Someone draw her a hot bath."

Molly and another maid went to work while Robert immediately concentrated on getting Sarah out of her cold, wet, blood-encrusted clothes. He had gotten her down to her petticoat when he was stopped by something other than the dictates of modesty and propriety. Sarah Pole had a mass of scars on her arms and thighs. Some were clearly old and faded, but others looked relatively fresh. Robert's mind reeled. *Had Sarah perhaps been bled by a doctor in the past? Could that account for the marks?*

While a doctor might bleed a patient from the arms, it was extraordinarily unlikely he'd bleed a patient from the legs, especially a female patient. Could Sarah have somehow been abused? But by whom? Molly announced the bath was ready, and they put her in it. Molly must have noticed the scars as well, but she made no mention of them. After her bath, Sarah was immediately put into bed to rest. It was some hours before Robert could confront her.

In the meantime, Bromley Hall was a whirl of activity. Man traps were, of course, legal. Landowners were well within their rights to protect their property from poachers. While Adam's demise did not mean any culpability for the Mandeville family, it was nevertheless a damned nuisance. At the news of her brother's fate, young Meg had run out, disbelieving, and took a look inside the sheet. She'd become hysterical and was administered a sedative by Dr. Healey before being retired to her quarters. The rest of the Riggs family and local authorities had to be notified of Adam's death. Provisions had to be made about the body. An inquest, if only as a matter of routine, was to be expected. Both Thomas and Mrs. Mandeville felt legitimately put out by the whole thing. Violet and Elinor were, at present, exiled to the schoolroom, where they let their imaginations run wild about the nature of the whole household disturbance. They understood something very bad had happened, involving one of the children from the huts, and that Sarah was currently "indisposed" and needed a doctor. *Had something in the woods attacked Miss Pole and the cottager child?*

Robert was interrupted by both adult Mandeville children. Hugh was the first to arrive. "I understand you're treating Miss Pole," Hugh said abruptly. "What's her condition? How bad is it?" There was a layer of urgency to his voice that could almost have been described as eagerness. "Any chance it could be life-threatening?" he added before giving Robert a chance to speak.

"She's had a horrible shock, I'm afraid, and stayed immobile too long in the cold, but she should be fine with a little rest."

"She will?" Hugh sounded disappointed. "Oh well, carry on then," and he sulked off. He made no mention of Adam at all. Robert found the whole meeting so confounding he almost wondered if he'd imagined it.

Alicia Mandeville was next.

"Oh, Doctor Healey, isn't it all just awful? They have the boy's body outside right now, covered in a sheet!"

"It's certainly a bad business," Robert agreed. "I'd hate to be the one who has to tell his mother the news."

"To have him bleed out, right in our woods," Alicia mused. "The Tudburys have their fancy ball for Twelfth Night, and I've spent ages planning my costume. You don't think this will interfere, do you?"

"Interfere with the Tudburys' ball?" Dr. Healey gasped. He had trouble believing his own ears. Adam Riggs was dead and covered in blood in an adjoining room, and Alicia was thinking about the Tudburys' party?

"Yes, of course, you're right. It wasn't even on their property, so it can't affect things for them at all. How silly of me!" Alicia cheerfully went on her way, oblivious to Robert's reaction to the callousness of her words. *Something must be wrong.* She must have been acting in a state of shock, just as Miss Pole was, he assumed. Alicia couldn't possibly be so shallow, so devoid of all real feeling and sympathy!

Could she? It suddenly occurred to him, with a start, that he didn't really know Alicia all that well. They'd had many conversations together, but he couldn't, in retrospect, think of one occasion in which they had truly talked about anything that really mattered. Oh, he knew Alicia's surface opinions and interests, but her deepest thoughts and dreams had always been closed to him. They'd been concealed. Or maybe they simply hadn't been. Maybe Alicia had always been this way, and this was the first time he had not overlooked it. It was a sobering consideration.

Then there was another young woman who Robert now realized he neither knew nor understood the way he thought he had. Sarah eventually woke.

"I wasn't dreaming, was I? It wasn't just a nightmare."

"No," he answered. "No, it wasn't."

"Adam's gone then. He's truly gone. My God, he was just a child," her face was intent. "Robert, do you think there was any way to save him back there? If I'd done something differently?"

"No," he responded immediately. "He'd lost too much blood out there. Even if I had found him, I couldn't have done anything for him. The only thing that could have made any difference was if he'd been found sooner. Much sooner."

"Oh, his poor mother. This'll break her," Sarah stirred. "And how will she get by? How will any of them get by without him doing jobs for extra pennies or catching game?" she looked quite agitated.

"Sar– Miss Pole, you mustn't get yourself worked up all over again," Robert told her. "You were in a bad state when they found you. You gave us all a fright."

Sarah wasn't listening, "Someone has to help them. I have to help them. I made a promise."

"A promise?"

"A promise to Adam!" she looked impatient. "I promised him I wouldn't let his family starve!"

"Well, they are wards of the parish now, and the parish will look after them," Robert pointed out. "It's really not your responsibility, and frankly, I don't see how you could help."

"I have a little money saved," Sarah looked thoughtful. "It's not much, but it would help. They could get through the winter at least."

"Sarah, right now, I'm worried about you," Robert came to the point.

"Worried about me? Whatever for? I wasn't the one who was hurt," her tone turned, becoming business-like. "I'm terribly sorry I frightened you earlier with my foolishness, but it won't happen again, I promise you," she gave a nervous laugh. "Perhaps I'm not really fit to draw for a surgery after all."

"I'm not worried about your episode of shock. That was normal. Sarah, you must tell me about the scars."

"The scars?" her face became furtive. "What scars?"

"Don't play games," he answered sharply.

She was silent for a long time after that.

"Sarah, who did these to you? Were they done by a doctor?"

She didn't answer the question.

"Sarah, if it was a doctor, then he's done a very bad job of the business, and if it wasn't a doctor... my God! Sarah, who's been hurting you?"

She was quiet a long moment and then, finally, in a very quiet voice, she answered, "Me."

"What?" he felt he couldn't have heard right.

"Me," she repeated, her voice louder and clearer, though it contained a tremor. "I've been doing it to myself. I cut myself."

Robert felt like he'd been punched directly in the gut. For a moment, he couldn't speak. Finally, he managed.

"For God's sake, why?"

She shrugged her shoulders, "What can I tell you, Robert? I have a very bad habit."

"A habit?" he grabbed her by the arm, hard enough to cause bruising, holding the scars up to clear view. "You call this a bloody bad habit?" he wanted to throttle her at that moment. He had never felt such fury and frustration before in his life. It was only later he'd come to question why that was so.

"I don't know what you want me to say, Robert. I'm not proud of it."

"But why?"

Sarah shrugged her shoulders again, "I don't know. It's difficult to explain."

"Try." It was a command. He seemed, at that moment, to be torn between rage and tears.

Sarah struggled to come up with the right words, "Have you ever felt angry? Or sad? Or in pain? I feel that way a lot. And when I do, I hurt myself. Because, somehow, pain on the outside makes the pain on the inside go away. Does that make any sense to you?"

"No, Sarah," he spoke quietly but firmly. "No, Sarah, I'm afraid that doesn't make a damned bit of sense to me at all." Healey turned around and walked away without saying another word or giving so much as a single look back, which is why Sarah never saw the tears spill out of his eyes nor that he punched a wall in the hall as hard as he could. Only later, with his hand smarting, did he reflect on the irony of that moment and did he feel the faintest glimmer of understanding for Sarah's "habit."

Sarah's Journal

I'd lost him. I realized that when Robert left. I think, deep down, I knew from the moment I saw the way he looked at my scars, I hadn't just lost whatever chance , however forlorn, but I'd lost him as even my friend; even as someone to just talk to. He would forever look at me with scorn and disgust. Worse still, perhaps he was right.

I had never really before examined my scars full light, but I did so then. For the first time, I realized how ugly they were, and of what an awful story they would tell anyone who cared to look at them. I honestly had never thought about this before because I had been determined that no one else ever would see the scars. Who was to see me undressed? Of course, if I ever married, such a discovery would be inevitable, but I had spent many years convinced I never would marry, and even when I'd dared to nurture private pathetic little hopes about Robert, I had never considered a marriage ceremony or a wedding night. Perhaps because if I had I would have needed to think about the scars and what any man who saw them would think.

It was then that I also began to understand what a fool I'd been, how deluded I truly was. My prospects for matrimony had always been unlikely, but with the efforts of that little pouch, I had made myself completely unfit to be any man's wife. Worse than that, women were shut away every day for sins far less grave than mine. At least Robert wouldn't tell anyone else. Somehow, I just knew he wouldn't. At least I'd be spared the madhouse. For now.

But what should I do? I thought about what my life would be like at Bromley Hall now that I no longer had Robert's companionship, how Alicia and Hugh both loathed the very sight of me, and while I tried to keep him from my mind, I thought about Adam. About how different his face appeared in death. About what happened to his eyes. And with that came a feeling of not only sorrow but of guilt, too. For wasn't I, in part, responsible for what had happened? Hadn't my inaction helped bring this about?

Even if there'd been nothing I could have done in the woods to save Adam, perhaps I could have stopped him from poaching. If only I had done more to help the Riggs family, he might never have felt the need to go hunting on Mandeville property. Or if I'd warned him about the traps. I could have done something, I was sure. I should have done something. It wasn't like I was a child anymore, helplessly watching everyone succumb to fever.

Then I began thinking of something else I hadn't thought about in years—something I'd deliberately kept away. I thought about my family, and how they died. I thought about Father and Mother and their final hours. I thought about little William and how hot his face had been with fever when I touched it. I thought about how I'd prayed so very hard to God to spare him and to take me instead. But God took William, and I never prayed again. In all these years, I've never been able to understand why God spared me; why God wanted me to live. They say he has a plan for everything, but I really couldn't possibly see what, if anything, his plan was for me. Why was I alive?

Or was I alive at all? Wasn't I rather just existing and not truly living? And wasn't that a sin in its own way? When life is so short – so very, very short – to not live it fully was surely a sin, too. A sin of wastefulness. I'd considered Alicia to be spoiled and self-centered, but was it not just as selfish to shut myself away somewhere to wallow in misery? It certainly wasn't very attractive, I concluded. But how was I to change that? How does one go about living - truly living - life?

I wasn't sure. I knew, however, that I was never going to find the answer as long as I stayed at Bromley Hall.

Twenty-Two

"There is nothing permanent except change."
—Heraclitus

If Hugh Mandeville had been disappointed to learn Sarah was expected to make a full recovery, he was downright distraught to have her corner him in the library for a private conversation.

"Adam Riggs must be buried," she told him. Her eyes were rimmed with red, but there was a firmness in her shoulders, and she bore an air of determination.

"What?" Of all the things he'd expected her to say to him, this was the last.

"He must be buried, properly buried. He should have a decent funeral and a headstone to mark him, not just a nameless cross. Let his mother have that, at least."

"Wait, do you want me to pay for Adam Riggs's funeral? The boy was poaching in our woods!"

"And it was in your woods he died. You, or rather your father, decided to set potentially lethal traps for the sake of pheasants. That has consequences." Hugh opened his mouth but before he could get in a word, Sarah continued. "And not just the cost of the funeral. I need assurances from you, or rather Mrs. Riggs needs your assurances. First, that you'll never evict them. Second, you won't let them perish."

"You're telling me you want me to support the entire Riggs family for life? Are you mad? Why the blazes should they be my responsibility? I had nothing to do with the boy's death."

"Because. I. Saw." Sarah looked Hugh directly in the eye. She said nothing more than those three words, each enunciated with a sense of poison. The threat hovered in the air. "It won't be too much of a burden for you. Just a few coins a month for food and supplies," she pointed out, "and as Mrs. Riggs's daughters get older, they can be sent out for service or apprenticed anyway. Consider it handling the hall's staffing needs in advance. For that matter, once her youngest is a little older, Mrs. Riggs might be willing to take in washing or piecework or such. I'm sure you'll be able to find them something."

Hugh stood still for a moment, then finally he gave a belligerent nod.

"All right. I'll make sure they're provided for one way or another. You have my word."

"Good. I shall hold you to it," she quietly walked out.

Adam Riggs was buried by Reverend Graham in a simple ceremony attended by his mother, his sisters, a few of the other cottagers, and Sarah. It was on the north side of the cemetery, traditionally where they buried strangers, unbaptized babies, and suicides. Still, he did get a proper service and a headstone. When the last handful of dirt was heaped upon his grave, Mrs. Riggs finished a spell of weeping in Sarah's arms. After the burial, Mrs. Riggs, to her astonishment, was presented with a small purse from Hugh Mandeville.

Sarah visited the local postmistress with several letters in hand. All three letters were addressed to locations in London. The days slowly crept by as she waited for replies. Finally, the postmistress announced there was a letter for her. She did not wait to get back to Bromley Hall but rather tore open the letter on the street and eagerly read its contents. It contained for what Sarah had hoped.

The next day, while the girls took their music lessons, Sarah walked in on Mrs. Mandeville. Mrs. Mandeville was, at that moment, engrossed in reading a French novel. She waited quietly until Mrs. Mandeville's gaze lifted from her book for a moment. At the sight of Sarah, she gave a start.

"Dear God, how long were you standing there?" Mrs. Mandeville managed once she caught her breath. She'd never admit it but right then she had some idea of why Alicia had found Miss Pole's quietness so unsettling.

"I'm sorry to disturb you, ma'am, but I wanted to let you know I'm leaving."

"Leaving? Like leaving to go to town for a bit?"

"No, as in I'm leaving Bromley Hall. Permanently. I'm officially offering you my notice as a governess. I plan to quit this house within the week."

A lengthy pause followed, but then Mrs. Mandeville began to sputter, "But the girls! Their lessons! Who will mind them? I mean, teach them. How am I to get a replacement in promptly?"

"I thought you might have concerns. So, I took the liberty of writing to an employment agency in London, asking about my potential replacement." Sarah handed her a letter. "As you can read here, the agency happens to have at least two candidates with excellent references available right away. A Miss Gardiner and a Miss Rollins. They describe them both along with their accomplishments. All you need do is write back which lady you'd prefer. You could have one arrive the very same day I leave."

"Yes, well," sputtered Mrs. Mandeville, "I appreciate your taking the effort, but this is still most irregular."

"I understand. By the way, you need not trouble yourself to write any letters of introduction for me," Miss Pole stated calmly.

"Why? What do you plan to do now?" A bizarre and unlikely scenario occurred to Mrs. Mandeville then. "Miss Pole, have you found yourself a fiancé?"

"No, ma'am, but I've made up my mind to resettle in London. My tenancy here is drawing to an end." And with that cryptic comment, Sarah left the room.

Mrs. Mandeville remained in shock for a few minutes. At last, she gathered her wits enough to examine the letter from the employment agency and consider the respective merits of Miss Rollins versus those of Miss Gardiner.

The final set of interviews at Bromley Hall were the hardest. When she informed Elinor and Violet that she'd be leaving them, there were tears and cries of, "Don't go! Don't go!"

"I'm terribly sorry to leave you both," Sarah said sincerely, "but I must."

"But why must you go?" Violet wailed between tears.

"It is difficult to explain," Sarah said carefully, "but this is just something I have to do."

"I hate you!" Violet stamped her foot violently and ran from the room. Elinor, stiff-lipped and eyes lit with anger, joined her. Sarah was left alone in the schoolroom.

Sarah got up early the morning of her departure to say goodbye to the girls. Violet hugged her fiercely, making her promise to write long, long letters, while Elinor maintained a cold dignity. Only at the last minute did she allow Sarah to kiss her and then turned her face away once more.

"It'll be all right, girls," Sarah told them. "I'm sure Miss Gardiner will be lovely." The girls looked doubtful.

Once again, George complained about the weight of Sarah's trunk, though, this time, at least he was carrying it down the stairs. A donkey cart conveyed Sarah and her trunk to Greenberry's town square. After a ten-minute wait outside with a showering of hail, Sarah boarded the coach for the twenty-mile journey to London.

London was foggy and dirty. The streets, many of them unpaved, were covered in horse droppings. It smelled like a stable long overdue for a cleaning. Most of all, it was noisy. The sound of wheels and horses' hooves was incessant. Boots and pattens clicked and clacked on stone. There were street peddlers hawking their wares at the top of their lung. It seemed as if there was someone ringing a bell or playing an instrument on every corner. Most surprising were the sounds of children everywhere. London was a youthful city, full of street urchins, messenger boys, crossing sweepers, children who begged, children who stole, and children who mined the streets, grubbing the dirt from between stones, looking for nails, coins, rings, and other treasures.

Alongside all this poverty were also displays of fantastic wealth. Carlton House, home to the Prince Regent, was a wonder, and so was John Nash's ongoing work on Buckingham Palace. Nor was it just members of the royalty or nobility who were living large. A whole new merchant class had risen with money to burn. Nabobs who'd accumulated enormous fortunes in India were now determined to display their newfound wealth in the most ostentatious style possible. They bedecked themselves in rich garments and jewels then rode out at top speed in phaetons and barouches pulled by Arab steeds who were better fed than many street urchins. The contrast between rich and poor in London was even greater than what it had been in Greenberry, and even more strikingly, some of London's most wretched could be found in the alleys of some of the finest, most fashionable places in town. In Greenberry, the poor had usually lived some distance from the great houses.

All of this, Sarah marveled at, but her first priority was putting a roof over her head. She carried a paper with a list of potential places she could room. The first boarding house she went to told her up front they didn't board young, single ladies, clearly to avoid taking in women of "low character." The second place she tried didn't have any problem with young, single women at all. Indeed, they seemed to make a habit of boarding exactly the sort of lady the first house so assiduously avoided. As she left, Sarah found herself fending off propositions from male admirers as she trudged along with her trunk. It was cold and damp, and dragging the trunk was becoming quite wearisome when Sarah finally came to the third establishment.

It was a none-too-clean coffee house, which attracted a none-too-clean clientele, run by a Mrs. Mundy. She was a thin woman, somewhere between the ages of forty and fifty, with eyes like knife slits and arms that were perpetually crossed. There had been a Mr. Mundy once, a useless miserable old drunkard who'd lock her outside in the rain and beat her. Eventually, she'd taken a poker and gave him a series of blows, leaving him bleeding. He'd fled and never came back. Whether he was still living or dead was all the same to Mrs. Mundy. She planned never to have another husband anyway. She had, though, needed to find a means of supporting herself, and to that end, had turned what had once been an especially wretched tavern into a coffeehouse, reasoning that it would be easier not to have deal with all the drunken fights on her own. The profits weren't very large, though, and the extra income from renting that spare room was of no small importance to her.

"You're here about the room? What's your name?" Mrs. Mundy inquired.

"Crow. Sarah Crow," she stated firmly. "I'm an artist," she added.

Mrs. Mundy thought the name fitting. She certainly looked a bit like a crow with her dark hair, thin build, and that nose. As for her being an artist, well Mrs. Mundy hadn't had one of those before. *Could you trust that sort to pay their bill?* Of course, it was always possible she wasn't an artist at all, but that sort of woman.

"Mind you," Mrs. Mundy commented, "I don't want a lot of folks coming all hours, day and night. It's not that I judge me lodgers' morals – that's their own business – but it's too much trouble it is to have blokes making noise at three o'clock in the morning."

Miss Crow actually smiled, "Believe me, that won't be a problem."

"Well, just so we're clear. I suppose you'll be wanting to see the room now? Right this way then. It's the top floor. Just leave the trunk for now."

Sarah rather uneasily did so and followed Mrs. Mundy up long, winding, and noticeably rickety stairs.

"Watch your head," Mrs. Mundy warned her as they stepped into the little room. It was the attic area, with a low ceiling that barely rose above their heads. A taller person would have needed to stoop over like a chimpanzee. It was dusty, and the rafters looked raw. There was, however, a little bed and a skylight over top it. On the skylight sat a pair of plump pigeons. On the back wall was a little fireplace that, at present, lay cold and inert.

"This'd be it then. If you want a fire, you have to pay for your own fuel."

"It'll do nicely," Sarah assured her.

"Hmmmph..." Mrs. Mundy eyed Sarah suspiciously. "This ain't a charity here. I'd need payment up front."

"I can do that," Sarah replied calmly, "but what exactly are the terms?" Negotiations commenced, and Sarah soon hammered out a rate for her first month's rent, including meals. Once Sarah produced the money from her thin purse, and Mrs. Mundy had reassured herself the coins were real, her whole countenance changed. She grandly invited Sarah to join her for some refreshment. The two enjoyed a hot cup of tea and some plain fare. Mrs. Mundy had one of her patrons bring Sarah's trunk upstairs. That night, she found herself putting extra clothes on over the thin covers to keep warm and reflected that first thing in the morning she'd need not only to purchase more coal, but an extra blanket.

Sarah's Journal

Of course, I took a new name. If you're trying to change things, if you're trying to change yourself, then your name is a good place to start—and my kinship with the crow also seemed part of who I was. It was a change for me but also an affirmation of my past.

London was so new. So strange. Overwhelming, really, with all its noise and stink and people. More people than I'd ever realized could be alive at once. Immediately, I questioned my decision. What had I been thinking? London was a hubbub of vice and crime. Everyone knew that. I must have been mad to leave a comfortable home and steady paid position to come here on my own. I already found myself missing Violet and Elinor, who would soon be taking lessons from their next governess. A pile of expenses in the future and I had so little money to spare. I knew I'd have to start finding work right away.

I woke up confused in the middle of the night. Then I remembered everything and found myself groping in the dark for the pouch, which I'd hidden under my pillow. I clasped it in my hands and fingered the glass, but then I closed it up again, chanting, "I will not. I will not. I will not."

When morning came, I was determined to throw the pouch away. I walked to the river and prepared to toss it into the black water, but I couldn't do it. I just couldn't. Instead, I brought it back and kissed it once before tucking it under the mattress.

Twenty-Three

"By seeing London, I have seen as much of life as the world can show."
–Samuel Johnson

London was a very different city depending on whether one had money. All the attractions of London that Alicia Mandeville enjoyed – concerts, museums, art – were closed to Sarah, let alone balls or being presented at court. She was, however, able to pay pilgrimage to the Royal Circus and Covent Garden, at least from the street outside. If you wanted an impression of places abroad, you could go to Leicester Square to see the panoramas. Dublin, disappointingly, seemed but an even dirtier and grittier version of London. Cairo, though, was quite impressive with its sandy deserts contrasting against the green of the Nile. Sarah quite admired the efforts of those responsible, and then there was the Temple of the Muses, a magnificent bookstore in Finsbury Square whose collection could put many libraries to shame.

Over time, Sarah became acclimated with a different side of London. The London of slums and rookeries. A London where some of the finest buildings on the street would turn out to be gin palaces constructed with all the finest gaudy accessories and gas lighting. A London where pickpockets, dressed as sharply as aristocrats, brazenly roamed the streets. A London where former heroes of the Napoleonic wars begged in the street. She once saw a huge crowd gathered around a yard. When Sarah pushed her way through to see what all the fuss was, it turned out to be a fight to the death between two bull terriers. She strolled through Covent Garden to observe London's variety of prostitutes, from elegant courtesans who could command as much as five pounds for their services to common drabs available to anyone with a few coppers. They were a chilling reminder of the inevitable fate of any young girl without family or means who could not find paying work.

Sarah also noticed a number of very handsome young men who seemed to seek the attention of older, male passersby. These, she would later learn, were London's "rent boys," and no doubt the ubiquity of their presence was one reason for Hugh Mandeville's fondness for the city. She thought of Hugh from time to time. Despite what she'd said, she never had any real intention of exposing him. He may not have been the most amiable of gentlemen, but he certainly did not deserve to have his whole life ruined—at least not because of a preference for men over women, and the consequences would have been even worse for sweet Joe, whom Sarah liked very much.

Having lived in small English villages all her life, Sarah had never seen a foreigner before, let alone anyone who wasn't white. London, particularly the dock areas, was full of people from all countries and all races. Spaniards, Indians, Blacks, even an occasional person from the Far East. Black people, she'd soon learn, were in particularly high demand as servants. A black footman was considered a great acquisition for a wealthy, fashionable household. England housed thousands of Jews, and more than half of them lived in London and were a common sight.

Sarah came upon the Bevis Marks Synagogue, built over a hundred years earlier. It was not, from the outside, a particularly interesting structure. It was simply a red brick building with a lot of windows that could have been any normal office or warehouse, yet it had once received a royal visit from the Duke of Cumberland. Life in London was, in its own way, as educational as the years Sarah had spent at Parsley School. Perhaps even more so.

London, she noted, was also a place where the church was far less relevant. In the country, everyone - rich or poor - attended services on Sundays, even if laborers sometimes resented using part of their one day off to hear a sermon. But in London, the Sabbath was treated generally as a day of leisure. Public worship services, in even the grandest churches, were often sparsely attended.

Sarah once treated herself to a hot drink called salop, served by a woman operating a still. It tasted like nectar and warmed her from the inside out, but she didn't dare treat herself to a second such drink. When one of her stockings developed a hole in the toe, she didn't think of replacing it. Not just yet. Even with the strictest economy on her part, money still seemed to melt away like snowflakes on the tongue. It was a cold winter, and fuel for the fire was not cheap. Of course, there was the cost of supplies for her craft, too. One of her first tasks upon arriving in London had been to find a portable easel. She hadn't dared to pay the cost of a shiny new one but bought one secondhand. Thanks to Dr. Healey, she had a good supply of brushes, but paper, paint, and ink all had to be steadily replenished. And then there was rent. Work had to be found quickly, but she wasn't finding any.

The days, for Sarah, were a depressing routine of tramping all over London to the offices of art agents and sellers. She walked the streets until her feet were sore and her face chapped by the wind. Originally, it had been her hope that she might, just maybe, sell something to someone, or at least get a commission. But as doors continued to slam in her face, Sarah began to revise that goal to just getting any of the gentleman in London's art community to talk to her. They wouldn't. An amateur artist? An amateur woman artist without any letters of introduction or reference? She was beneath their notice.

"No luck again, eh?" Mrs. Mundy asked Sarah one afternoon as she sat at one of the coffee house's tables, her chin in hand while she stared out at the distance. "Not my place to tell you what to do, dearie, but you are gonna have to make next month's rent. You're a nice, quiet tenant, and I'd hate to have to evict you," she said with perfect graciousness.

"Thank you," said Sarah, rather dryly. Sarah could not help but remember a horrific newspaper article of the death of a governess who could not find work and wondered if her story was to have a similar trajectory.

"But I'd have no choice if you can't raise the bob," Mrs. Mundy gave a firm, decisive nod before her tone turned conspiratorial. "Now, if I were you, I'd give the whole artist thing a rest for now and try to get my bread first."

"I suppose I could continue to work in the day for now, and paint and draw in the evenings," Sarah mused. "I understand people employ day governesses to come and teach their children while living elsewhere. Or some school in London perhaps? I could offer my services as a drawing instructor?"

"There's the spirit! Now, let's see what's posted in the papers, love," Mrs. Mundy began looking at a series of notices left behind by another patron when Sarah sat up suddenly with a glint in her eye.

"Newspapers! Does anyone know the address of The Charing Cross Courier?"

Sarah came to a soot-covered old stone building that did not possess a particularly appealing appearance. It was squeezed into a neighborhood that didn't seem like the sort of place you'd want to walk at night. People came and went through the main door freely, and so Sarah walked in.

The newsroom was, if anything, even noisier than the street. The sounds of printing presses and editors yelling at copy boys and copy boys yelling at the printing press operators. Everything smelled so strongly of ink that it made her dizzy, but it was better than the underlying scents of tobacco, paper, and dust. Some of the employees, when one got within arm's length of them, smelled of cheap gin.

"Excuse me? Can someone help me find Mr. Clarkson?" Sarah called out but couldn't make herself heard above the general roar. Eventually, she resorted to grabbing one of the copy boys by the shoulder and demanding assistance. He led her to a corner in back where hidden behind a screen and some shelves sat Rufus Clarkson, furiously scribbling away a diatribe on the latest parliamentary shenanigans.

"Miss Pole!" he paused and looked her over with evident surprise and delight. "So, you came after all."

"You are the one who said I should," she reminded him.

"I did," he admitted, "but tell the truth, I wasn't sure you'd have the nerve to quit that beastly family and come out here by yourself." He whistled. "It was bold of you. Consider me surprised."

"I'm rather surprised with myself as well," she said dryly.

Mr. Clarkson gave Sarah a shrewd glance, "Something's changed for you, hasn't it, Miss Pole? You're different from when I saw you last."

"Something has changed," she said simply. "I don't go by Miss Pole anymore. It's Crow now. Sarah Crow."

Mr. Clarkson waited, but when it became apparent that Sarah wouldn't elaborate, he shrugged his shoulders. "Suit yourself, then. It's almost closing time today. Why don't we go out for supper? My treat," he added after noting the worn condition of Sarah's boots.

They went to an establishment down the street known as The Goat and Grapes, which had evidently been a long-time favorite of Courier staff. Once seated, Clarkson told the server, "A pint for each of us and some broil. Heave to."

"I am capable of ordering for myself, you know, Mr. Clarkson," Sarah noted.

"You need a little fattening, girl," he told her.

"And I don't make a habit of drinking pints either."

"Be careful who you tell that to or you'll be banned from London as a foreign spy," he gave her a shrewd look.

"Now, is there a reason you wanted to see me – besides the pleasure of my company, obviously?"

Sarah told him about seeing Adam bleed out in front of her and about how she'd felt compelled to leave the Mandeville house, and about her struggle to find work in London as an artist.

"I should have known it would never be so easy," Sarah concluded.

"Well, not without knowing anyone, it's not. Blast it, girl, you should have come to me on your first day here."

"Why? Are you commissioning a painting right now, or do you know anyone who is?"

"Not personally, no. But I reckon I know a fellow who would. His name's Levi. Isaac Levi, and he deals in pictures. Tell him I sent you. He'll at least hear you out," Mr. Clarkson scribbled an address for her on a notepad.

"Oh," said Sarah, "well thank–"

Mr. Clarkson interrupted, "I can do something else for you as well. How about a little advertisement in The Courier announcing the services of a miniaturist and portraitist available right now for whomever wants her. Just inquire at Mrs.

Mundy's? That's what they all do these days."

"It might work, but how much would that cost?" Sarah asked warily.

"Absolutely nothing. Consider it – and tonight's meal – payment to you for providing me with all that free nursing for days on end."

Sarah was astonished, "Oh, really, Mr. Clarkson, you're being far too generous."

"Really, I'm not," he waved his hand. "I owe you and that Irish doctor a debt, and now I'm just clearing it away. How is old Healey doing anyway?"

"I really don't know. I didn't get a chance to speak to him before I left."

"And you haven't written to him since?"

"Uh, no," said Sarah, biting her lip.

Clarkson just nodded.

Sarah got up at the crack of dawn the next morning, and after a quick wash in freezing water to try to look and smell presentable, she set out for the address Mr. Clarkson had given her. It was a long distance, and she had to stop and get directions from strangers at several points, but eventually she made it there. The whole street smelled of fresh bread from a bakery. At the far end, tucked behind the corner, was a little shop with windows displaying several oil paintings of ships at sea and heather filled moors. On the door was a brass plate, announcing it to be "Isaac Levi. Art Purveryor and Agent."

Sarah knocked, but there was no answer. She then tried the door itself and let herself inside. The walls were covered in pictures. The smell of paint and varnish was almost overwhelming. In the back, there was an old wooden table, and behind the table was an old wooden stool on which sat the figure of a man engrossed in his newspaper, The Charing Cross Courier, in fact, where today's edition announced vivid details about a shocking murder in Southwark. She stood silently for a while, but the newspaper didn't move, and its reader remained hidden. Finally, Sarah cleared her throat as loudly as possible. The paper fell away to reveal a man of indeterminate age and slender build with a shining bald skull behind an enormous pair of spectacles. Around his neck, he wore the Star of David. Sarah cleared her throat rather loudly. No response. Finally, she mustered up the nerve to address him directly.

"Are you Mr. Levi?" she asked.

"I am," he did not look up from his newspaper. There was a long pause. Finally, he spoke again, "You're still here." It was a statement, not a question.

"Yes," Sarah answered. "I was hoping to conduct business with you."

Mr. Levi slowly and deliberately folded up the newspaper and put it down to better examine her. His eyes stared owl-like from the spectacles at Sarah, "Do you wish to buy any of my paintings? I have some lovely flower illustrations, most appropriate for a young woman such as yourself."

"I'm not here to buy," Sarah explained, and he was visibly disappointed. "Actually, I was hoping to sell. I have some drawings and watercolors to show you."

"Oh, another amateur hoping to make a few coins." He gave a melodramatically weary sigh as he went on, "Let me guess. You were first taught by your governess and your former instructor said you showed some promise, and your parents delight in your work, so now you fancy you can be a professional, don't you?" His eyes practically rolled out of his head.

"Actually, I've been the governess and drawing instructor, and my parents are dead so they can't offer me their opinion on my work." Sarah felt herself getting heated, "But other people who aren't related to me at all told me I had some talent. One of them, Mr. Clarkson, referred me to you." At the last words, Mr. Levi's expression changed.

"Mr. Clarkson gave you my name? Rufus Clarkson of The Courier?"

"Yes. He told me you were an art purveyor."

"Hmmm..." he surveyed her with new interest. "Do you have any samples of your work to show me?"

Sarah handed him sketchbook, and Mr. Levi went through the contents carefully, one at a time. He took his time, saying nothing, but making an occasional murmur or grunt. Sarah couldn't tell whether it was good or bad. Finally, he spoke.

"You haven't received a classical arts education, obviously."

"No," said Sarah, her heart sinking. "No, I haven't."

"It shows. But these," he tapped on the sketchpad, "are not entirely without merit. In fact, some of them properly framed..." he pulled out from the group a watercolor of Bromley Hall's gardens and another of mounted men in fox hunting uniforms, "could probably be sold to those looking for the usual popular fashion. Some of these others..." he pulled out a sketch of a crumbling stone toll bridge with a troll sleeping underneath, "are a little harder to categorize. But they might well appeal to persons with a sense of whimsy." His lips twitched. "I must warn you, though, as an unknown, I can't pay you very much. Also, watercolors and drawings cannot command the same prices as oils."

"But you will pay?" Sarah's voice seemed to tremble a bit.

"For some of them, yes." He named a price, and Sarah agreed immediately without any thoughts to negotiating. "Also, Miss..." he hesitated.

"Crow. Miss Sarah Crow."

"Well, Miss Crow, I'll keep you in mind if anyone asks for a referral from me. Also a word of advice: the city is full of museums and collections of some of the finest artwork in the world. I cannot recommend highly enough that you avail yourself of this advantage. Careful examination of the works of past masters will only improve your craft. The Royal Academy will hold its annual exhibition in May. You will be able to examine offerings from the finest painters in all of England. Moreover, they offer lectures and catalogs to help elevate public taste."

"It sounds wonderful!" Sarah exclaimed.

"It is," Mr. Levi gave a crooked smile. "And, Miss Crow, welcome to London!"

Sarah's Journal

When I left Mr. Levi's that day, I felt like I was pulled along by a heavenly cloud. Things were, as they say, looking up. For the first time since I came to London, I started to feel that, perhaps, I had done the right thing in coming here. I was now a real artist. A low-paid, obscure artist who was just barely scratching out a livelihood, but an artist nevertheless.

I may have been less "respectable" as an artist than as a governess, but I enjoyed far greater freedom as well. I was, for the first time, independent. No one to order me around. No one to watch my words. I started to explore London a bit and sketch out scenes of street life, which I enjoyed doing. Mr. Levi thought the work all right. In some ways, I was better off than I'd ever been before.

Of course, I'd soon learn that the life of a portraitist is not all jam and cake.

Twenty-Four

"There are only two styles of portrait painting; the serious and the smirk."
—Charles Dickens, *Nicholas Nickleby*

Not long after her meeting with Mr. Levi, Sarah received her first commission. A man by the name of Mr. Burns came to Mrs. Mundy's inquiring about a portraitist who lived on the premises. He was a middle-aged fellow with a wig of grey hair and a large, bulbous, red nose. He worked as a silversmith. His wife had been nagging him to get a family portrait done, though he personally hadn't felt the expense warranted. One reason he picked out the advertisement for "S. Crowe," was that it had stated outright that the painter in question was cheap. They quickly settled on a fee and arranged a time and date for the family to sit for her.

The Burns' occupied the second floor of a townhouse, and the sitting was to be done in the parlor where Sarah was introduced to the whole family with all of them wearing their Sunday best. Sarah arrived with watercolors, brushes, and her easel. Besides Mr. Burns, there was his wife, Mrs. Burns, who used as much paint on her own face as Sarah would use on a canvas. Kitty Burns was a saucy, pert little creature at sixteen years old, and in complete contrast to her younger sister, Augusta Burns, a heavyset girl of fourteen with spots on her face. Finally, there was young Ronald Burns, the baby of the family, who was five years old and his mother's favorite. Ronald did not want to model for anything and made these views quite public.

"NOOOO!" he roared as his mother tried to comb his hair.

"Ronald, angel," his mother cooed. "Please, if you could just stand still for a while and show her your lovely smile. Augusta, don't slump like that." Augusta had her feet apart and hands clasped awkwardly behind her back, face sullen.

"I don't see why Augusta has to be in the portrait at all," Kitty spoke. "She's so ugly." Augusta stomped on Kitty's foot, causing her to wail. "Mother, look what she did!"

"Girls! Girls! You shame me. Remember above all else your manners."

In the meantime, Ronald had begun sticking out his stomach and then held in this breath until his face turned blue. When his mama went to check on him, things between Kitty and Augusta escalated into hair-pulling. The sitting had to be cut short. The next time Sarah arrived, the family was, however, grudgingly willing to stand in place while Mrs. Burns took the trouble to advise Sarah on how to do her job.

"Now remember, Miss Crow, I want a picture to show just how lovely this family is for everyone to see!" Mrs. Burns instructed Sarah, who said nothing but continued to work at the problem that had been the bane of countless artists in the past. How does one render one's subject recognizable but at the same time flatter them?

Well, for Ronald, one simply tried painting him accurately to physical type but minus all the scowls and howls. In fact, with the Burns family, it seemed wiser not to convey too much of their actual personalities. The redness in Mr. Burns's face that suggested a certain fondness for grapes was evened out. Mrs. Burns's copious use of cosmetics was not included but the intended effect, a more youthful appearance for Mrs. Burns, was achieved. Augusta's spots were not drawn, and her complexion was much improved. Kitty's own likeness was left relatively unchecked but with perhaps less impudence in the natural expression. Ronald was depicted with cherubic charm and calmness. Mrs. Burns proclaimed herself well pleased with the final product.

"Well, it's all right for me," said Kitty, "but it don't look like Augusta. She looks too nice."

"Oh, nonsense! This is just Augusta at her best! It's all of us at our best." Mrs. Burns proclaimed in delight as Ronald, sadly indifferent to the whole matter of his portrait, began kicking the walls of the room and wailing for supper.

Other people besides Mr. Burns saw the ad as well and came to employ Sarah. She managed to satisfy them, and before long, she was serving more clients recommended to her by other clients. These clients were invariably tradespeople from drapers to attorneys. Even, at one time, an especially prosperous butcher. Sadly, he did not pose with the apron and cleaver of his profession, but insisted he was depicted wearing his best clothes. Isaac Levi was able to arrange other valuable introductions for her as well. Mrs. Mundy was quite gratified to learn she wouldn't have to throw her latest – and as of that moment, quietest – tenant out on into the street after all.

Along with portrait painting, Sarah continued with her own original works. She soon learned that pictures of sprites and fairies sold particularly well. London was full of sentimental souls who found such visions charming. And there was also the advantage that, with fairies, you didn't need a live model. You could just imagine them as whatever you thought a fairy should be. An advantage since the only models she could afford at first were two pigeons roosting on the skylight. She named them Percival and Peck. As more and more work came in, Sarah was able to replace her stockings, buy candles, and even afford some additional comforts, like a daily copy of The Courier. She joined a lending library and began to visit some of London's museums. Bullock's was her favorite. Not only for the Egyptian room, of course, and the chance to see all the incredible stuffed animals, but they had such a collection of fine art there as well. It was enough to make one's head spin. While observing the paintings, Sarah took note of the brush strokes and techniques used by past masters and polished her craft even further.

Sarah's Journal

Things were going well. Things were going very well, even if my subjects could be a bit challenging from time to time, but I learned it was much easier to tolerate difficult people when you know you can leave them at the end of the day, instead of living under their roofs in a state of utter dependence. In that sense, the Burns family were, in fact, an improvement over the Mandevilles – the older Mandevilles, at any rate.

I was also having such a good time exploring the great city. I'd even become attached, in a way, to my little attic, and I was beginning to outfit it as a studio according to my tastes and specifications. There had been no chance of that at Bromley Hall, and even at Weberley I'd been restricted by having roommates. Mrs. Mundy said it was perfectly fine for me to keep the space in any sort of order I saw fit as long as I didn't expect her to clean it. Here, I could hang pictures of any style I wished and hang them anywhere I wished. I could leave paints and books piled up any old way.

Yet, I was still lonely during the night, and I found there were some things about Bromley Hall I missed. Not the adults, to be sure, but I missed the girls. I missed Robert, too. And worst of all, I still felt the urge to hurt myself. I resisted cutting at least, but I'd pinch myself until I was black and blue. I didn't know how long it would be before I succumbed again. I knew I needed help.

Twenty-Five

You shall not make any cuts on your body for the dead or tattoo yourselves:
I am the Lord.

–Leviticus 19:28

One day, Sarah was walking back to Mrs. Mundy's, following a sitting for a miniature. An iron-faced, grey-haired solicitor named Mr. Bates had hired her to paint a frightened looking young woman named Dora. Sarah had originally assumed the young lady was his daughter or even granddaughter, but to her surprise, Dora turned out to be his wife. At first, Sarah had thought the young bride might be mute since she never uttered a sound while her husband was in their drawing room, overstuffed with very respectable, but very ugly-looking, old wooden furniture. Eventually, though, Mr. Bates left. The moment he did so, Dora gave a big whooshing breath of relief.

"Well now! Ms. Crow, was it?" she spoke animatedly. "What's the latest gossip in London?"

"Gossip?" Sarah repeated. "I am afraid I do not have many people to share gossip with."

"Well, what have you read in the papers then?" Dora exclaimed impatiently. "I used to love reading the papers. So many stories about dances and balls and gentleman's wives who run off and the like. Mr. Bates, though, he don't let me read the papers. Least not the ones I like."

"He doesn't?" Sarah asked. "Why ever not?"

"He's afraid I'll read something inappropriate," Dora replied with undisguised resentment. Her mouth actually twisted at the word "inappropriate."

"Well, I do keep up with The Charing Cross Courier," Sarah admitted.

"Oh," Dora's eyes sparkled, "any good murders lately?"

Sarah related all the lurid accounts she could remember while sketching out Dora's features. She also promised to smuggle her a society magazine or two on a future visit. As she walked home that day, she reflected that, contrary to what Mrs. Mandeville had taught her daughters, there might well be worse fates for a young woman than spinsterhood.

On her way home, Sarah cut through a side street and came upon a church. There was nothing particularly noteworthy about the church in question. True, it had some nice stained glass windows, but so did a hundred other places as well. It was a Catholic church rather than Anglican, which was more of a rarity in London, but at the end of the day, it was just another bloody church. There was no particular reason it should have caught Sarah's eye that day, but as Sarah passed by it, she saw a trinity of crows on the church's main spire. Something prompted her to go inside. Once she was within the chapel, she breathed in the smell of incense mixed with plaster.

Sarah caught Father Gorman's eye the moment she walked into St. Anne's. She was a stranger to the church. He was certain he'd never seen her before. He'd have remembered her if he had, with those queer big eyes and pale skin. She sat stiffly in a far back pew, looking uncomfortable and out of sorts. Over thirty years of experience as a priest and his own natural intuition told him this was someone who needed to speak with him. She saw him approach her and watched him in a way that was wary and expectant at once. He was a heavyset met man of about fifty with red hair and a beard now sprinkled with grey, and a voice that carried well. A most useful attribute in his chosen calling.

"I was admiring the stained glass, Father," she gestured to the windows displaying various tableaus, from St. Francis with the birds to St. John the Baptist, and finally the Virgin Mary, clothed in blue. Light poured in through the glass and cast luminous rays of color across plaster walls and stone floors. "They're all so beautiful. Perhaps I should consider painting religious subjects."

"Perhaps you should, but did you come in here today just to admire the windows?" She didn't answer and he went on, "When I saw you, I thought you looked troubled."

There was a long pause, but finally she spoke, "I'm not sure why I came here, Rev– I mean, Father. I'm not even Catholic."

"Well, nobody's perfect," he magnanimously declared. Sarah couldn't help but laugh as he continued, "Our doors are open to any who need guidance, even you heathen protestants." He added that last part with a twinkle in his eye.

"And do the rules of confession apply to everyone? Catholic or otherwise?"

"Well, I cannot actually do the rite of confession for you, my child. That would be violating the sacrament."

"Oh," Sarah looked disappointed.

"But even if I cannot offer you a formal confession, I can still listen to you, and I give you my word anything you tell me stays between the two of us."

"So, if I said something to you that made me sound mad, you wouldn't just call to have me committed?"

"You could tell me you'd murdered someone, and I wouldn't tell a soul. I promise."

She stayed thoughtful and silent for a long moment, and he was about to suggest it might be easier for her if they used the confessional booth when she finally spoke, "I have something to show you that you'll probably find hard to believe." She rolled up the sleeve on her dark dress and showed him an arm with a multitude of scars. "I–I–" her voice was choked with shame and despair, "I did these to myself."

Father Gorman nodded, "Ah, did you use a knife or a razor?"

She blinked, baffled, before answering, "A razor and other things."

"Ever stick yourself with a needle perhaps?"

She looked dumbfounded, "Yes. Yes, I have. How did you know?"

"You're not the first, my child, to be afflicted with your condition. There've been others. Mostly young women, though we do get an occasional man. Believe me, if there's one thing we've a long tradition of in Catholicism, it's people trying to make themselves hurt."

"So, you're not shocked?" she said slowly, in disbelief.

He guffawed, "Goodness, child, I've heard things. My Lord, I've seen things that far dwarf this. If I told you even a fraction of them, your hair would turn white! Now, tell me, when did this all start?"

Sarah took a moment to collect herself, "When I was a child. It was right after my parents and brother died." Father Gorman gave a slight nod as if to say this confirmed his suspicion. "The day of their funeral. I was so upset, and I saw the knife, and somehow…" she trailed off.

"You thought you'd feel better if you cut yourself?" he suggested. "Bleed on the outside a bit, just like you were bleeding on the inside?"

"Yes. Yes! How did you know?"

"It's what the other girls told me, too. Now, let me guess. You did feel better at first, but later you felt bad about what you'd done. Probably thought you'd never do it again. Only you did. You wanted to stop, but you didn't know how."

"Yes, my God. Yes, that's exactly how it's been," Sarah gave a sad smile. "I didn't realize my particular condition was so common."

"All man's sorrows feel unique to him alone, but all sorrows have been shared," he told her, not unkindly. "Now you don't have to tell me anything more about yourself if you don't want, but a lot of people do like to tell their stories. Would you?"

They sat there for what seemed an eternity. The light pouring in through the stained glass left pools of colors on the whitewashed walls. She talked about how her life had seemed divided into stages. Before, when she was a vicar's daughter in comfort, and after, when she became a penniless orphan. About Parsley School and how she'd had to leave. About Bromley Hall and being neither family member nor servant. About never feeling like she had a settled home, anywhere. She teared up when she spoke of Adam. She even found herself telling about Hugh Mandeville and how she'd blackmailed him into caring for Adam's family.

"I suppose that was sinful of me, Father," she concluded.

Father Gorman looked at her curiously, "If you'd been trying to feather your own purse, well yes, I'd say you were in the wrong, but you had made a promise to the boy you needed to keep. And this Hugh Mandeville's got his own sins for which to atone. Perhaps you did him a favor by giving him the chance to show charity to others. But I still think you should do at least ten Hail Marys for it."

"I don't know any Hail Marys," Sarah confessed.

"Oh yes, of course, you're a protestant," he stroked his beard. "Do you know Our Father then?"

"Of course," said Sarah.

"Then do ten of those," he proclaimed with satisfaction. "Is there anything else you'd like to tell me, though? Is there a young man involved, somehow, in all this?" he asked shrewdly, and the twitch of Sarah's mouth reassured him that, once again, he'd guessed true.

"Well there was a young man, but I don't know if you could call him involved. We never– I mean, there was no hint of anything like courtship."

"Did you love him?" Father asked softly.

"Yes. I did. I think I still do, but it's hopeless. I'll never marry now. Not with the scars."

"I wouldn't be so sure about that, my child. It's hard to know what our destiny is or what plans God has for us, but one thing I'm sure of: He doesn't want you hurting yourself. Corinthians tells us the body's a temple, and we're not supposed to be vandalizing temples, now are we?"

"I can't say I ever considered myself a temple before," Sarah observed.

"Well, it's high-time you started then. Now, there's a number of things you can do next time you feel like hurting yourself. Prayer, of course. Some girls grab rosaries and do special appeals to St. Dymphna."

"St. Dymphna? I've never heard of her."

"She was the daughter of a pagan king and a Christian woman. Her father wanted to marry her. When she refused, he murdered her."

"That sounds dreadful."

"But she became a martyr and the Lily of Eire, due to her spotless virtue and for the miracles that happened at her tomb. People with epilepsy or other sicknesses in the mind found themselves cured. So, she was named the patron saint of those who are nervous or disturbed," Father Gorman explained. "For folks who are, well, out of their minds – to be blunt about it," he tapped his skull a moment for emphasis.

"A patron saint for madness? I never knew." Somehow, Sarah found herself less offended than bemused. "Perhaps, I should do a picture of her."

"We'd be glad to have it here if you did. Or perhaps you could keep it to pray to her. Many young women find regular confession helps. They've found a few other tricks as well. One girl told me whenever she felt the need upon her, she'd go and beat a carpet for a time until her arm was sore, and then she'd feel better. Another would go down to the coal cellar to scream and kick the walls until the fury left her."

"A pity then, I don't have carpets. Or a cellar. Though maybe there is a cellar, but I doubt my landlady would let me put it to such use."

"Well now, would you consider keeping a journal then?"

"A journal?"

"I knew at least one girl who used to pull out her hair who said writing in a journal helped her. She said when she wrote down whatever was eating at her at the time, it felt a bit better."

"Well," Sarah replied, "I suppose it's worth a try."

"There's the spirit!" Father Gorman proclaimed. "Now, how about those Our Fathers, child? Penitence is good for the soul."

Sarah's Journal

After seeing Father Gorman and reciting ten Our Fathers, I found a stationery store and bought the biggest, fattest journal I could find, bound in black, like a crow's back. I started writing after dinner, and hours later I'm still at it, wasting this candle long into the night. I've written so much now that my hand's starting to cramp up, but tonight I didn't feel the need. For the first time ever, I feel free to say — or rather write — everything that's on my conscience. Even though no one will ever read this, it feels good to unburden oneself. In fact, it's precisely because no one will ever read this that I can unburden myself. I can bleed on the page instead of bleeding my body.

Will writing in this journal help every night I feel the need? I do not know. But it is worth trying and worth the candles and ink.

Addendum to last night. This morning, the first thing I did when I awoke was take the pouch outside and throw it in the dust bin.

Second addendum. I fished the pouch out of the dust bin. I haven't used its contents, but I'm not quite ready to give it up just yet.

Twenty-Six

"Friendship is certainly the finest balm for the pangs of disappointed love."
–Jane Austen, *Northanger Abbey*

Dear Sarah, you naughty creature!

You go months and months without writing me, and then you pack it in as a governess and go off to London to be an artist like some romantic without telling me first? I'm quite shocked, I tell you. If nothing else, you could have asked me for help or for money – or could have come to Portsmouth and stayed with me and baby Francis. We've got oh-so-many things here you could draw and sketch. What captain doesn't want a picture of his boat?

Oh well, it's all done with now, and I suppose London is most exciting. Is it really so filled with crime as all the papers say? You must tell me all your adventures living in the city. And if you don't have any shocking adventures to tell, then do make some up!

Your ever loving,
Geraldine

P.S. Who's this Mr. Clarkson you ever so tantalizingly mentioned?

To Miss Pole,

Poor Sarah. I was relieved to hear from you again after so long. I feared your trials in the schoolroom may have put you beyond the reach of maintaining any social connections at all. I must confess, though, I also have my concerns about your present course of action as well. While I understand completely why the death of that poor child may have turned you against Bromley Hall, London is no place for a respectable young woman to be living alone. I think it would have been far better had you asked to stay with me and painted the countryside. But at least it sounds like you're making your way at present. I only ask, for your own sake, that you be careful. A woman in your position is vulnerable to malicious slander.

My father-in-law, Lord Lomberdale, prefers the country, as do Paul and I. But Paul's elder brother, William, is in London for the season, as well as Paul's eldest sister, Elizabeth, and her husband, Ronald Cheviot. I took the liberty of informing Elizabeth about you and recommending you to do miniatures of their young twins. You should hear from them soon. I rather hope that success with the Staffords – I have full confidence you'll satisfy Elizabeth – will help you procure further commissions among people of quality. I gather, my dear, your connections as of late haven't been of the very best sort, and I hope this helps move you into a better circle of acquaintance. By the way, who's this Mr. Clarkson you mentioned?

–Mrs. Stafford

No respectable boarding house would ever send a male visitor up to see a single young lady living alone unless that visitor was a relative. Sarah, though, was not living in a particularly respectable sort of house. Mrs. Mundy only wanted her tenants to pay their rent on time, not disturb her sleep, and not bring trouble or Scotland Yard to the premises. Beyond that, she didn't much care. So, when Rufus Clarkson came to call on Miss Crow, she sent him right up to the top floor with just a warning, "She's busy with painting right now, and she might not be in the mood to talk."

Sarah had set up her old easel in a corner and was seated in front of her latest endeavor on a rickety old chair.

"Halloo," Mr. Clarkson greeted her, and she turned around, revealing a speck of green paint on her nose.

"Mr. Clarkson!" she looked surprised.

"Sorry for barging in like this, but I was curious to see how you were getting on."

"Surprisingly well," Sarah answered.

"What's that you're working on now?" he pointed to the canvas where there seemed to be the beginnings of the form of a young maiden in a medieval style dress with a green skirt. She wore a white shawl and what tendrils of hair that the shawl did not cover were the color of fine bronze. She was carrying a green Irish cross and there appeared to be a halo around her head, but in the corner of the painting, ominously close to the maiden, was a large and terrible sword.

"Oh, this is something new," Sarah explained. "I've decided to do a representation of a saint which, if it's any good, I plan to donate to a certain church."

"I didn't know you were a Roman," Clarkson commented.

"I'm not. It's a personal matter," was all Sarah said.

"Can you even afford to be giving your work away? You're no amateur gentlewoman taking this up as a hobby." Only Rufus Clarkson would have been so blunt.

"Mrs. Stamford not only paid well, but now that I've painted miniatures of Lord Lomberdale's grandchildren, I've gotten a number of inquiries. I just met one this morning, and I'll start sittings with them the day after tomorrow, and tomorrow I'm meeting with the other inquiries." Her lips twitched, "St. Dymphna may be my last chance for quite some time to paint a subject who won't talk back."

"Do you think you and your Saint... what's it?"

"St. Dymphna."

"Well, do you think you and Dymphna can stand to be parted for a bit? By the way, you've got a little smudge on your nose. Here," he produced a handkerchief and proceeded to carefully polish Sarah's beak. In doing so, for a single moment, one finger grazed her left cheek.

A little water and a dab from Mr. Clarkson's handkerchief removed the paint from Sarah's face. Rather than stay at Mrs. Mundy's, they took a brisk walk through town and through a nearby park. They bought meat pies off a street vendor and ate them seated on a public bench.

"These are good. The crusts are nice and flaky," Sarah observed as she consumed her pie.

"Aye, but they could have been more generous with the meat filling," Clarkson grumbled.

"Seems like enough meat to me."

"But you're built like a bird! Now a Yorkshire fellow like me needs something solid, especially when he's pursuing journalism. It is hungry work, you know! Takes a lot to keep going."

"Listening to meetings of parliament is so hard?"

Clarkson snorted, "It's not just sitting and taking notes like a damned secretary girl! It's about figuring out what angles everyone's playing, why things are happening at all. And then there's the benefit of my political analysis."

"You've got some crumbs there on your coat," Sarah noted. Clarkson brushed them off.

"So, how does one go about analyzing the motives and angles of everyone in parliament?"

"Well, for starters..."

They continued to talk for quite some time on the bench. The conversation flowed easily, as Rufus Clarkson was a born storyteller. Sarah even caught herself laughing once or twice. Mr. Clarkson marveled at how much gaiety seemed to transform her appearance. Really, she seemed quite a different creature altogether since she'd left that hideous family and that awful hall for London. He, for one, heartily approved. Sarah was a peculiar sort of companion to be sure, but he, for one, preferred her to a great many other, more ordinary people. As for the nature of his intentions, well, suffice to say he would not at all mind becoming more familiar, even on intimate terms, with Sarah. In the meantime, he genuinely enjoyed her conversation and companionship, even if it were, alas, strictly platonic for now. It was only to be expected that he'd make a habit of calling on her regularly and help introduce her to the great metropolis.

"You certainly see a lot of that newspaperman," Mrs. Mundy noted one morning over toast and tea.

"I suppose we have been spending an awful lot of time together."

"Hmm," Mrs. Mundy murmured, boring holes into Sarah with her stare.

"What?" Sarah finally asked.

"Do you think he's courtin' you?"

"Courting me?" Sarah nearly choked on her tea and had a coughing fit. Mrs. Mundy gave her a good firm clap on the back to clear her airways.

"Thank you," Sarah murmured. "That was a bit of a shock. You can't honestly believe he thinks of me like that."

"Dunno why he shouldn't. You're young, and you're not half bad looking. Neither is he."

"We're friends. We're just friends. There's nothing else going on."

"Isn't there?" Mrs. Mundy gave Sarah an inquiring look that made her feel uneasy. "Well, he's certainly been very friendly where you're concerned. Helping you find work and all."

"He only felt indebted because I nursed him after an accident."

"Oh, you've nursed him, too, have you?" Mrs. Mundy cocked an eyebrow, and Sarah's cheeks flushed.

"That was– I was just in the right place. There's never been the slightest hint of an understanding," Sarah stammered.

"Understanding! That's a fancy way to put it." Mrs. Mundy shook her head. "Now, mind you, I say from experience, men are usually more trouble than they're worth, but if a girl must marry... well, you could do worse. A lot worse. I would know," Mrs. Mundy added that last part grimly.

Sarah was stunned and speechless. Sarah had been raised since childhood to see herself as undesirable and destined to be an old maid. Her first hopes of romance had met with a bitter rejection that still stung. So, the idea that she might have, unintentionally, made a conquest was a genuine thunderbolt. It seemed to upend her entire perception, not only of Mr. Clarkson, but also of herself as well. Who ever heard of anyone courting a crow? Except for crows courting one another, of course, which had to happen with some regularity, or there'd be no new crows.

"Lot to take in, isn't it, dearie? Now, now, just think about it a bit. And another word of advice: Even decent men like to get as much as they can for free you know. Don't be letting him take any liberties until after the vows have been said." After imparting this piece of wisdom, Mrs. Mundy tottered off to settle accounts with a regular she'd spotted in the corner, leaving Sarah's mind in a whirl.

Unbeknownst to either of them, Mr. Clarkson was, at that very moment, experiencing a predicament of his own. He could not deny his passion for Sarah. More importantly, he valued her for reasons beyond the sensual as well. He truly liked and respected her. She would, he thought, make him a good wife. But for all that, Rufus Clarkson knew marriage to Sarah was simply out of the question for one very good reason. He already had a wife.

Her name was Martha. There was a child, too. A little boy named Samuel who took distressingly after his mother's blood. They lived in Yorkshire with Martha's kinfolk. He sent them money from time to time, but the husband and wife had not seen each other in years. He had been a newspaperman in the city of York before getting a lucky chance to work in London, which he had grasped with both hands. Martha had no desire to live in London, considering it an unhealthy, stinking den of vice, utterly unfit to raise a child in. Indeed, she did not like cities much at all. She preferred the country. He, in the meantime, had found his wife's increasingly devout Calvinism – she started attending church twice a week – completely intolerable. Separation had suited them both admirably. Rufus had considered himself a bachelor again, if not according to the law, then certainly one in spirit. He'd had his share of casual dalliances since moving to London, but none of those past trysts had caused him anything like the genuine crisis of spirit he was having now. Obviously, a man shouldn't be toying with a woman's affections when he had a wife. *But did he really have a wife? Wasn't his marriage, for all practical purposes, over already – no matter what the law or church might say?*

No, he decided it was all right for now to continue his acquaintanceship with Sarah. Rather, the question was how he should go about it. Should he simply tell her the truth? She might be willing to accept a less conventional state of affairs between them. Such living arrangements were not at all unknown among artists, and he heartily approved of them. Then again, Sarah had been raised the daughter of a clergyman. Perhaps it was better not to force her to pretend she was more modern than she truly might be. No, for the time being, there was no reason to press the issue, he concluded. After all, she had never asked about his marital status so he wasn't really lying. That was what he told himself. Besides, absolutely nothing of any kind of romantic or physical nature had even transpired between them as of yet. More the pity.

Sarah's Journal

I had begun to make one progress as an artist only to have another difficulty arise, and such an unexpected one, too. It's a distressing thing in this world that no woman can enjoy any man's company without inviting gossip, and it doesn't take much to be labeled a fallen woman. Even I know that. That's bad enough, but in this case, could there be anything in it?

Could Mr. Clarkson actually be interested in me that way? This is something I'd never asked myself before Mrs. Mundy brought it up. The possibility simply never occurred to me at all, but now I can't get it out of my mind. He has been most helpful, it's true, and he's sought out my company quite a bit now that I think on it. Suppose it's possible he believes he is courting me? Or that he hopes – or expects – something other than friendship to develop? Oh, how unfortunate that would be.

It's not that I don't enjoy his company and conversation - I do - but it's impossible for me to imagine anything beyond that. Now, I know Marianne was very happy with Colonel Brandon after Willoughby deserted her, but I don't know that I'm there yet. And even if I were, well, look how Robert recoiled at the sight of my scars. Why would it be any different for Mr. Clarkson? I know myself to be unworthy of marriage, but other people don't know that. It would be most cruel to give Mr. Clarkson reason to form an attachment to a woman if the sight of her naked flesh would repel him, and while I have no personal experience in such matters, even I know it's customary for women to disrobe before their husbands and lovers. Maybe I'm worried for nothing. Mrs. Mundy might have gotten it all wrong. Indeed, it's likely she has. I've never been one to catch men's eyes, much less their hearts. Why on Earth should that change now?

I don't know what I would say if he should propose marriage. Though I suppose it is possible he might have things in mind other than marriage or mere friendship. Other men have never had any designs on my virtue, but Mr. Clarkson is not like most other men I have known. I honestly do not know if he did have any such intentions whether I should be insulted or flattered by the attention. I do wish I had more experience in these things, or a mother to advise me. Even an aunt or elder sister would do. For now, though, I suppose I must make do with Mrs. Mundy.

Twenty-Seven

"*Maria was married on Saturday. In all important preparations of mind,*
she was complete, being prepared for matrimony by a hatred of home, by the
misery of disappointed affection, and contempt of the man she was to marry. The
bride was elegantly dressed, and the two bridesmaids were duly inferior. Her
mother stood with salts, expecting to be agitated, and her aunt tried to cry.
Marriage is indeed a maneuvering business."
–Jane Austen, *Mansfield Park*

Life in Greenberry did not come to a grinding halt with the departure of Sarah Pole, or even with the death of young Adam. Indeed, things continued along in a quite orderly fashion. The Twelfth Night ball at Gaskell Park was a huge success. Alicia Mandeville dazzled, dressed as a wood nymph, all the better to let her radiant beauty shine. Within a week's time, George Tudbury made the expected proposal, which Alicia was delighted to accept, and both families were well pleased by the match. Gaskell Park was quite happy to receive such a charming new future mistress. Sir Tudbury, meanwhile, began mentally planning all the improvements and additional comforts Alicia Mandeville's thousand pounds a year could bring to the estate.

Thomas Mandeville and his wife were quite happy Alicia was to be so well settled. Mrs. Mandeville was practically skipping through the main hall at the thought of her stepdaughter moving out. The elation was mutual. Seldom, indeed, does a contract thoroughly satisfy all parties to this extent. It was, in fact, to be a double wedding.

Maria Tudbury, having finally forsaken Hugh Mandeville as a lost cause, had accepted the proposal of Reverend Graham. No, wife of a clergyman was not the most desirable outcome, but she wasn't getting any younger, and the specter of old maid status hovered above her. To be an old maid with a sister-in-law, particularly one like Alicia, would be especially dreadful. Even life in a parsonage would be superior to that. Besides, another living had just become available to the Tudbury family to award Reverend Graham. All-in-all, between his own small inheritance, her dowry, and the income from the two livings, the future Mr. and Mrs. Graham would have almost two-thousand a year, which would certainly provide a few comforts, though it was nothing to the splendor of Gaskell Park. Alicia's triumph was thus made all the sweeter for knowing she wouldn't have to share a roof with a sister, and for knowing that she'd caught the bigger fish, even though Maria might have been born to higher birth. Indeed, Alicia would be ascending to the rank Maria had once enjoyed.

Of course, for Alicia Mandeville, Sarah was the furthest thing from her mind. First, there were the arrangements for her wedding, which was the social event of the year in Greenberry. As a bride, Alicia was radiant as usual. She utterly eclipsed her bridesmaids. After the ceremony, bride and groom had departed immediately for London and the house in town. All the better for the new Mrs. Tudbury to celebrate her success. The only thing marring Alicia's triumph was her wedding night and the inevitable marital duties she had to suffer. They were, of course, every wife's cross to bear and Gaskell Park must have an heir someday, lest Maria's children inherit instead. God forbid! Nevertheless, as Alicia lay with her husband grunting away on top of her, she couldn't help but feel she was paying a high price for her current position indeed. These moments of sweaty unpleasantness never lasted very long, but she still had to look at him over the breakfast table and endure his conversation. Fortunately, London was full of distractions for George. Alicia was more than happy to encourage him to spend as much time at his clubs and other pursuits as possible. There was plenty for her to do as well. Shops to visit, theatre performances to attend, card games to play, and gossip galore. And of course, social calls to be made. London was always full of handsome, charming men, all of whom were more amusing than George.

A pity a lady is not supposed to flirt once she has married, but there was no rule saying you can't at least be friendly and enjoy the company of amiable gentlemen was there? Like the delightful Mr. Abbott, who had such amusing anecdotes and clever conversation. Though, sadly, she couldn't enjoy Mr. Abbott or other gentleman's company the way Alicia would have liked. George showed signs of a most vexing jealous streak, and Alicia found she had to watch herself more in public these days. Why, George seemed annoyed if she garnered too much attention even by providing musical entertainment. All in all, Alicia's prize marriage was not proving to be quite as glittering as she might have hoped. Still, there were consolations. Beyond a grand income and handsome homes, Alicia was, as the future Lady Tudbury, ascending into a finer set of circles than she'd ever climbed before.

Indeed, she had just been invited to call upon the home of Sir John Tudbury's cousin, Lady Fowler. This was, by far, the most important of all the social calls she'd been paying. Lady Fowler was not only an immensely wealthy widow but a viscountess. An association with her would open doors to the most fashionable and exalted circles in all of London. The night before, as George lie snoring beside her, Alicia was awake and worrying about their first meeting. She was determined to make an excellent first impression. She was equally determined to start using a separate bed chamber from her new husband as soon as possible.

Lady Fowler lived in an elegant townhouse in Mayfair with a big brass knocker on the door. She received visitors in her parlor where a Chinese vase displayed the cards of all the socially relevant people who'd called upon Lady Fowler in recent memory. It was an impressive list of names. Alicia had lovely visions of someday, when her father-in-law passed on and she was Lady Tudbury, of having a display of cards equally, if not more, impressive. Someday, she would be the one to whom eager young social climbers would wish to pay homage.

The footman brought her to Lady Fowler to be presented. The dowager sat on her favorite blue settee from which she examined all her supplicants. It was an exquisite salon, decorated predominantly in blues and creams in the French style with the occasional curio from the East thrown in as well. Alicia's eyes took it all in eagerly, gathering notes for decorating schemes of her own. Lady Fowler was resplendent in a silk gown made by one of London's most exclusive seamstresses. Her face was face heavy with powder, and she held a bejeweled fan, but what impressed Alicia most was how ugly the woman was. This was no mere ordinary ugliness but an ugliness rather of distinction. Lady Fowler's moles, her dry papery skin, her pursed lips, and sturgeon eyes posed an ugliness from which one couldn't look away. The footman announced her. Alicia entered the room, giving her deepest and most demure curtsey. The usual greetings were exchanged, and the usual dull conversation had commenced when they were interrupted by the arrival of a King Charles Spaniel, who ran into the room and began tugging at Lady Fowler's knee.

"Jeanne Marie!" Lady Fowler exclaimed, her hands instinctively pulling the dog into her lap, oblivious to the risk of shedding as the dog whined for her mistress's attention. "But you're supposed to be in the Green Room sitting for Miss Crow!"

"Sorry, ma'am. I think she missed you. But we've made good progress so fa–" A familiar voice had rung out from the chamber beyond, and it was followed by an all-too familiar face—a face which Alicia had never expected to see again and had never wanted to see again, but there was Sarah Pole, standing before her and staring at Alicia. Alicia stared back. Lady Fowler looked up sharply.

"Do you two know each other?"

Sarah was the first to recover, "I've had the pleasure of painting Miss Mandeville's likeness in the past. I've also painted other members of her family as well." It was true. Every word. And yet it didn't give an entirely accurate impression.

"It's Tudbury now," Alicia somehow managed to speak. "Mrs. Tudbury. I'm married."

"Miss Crow," Lady Fowler began, and Alicia immediately wondered at the change in name, "is doing a portrait of Jeanne Marie here." She gave the Spaniel an indulgent pat on the head. "I do hope she does justice to my little darling. I've never had such a fine little bitch before."

Lady Fowler was, to date, the most high-born client to hire Sarah. The fee she offered had been a tempting one indeed. However, when first presented to the viscountess, Sarah had felt a sense of dread. She wasn't sure even her abilities as a portraitist were up to the job of both flattering Lady Fowler's visage while still rendering her recognizable. It had been to Sarah's considerable relief to learn that Jeanne Marie was to be her subject instead.

"Well, I have some preliminary drawings for you to examine," Sarah had brought her sketchpad with her, and soon she and Lady Fowler were carefully examining images of Jeanne Marie while ignoring Alicia altogether. Lady Fowler fastened upon one sketch.

"There," she proclaimed firmly. "This one, here. You've captured her sweet nature perfectly. Can you make that the portrait?"

"Absolutely."

"I wager you'll want another sitting, though. Same time tomorrow?"

"Of course."

"Excellent!" the old lady's smile set the wrinkles in her face into a whole new set of lines. Jeanne Marie whimpered and whined.

"Are you tired, my little darling?" Lady Fowler asked Jeanne Marie, who gave a plaintive reply. "We're done for the day," Lady Fowler proclaimed and rang a little bell. "Josiah, see these young ladies out!"

And before she quite knew what happened, Alicia stood outside the townhouse next to Sarah. For a moment, she was too flustered to speak, but as Sarah turned to walk away in the other direction, she finally found her voice.

"And what the devil are you doing here? At Lady Fowler's house?" Alicia demanded. This was hardly the height of etiquette, but Alicia's shock put her beyond the point of caring. Besides, what need was there to be polite to a governess? Or rather a former governess. God only knew what sort of thing this bony, beaky creature was now. She might not even be a lady at all.

"I thought it was pretty clear I'm doing a portrait of Jeanne Marie," Sarah replied dryly.

"Oh, don't start with me. You know perfectly well what I mean. How are you suddenly doing portraits for nobility, or even their pets? And since when do you go around by the name of 'Crow?'" Alicia demanded. She was getting a chance to see Sarah more clearly, and while there was no notable change in her wardrobe or mode of dress, something seemed different about her. Her cheeks held more color and her gaze seemed bolder – even, one might say, impertinent.

"My life's changed, and with it, my name changed as well. The same could be said for you. Congratulations, by the way, on your marriage. A most suitable match," Sarah's voice and face remained calm, yet Alicia felt she detected a note of mockery. The idea that Sarah, of all people, might mock her was infuriating. Alicia summoned all the dignity she possessed to coldly answer.

"Thank you. I've never been happier."

"I can see that," Sarah responded with equal coolness. "How are your sisters by the way? Do they get on with Miss Gardiner?"

"How should I know? I was far too busy planning my wedding for the schoolroom, and since my marriage, I haven't set foot in Bromley Hall once."

"Of course, you haven't." As Sarah's eyes met hers, Alicia had a rare epiphany. She finally understood what it was she had never liked about Bromley Hall's former governess. Not her somber appearance or her quietness. Rather that, while quiet, she seemed to be secretly judging everyone and everything around her, including Alicia. To be judged by one's social inferior is a complete reversal of the proper order of things. Worse still, Alicia sensed the other young woman's conclusions were less than flattering. In fact, for a moment, she detected something like pity in Sarah's eyes. If feeling mocked by Sarah had been infuriating, to feel pitied by her was absolutely insufferable. Happily for Alicia, the moment did not last long.

"Well Miss Mand– I mean, Mrs. Tudbury, I have other appointments, and I'm sure you're equally busy as well," Sarah gave a slight curtsey and walked off in the opposite direction without a backward glance.

Alicia continued on with the rest of her day, determined not to waste another moment's thought on Miss Pole or Miss Crow or whoever she was. Yet, Alicia's mind would return again and again to the vexing matter and to that strange note of pity she thought she'd seen. It was unfathomable and unlikely, but it gave Alicia more sleepless nights than she would ever admit.

Sarah's Journal

Lady Fowler was easy enough to get on with, if perhaps a bit eccentric. There are some who might have been insulted by the offer to paint a lapdog, but I am not one of them. The fee's good, and Jeanne Marie is better looking and better tempered than clients I have had in the past. Perhaps I could become known as a portraitist for animals. A whole new market to explore!

No, the job itself was all well and good, but to come across Alicia again! You would think in a place as large as London you wouldn't have to worry about accidentally meeting people from your past. It makes me laugh. Alicia marries a title, and I become an artist, and we both are invited to the same house. Of course, she goes home to what is, I am sure, a comfortable home with servants and every luxury, while I come back to this little attic. But I feel I have the much better deal than she, poor thing. I won't pretend I ever liked her, but I felt a twinge of pity for her to learn she was married to George Tudbury. It doesn't appear to suit her. Oh, she's still beautiful, but her luminosity seemed dimmed. Though maybe that was my own imagination.

I didn't even try asking her about the Riggs family. I doubt she even remembers who they are. But it reminds me that I promised Elinor and Violet I would write to them, and so far I haven't. But now I'm just going to put this journal aside for a moment so I can write an extra long letter to the girls. Despite my attempts at a new life, I confess I am curious about what has happened in Greenberry since I left and whether Robert.... but I must not think of Robert. That's all over and done with.

Twenty-Eight

"*But he that dares not grasp the thorn should never crave the Rose.*"
–Anne Brontë

When Robert Healey first heard of Alicia's engagement to George Tudbury, he ruefully found himself completely indifferent to the whole matter. However strong his previous passion – or rather infatuation – with Alicia had been, it had somehow dissipated into nothing. He was now left only with bewilderment over what he had ever seen in her to begin with. Another woman, though, lingered in his thoughts. While he had returned to the Mandeville house between Adam's death and Sarah's departure, he had not seen her. She had kept away, and he'd handled Thomas's bleeding alone. At the time, this had been a relief. He had been so angry and confused, he did not know what he would have said or done had he seen her.

But then, he had heard Sarah had left very suddenly, and that a new governess had just been rushed in from London. The news had raised a few eyebrows. More than a few tongues in Greenberry wagged on the matter with speculation about the sudden switch. Had the young lady been caught stealing? Had she, as they say, gotten herself in the family way? Or had Mrs. Mandeville simply taken against her? Another item of curiosity was the way Hugh Mandeville had uncharacteristically taken up the welfare of the Riggs family by settling a small annuity on the mother and apprenticing one daughter to the village seamstress. It was all very good of him to do and certainly reflected the spirit of noblesse oblige, but before then, Hugh Mandeville hadn't been known for having much of a sense of noblesse oblige. Indeed, he had given the local cottagers the distinct impression of thinking all the oblige belonged on the other side of the equation. Perhaps he was turning over a new leaf.

Robert had a good understanding for why Sarah had departed. He also suspected she was somehow involved in Hugh's generosity to the Riggs family, though he wasn't sure how. The question which needed answering was where was Sarah now? Discreet inquiries at the hall had revealed only that she had taken the coach to London. But where in London? No one knew of any forwarding address, and in a city so large, there would almost surely be no hope of finding her, if she was really there at all. If she was even alive at all. She had proven herself a deeply troubled young woman, willing to resort to extremes. Now, set adrift in a world without family, friends, or any money to speak of, what might have happened to her? It was an anxiety that gnawed away at him. He found himself bitterly regretting not having spoken to her again to prevent her from doing something so foolish. What exactly he would or could have said, he didn't know, but he felt quite certain he ought to have done something.

As a country doctor, he was always busy. It seemed like half the town had come down with aches and chills. Then, Jem Howe, in a drunken stupor, somehow managed to impale himself with a five-inch knife directly into his chest. Demonstrating that there truly is a force that looks after fools and drunks, he had managed to miss every major organ and blood vessel. The wound never even become infected. Jem Howe took this as evidence that he truly was invincible. He would boast of his injury and show off the scar to anyone who would listen.

There were all the usual broken bones and amputations to be performed. Soon, Dr. Healey found his medical kit needed to be replenished. He told himself that was his only purpose in going to London, but deep down, he hoped, by some miracle, while he was in town, to stumble across a familiar pale face. But no one he met in London knew anything of a governess or artist by the name of Miss Pole.

His bleedings of Thomas Mandeville continued. One day in spring, as he was leaving, he came across Elinor and Violet Mandeville. Elinor held a large, fat envelope in her hand, and Violet was trying to snatch it away from her.

"Let me see it, Elinor!" Violet demanded. Elinor ignored her and was focused on reading the sheets of paper enclosed.

"Girls! Girls!" Robert interjected. "Where is your governess?"

"She's asleep in the schoolroom," Violet announced dismissively. "She does that sometimes after we've been outside." Miss Gardiner was a heavyset woman in her forties. She was frequently short of breath and found it most difficult to keep up with the Mandeville children. Moreover, she sometimes found herself waking in the middle of the night, which meant it was not unheard of for her to occasionally doze off in her chair in the schoolroom. Rather than rouse her, Elinor and Violet ruthlessly exploited these opportunities to wander around on their own.

"Miss Pole wrote us a letter," Elinor explained. "It's just been delivered."

"And she won't let me see it!" Violet was indignant at the injustice. Robert gave a start.

"Miss Pole wrote you?" he asked, carefully, and he felt something quicken in his veins.

"Uh-huh, she's in London now," Elinor helpfully replied.

"It's my turn!" Violet howled.

"I haven't finished reading!"

"Tell you what," Robert interjected, playing the part of peacekeeper with no one else around to take up the mantle. "Why don't we all find a seat somewhere, and we can read the letter together?"

The suggestion was agreeable. A comfortable sofa was found where Robert sat in the middle with a Mandeville child on either side of him. He began to read aloud.

Dear Elinor and Violet,

I am terribly sorry to have been so remiss in writing to you in the past, and I hope you may pardon the lateness of this letter. In my defense, I have been very, very busy. I live in London now, above a coffee house, with a pair of pigeons named Percival and

Peck. All three of us, birds together! I enjoy afternoon tea with both of them as they're quite fond of crumbs.

At this point, Robert stopped.

"Birds?" he wondered aloud. "What does she mean by all us birds?"

"Because Sarah's a bird, too," Elinor explained, exasperated and as if trying to get a simple concept across to a rather slow child.

"Sarah's a pigeon, too?" Robert was befuddled.

"No, Sarah's a crow, silly!" Violet laughed at him.

"Oh yes, a crow. That makes perfect sense," Robert replied. "How could I have failed to have seen that?"

"Keep reading!" This came from both girls at once. Robert obeyed.

Percival is the larger of the two. He has a head of fine white feathers. Being such a proud, handsome fellow, he likes to puff out his chest as far he can. Peck's feathers are all brown and grey, and he's a rather scrawny fellow. In fact, my landlady, Mrs. Mundy, compared him to a rat with wings, which was not very kind of her. We can't all be handsome birds, now can we?

I've been painting pictures for a living. A lot of people like having portraits of themselves, like the one I did of you dear girls. Sadly, not all people are as pretty or as easy to paint as you two were, but I had another client just the other day I liked almost as much as you two. Her name is Jeanne Marie.

"She likes a French girl nearly as much as she liked us?" Elinor was affronted. Robert continued to read aloud.

Jeanne Marie is a pretty young thing of about three years old with soft white and brown fur, long floppy ears, and a pert little tail, which she wags constantly.

"Oh, she's talking about a dog," Elinor and Violet's feelings were salved.

It's very wicked of me to say so, I know, but poor George always did resemble a monkey.

At that moment, both Elinor and Violet collapsed into hysterical giggles and Robert had to speak sharply to get them to quiet down, though he secretly rather shared their mirth.

He and Alicia must have seemed like a very mismatched pair walking down the aisle.

"They did!" Elinor laughed again.

Alicia and I did not speak long, and I did not get to ask her all the questions I had about your family and Bromley Hall. I do hope your mama and papa are not too upset at Hugh for not wedding Miss Ambrose or Miss Tudbury. I also hope your parents can make peace with the fact that Hugh will never marry.

"Well, that's odd. Why does she write Hugh will never marry?" Violet frowned.

"Maybe because all the girls around here have married other men," Elinor observed wisely. "There's no one left in Greenberry who is good enough for him, mama says, and he spends too much hunting and riding to meet anyone else." Violet nodded. That made sense. Robert harbored a different opinion on the matter but decided to keep such thoughts to himself.

London is very different from Greenberry, or any other place I have lived before. It makes me feel rather like a simple country girl from time to time. Fortunately, I have Mr. Clarkson here as my guide. You do remember Mr. Clarkson, don't you?

"He's the man who fell off the coach!" Violet declared, happy to know the answer.

"Yes, he was," Robert said slowly. "I didn't know he and Sar— Miss Pole had kept in touch."

He's become a very dear friend. I do not know what I would have done here without him.

At that moment, Robert paused in his reading, and much to Elinor and

Violet's surprise, made a sound like he was grinding his teeth. It was only after being nudged by Elinor that he continued.

> *I wonder if either of you girls could be so kind as to find out about the Riggs family and how they are doing since the death of poor Adam? I realize it would not be appropriate for you to visit yourselves, but perhaps you could ask one of the servants to make enquiries? I would be very grateful if you did so.*

With love,
Miss Pole

There was another page enclosed, and unfolded, it revealed a sketch of two pigeons, Percival and Peck, just as they had been described in the letter. The girls admired the picture and then Violet asked, "But how will we find out about the Riggs?"

"Maybe we can ask Mrs. Brown," Elinor mused.

"There's no need," Robert announced. "I'll visit them myself."

"Then you can tell us all about them and we can write to Miss Pole!" Violet said eagerly.

"Or maybe I could write to Miss Pole," Robert suggested.

"But she didn't write to you," Violet pointed out.

Elinor nodded and added, "She never mentioned you at all."

This stopped Robert cold. It was true. Sarah's letter had not said one word about him, nor had she asked about him. It was as if he no longer existed to her at all. It felt like a blow to the gut. Had their last meeting, harsh as it was, forever poisoned him in her eyes? Or had she always been indifferent? With Miss Pole, who could know? He had never been able to read her very well. In fact, he admitted to himself, ruefully, he was apparently not very good at reading women at all, going by his unfortunate infatuation with Alicia Mandeville. But, in his defense, Miss Pole really was a peculiar specimen altogether—a woman who called herself a crow, whose dark, simple attire hid skin that she had marked, and who gave up being a governess with apparently no thought at all to run away to London and become an artist!

Who could understand such a woman?

Robert did, however, visit the Riggs in their various quarters. He found the family still grieving, but materially, at least they appeared to be getting on all right. Polly and Meg were now clean, decently clothed, and comfortably ensconced in their respective new situations. Mrs. Riggs had lost some of the dreaded pinched look in her face, and even baby Rosie was now growing at an astonishing rate. He conveyed these impressions to Elinor, who included them in her next letter to Sarah. Elinor did not, however, think to mention Robert's role in ascertaining any of these facts.

Twenty-Nine

"There is nothing on this Earth more prized than true friendship."
—Thomas Aquinas

Geraldine's visit to London was unexpected, though it was a good time to visit. Winter had melted into a glorious spring, and London was at its finest. The letter announcing her visit with her baby arrived only days before she did. They met inside Sarah's attic room and embraced. There was much shouting, laughter, and cries of delight. Baby Francis was *oohed* and *aahed* over like the little princeling he was.

"What on Earth brings you to London, dear?" Sarah asked.

"Joel had business in town, and I decided to join him so I could call on you," Geraldine embraced Sarah tightly before taking a step back to examine her. Her eyes examined Sarah from head to toe, just as Sarah's eyes examined her.

"London air is said to be unhealthy, but it certainly seems to agree with you," Geraldine proclaimed.

"Marriage has certainly agreed with you as well," Sarah replied.

Sarah marveled at the subtle changes in Geraldine's appearance since she had last seen her more than two years ago. The changes in face and figure, which would have come imperceptibly over the years if she had seen her on a daily basis. Geraldine Nesbitt, the troublesome schoolgirl, was a different creature from the new Mrs. Harris. Her face and shape had both filled out more, the inevitable consequence of her new status as wife and mother. She bore a more matronly countenance as well, but some spark in her black eyes hinted that the mischief-making vixen who Sarah remembered had not entirely vanished.

Meanwhile, Geraldine reflected on how different Sarah seemed. Oh, she still had the same unfortunate beaky nose, but her face had managed to catch up to it more. There was some color in her cheeks, and even her figure had improved as well. Sarah was not, nor ever would be, a great beauty, but she was a far cry from the drab, bony creature she had once been.

Geraldine's eyes did not miss the simplicity or shabbiness of Sarah's new surroundings, but she didn't say anything on the matter. She did, however, have many appreciative comments to make on the paintings on display.

"Blazes, we've both come a long way, haven't we?" Geraldine threw her head back and laughed. "You're an artist now, just like you always wanted to be. I never got to be a pirate," she said. Did Sarah detect something wistful in Geraldine's tone?

"But I may yet raise one! Francis here could be quite the buccaneer someday, eh?" Francis's only comment was a sleepy yawn. "Both the men in my life certainly keep me busy," Geraldine prattled on with evident self-satisfaction. "And what about you, dear?" she asked slyly. "Are there any men in your life?" A sudden flush in Sarah's cheeks let Geraldine know she'd struck gold. "Ha! I knew it! It's that Rufus Clarkson fellow, isn't it?"

"It is," Sarah admitted. Geraldine gave a very un-matronly squeal.

"Well, now you must tell me all about it!"

"I will, but let's go downstairs first and get some tea." They did. Baby Francis was left to the care of Mrs. Mundy so the young woman could better converse uninterrupted. Sarah relayed to Geraldine all her adventures since arriving in London and her acquaintanceship.

"A newspaperman! Oh, Sarah, you do things so differently! It must be because you're an artist. Most girls of your upbringing would set their sights on a clergyman."

"I didn't set my sights on him," Sarah protested.

"I know, rather he is the one pursuing you. Is he courting you in earnest," Geraldine asked, "or is he simply amusing himself?"

"I really don't know," Sarah confessed. "He's been attentive, but he's never spoken anything of engagement or marriage. To be honest, I don't know if he's even the marrying kind."

"Hmm..." Geraldine trilled. "Well now, he's got a bit to explain, doesn't he, if he's leading you on with no thought of putting up the banns? Hardly gentlemanly of him, is it? And you do have your reputation to consider."

"My reputation? You sound just like Clara!" Sarah laughed, and Geraldine gave an exaggerated shudder.

"Bollocks! I do, don't I?" she laughed.

"I am a penniless woman living alone in London and earning my own bread," Sarah reminded Geraldine. "I think I am a bit beyond caring about my reputation at this point."

"Never say that to Clara, or she'd cut you out of her life altogether. She may have to anyway, once she becomes a noblewoman." At Sarah's expression of confusion Geralidine asked, "Haven't you heard?"

"Heard what?" Sarah responded.

Geraldine was happy to enlighten her, "Paul Stafford's older brother, William, has had his health absolutely wrecked. Too much drink and debauchery. He's back at his family estate, under constant nursing, but no one thinks he'll live out the year, which means his brother will get the title and the estate, and Clara will be the next Lady Lomberdale."

"My, my... she's never written anything of the matter to me."

"She probably thought it wouldn't be proper, dancing on her brother-in-law's grave while his body's still warm," Geraldine noted shrewdly. "From all accounts, William's been the disgrace of the family for years, but enough about all that! The fact remains, Sarah, you and your newspaperman are due a talk. Find out exactly what his intentions are."

"It would probably be prudent," Sarah mused, "except there is one problem."

"Oh?" Geraldine cocked her eyebrows.

"I am not entirely sure what my intentions are toward him either. Even if he did wish to marry me, I don't know if I would have him!" Sarah blurted out. "Do not misunderstand me, I greatly enjoy his company, but as for marriage, I'm just not sure."

"Now, don't be too modern and bohemian here, Sarah!" Geraldine warned. "You don't want to end up like any of Lord Byron's former mistresses. One of them, Claire-something or other, was sister-in-law to Shelley, who had Byron's child. Byron took the girl away from her! She never saw her again, and then the child died. Or look at Lady Hamilton after Lord Nelson perished at Trafalgar, left to die slowly from poverty and drink. I couldn't bear to see anything like that happen to you!"

"Don't worry. I assure you, I have no intention of being anybody's mistress," Sarah was quite firm.

"Then what do you intend?"

"I don't know. I like him. I like him a lot, but it would be a lie for me to say I loved him. At least at present," Sarah confessed. There was a long pause.

"Is it simply a matter of time before you do feel that, Sarah? Or does Mr. Clarkson have a rival for your affections?"

"A rival? No, no," Sarah emphatically shook her head. "No, I mean, the idea is just nonsense. What rival could there possibly be?"

Geraldine looked skeptical, "London is a big town. It would not be so strange for you to have met more than one gentleman. I would understand if that confused matters for you."

Sarah was adamant, "I promise you, Geraldine. There is no one in London to, as you say, 'confuse matters.'"

"And what about the doctor you met in Greenberry?" Geraldine came to her main point. "You mentioned him more than once in your letters."

Sarah was quiet for a moment. "Dr. Healey and I have had no correspondence since I moved," she finally declared. "I doubt I will ever see him again."

"Well, if that is the case," Geraldine pronounced, "then I say, presuming Mr. Clarkson wishes to marry you, you should!"

"I should?" Sarah was nonplussed.

"Indeed," Geraldine nodded. "You are at least friends with him and, given time, if you were wed, I think you would grow to love him. I understand why you left being a governess and decided to come here and paint, I really do. But Clara and I both worry about you. We've both started families while you're all alone."

Sarah bridled at that, "I have my clients. I've made friends since coming here."

"A landlady and a pair of pigeons are no substitute for a husband and children, believe me. Can you honestly tell me you never feel alone at night? Sleeping all by yourself?" Sarah colored once more, and Geraldine pressed on, "You, my dear, are simply too good with children never to be a mother yourself, and Sarah, dear," Geraldine paused as if embarrassed, but then went on gingerly, "it is so difficult to say this! You know how I adore you, but well, fact is, a lady in your position is unlikely to have any other offers."

"Oh," said Sarah. "Oh."

"Not that you don't deserve them, but you have no dowry and no family."

"I understand. I said as much myself when we were children. Have no fear of offending me."

Geraldine was relieved. Not only that Sarah was not taking offense, but more importantly, she was realistic about her prospects. Geraldine looked Sarah directly in the eye.

"Now, you have no mother to guide you here, but you are like a sister to me, and as a sister, if Mr. Clarkson does propose then please, please, Sarah, for your own sake, accept him!"

"Well, I'll certainly consider it," Sarah promised.

"Good. One reason I'm telling you all this now is we might not have a chance to converse again for some time. I told you Joel was in town on business, right?"

"You did."

"Well, the business is there are plans for a voyage to India, and when he goes, baby Francis and I will go with him," Geraldine grinned. "You know I've always wanted to travel. Travel outside of England, I mean. Now here's my chance!" And the two former school friends spent the rest of their time together discussing elephants, oppressive heat, ancient temples, snake charmers, armed uprisings, and all the other things Geraldine could look forward to in her future home.

Sarah's Journal

Is Geraldine right? Are they all right? Not just Geraldine, but Mrs. Mundy and Clara as well? The "hints" Clara dropped in her last letter were broad enough to flatten me. If Mr. Clarkson were to ask for my hand, should I accept him, even if I do not, at present, feel anything more for him than esteem and friendship?

But perhaps that is a good thing. Perhaps being passionate about someone is always doomed to fail. Look at Guinevere and Juliet. Marianne Dashwood lost Willoughby, but she was happy with Colonel Brandon, and, in time, came to love him with all her heart. Perhaps it would be the same for me? It may not be flattering to think I would never have any other suitors in life, but it is perhaps true. I am not getting any younger, after all, nor am I much of a prize to begin with. Certainly Miss Austen would argue it was better for a woman to marry someone she at least esteemed rather than be an old maid and penniless. Of course, Miss Austen's heroines never had a secret vice like mine. It would be impossible to hide my scars from a husband.

And while I keep busy enough here in London and have no shortage of people to talk to, it does get lonely at night. Cold, too, in winter. I would most certainly prefer not to spend another long, dark winter sleeping alone in a cold attic. And there's the consideration of my social circle. I'm happy for Geraldine, I truly am, but I know I'll miss her. And if Clara does become Lady Lomberdale, as Geraldine thinks she will, the odds of my ever visiting with her again go down precipitously, too. Doubtful Clara would even have time to correspond with me at all if she were to take on the duties of a great lady.

Then there's the question of children. It is not something I have thought of previously. It seemed so beyond my reach, but I did love my little brother William very much. I was quite fond of Elinor and Violet as well.

If I did marry Mr. Clarkson, I could have a family of my own. I could have a fine, handsome little boy. I could have a darling little daughter. Maybe they would look like me. Poor things! Or maybe they would take after their father. Or perhaps they would look like William or my parents did. Oh, how wonderful that would be! No, Geraldine is right. If I were to get a proposal, I would be a fool to refuse.

Now it is simply a question of whether he will propose.

Thirty

"The sunlight claps the Earth; and the moonbeams kiss the sea:
what are all these kissings worth, if thou kiss not me?"
–Percy Bysshe Shelley

"Dear God, this city reeks," Sarah proclaimed over tea one afternoon with Mrs. Mundy and Mr. Clarkson. The latter had been particularly busy as of late with writing about Robert Peel's new Judgement of Death Act, which would allow judges to commute sentences for crimes other than murder or treason to mere transportation or life imprisonment. It was one week after Geraldine and Francis had returned to Plymouth. Geraldine's timing had been impeccable. As the weather grew ever hotter, the odor of thousands of daily privies became overwhelming. Moreover, it wasn't unheard of for poor folks to urinate or defecate right in the middle of side streets and alleyways. On top of it all, there were animal carcasses from the slaughterhouses everywhere as well. It all combined to make a stench fouler and more malodorous than could be imagined. Finally, one was faced with an increase of sweating as well and a constant feeling of stickiness. Small wonder that many considered London, with its effluvia, to be a place of sickness. At times such as this, Sarah looked back fondly on Weberley and the briny smell of the sea, or Greenberry's fresh country air. Mrs. Mundy, however, was unsympathetic.

"It's only July, love. If you think it's bad now wait 'til August. Parliament will be closing soon for the season, and all the gentry will flee the season with them."

"Then what'll we do?" Sarah exclaimed. "You," she addressed Mr. Clarkson, "you won't have anything happening in parliament to write about, and everyone who can afford to have their portrait done or buy pictures will be gone. Even Mrs. Mundy's business will be slower." Her companions were unfazed.

"I don't serve gentry, dearie," Mrs. Mundy noted. "Though it's true folks drink less coffee and tea this time of year than winter, when they need warming up."

"London still gets plenty of crime during August," Mr. Clarkson pointed out. "More, actually. Everyone's in shorter temper. I'm sure I'll find plenty of murders and hangings to entertain my readers with," he concluded nonchalantly.

"Still doesn't solve my problem, though," Sarah noted gloomily. "Business is already slowing down, even those who stay in town will have less and less patience for a long, hot sitting. For that matter, I'm not sure I will either. Maybe this is a good time for me to take up Geraldine's invitation to Portsmouth or visit Clara. She writes so lovingly about the parsonage at which she now resides."

"A country parsonage!" Mr. Clarkson snorted rudely. "Dullest places on Earth. I'd take a prison first!"

"I grew up in one," said Sarah. "A country parsonage, that is. And while I have no experience of the latter, I feel quite sure the former was more desirable." Though Sarah's tone was calm, her back stiffened. Mr. Clarkson suddenly felt a change in topic would be in order.

"What I mean to say, Miss Po— Miss Crow, is that you've barely begun to taste the delights of the great city! There's so much more of London to see. The Tower of London! Covent Garden! Rotten Row! Public executions!"

"She's not even been to Vauxhall yet," Mrs. Mundy helpfully added.

Mr. Clarkson was astonished, "Never been to Vauxhall! I've never heard anything so outrageous in my life!"

"Everyone goes to Vauxhall," Mrs. Mundy chimed in again.

"Well, not everyone, obviously, because I haven't gone. I've read quite enough about it in books," Sarah retorted, thinking of Frances Burney's novel, *Evelina*, and the misadventures the titular heroine had endured in Vauxhall and other pleasure gardens. Since coming to London, she'd seen and heard things arguably more shocking than anything in the novel. Still, the impressions she'd formed as an early reader had left her with little desire to visit the notorious gardens.

"Well now, then I'm taking you! I've got business tonight and tomorrow, but day after tomorrow, we're going." Sarah looked ready to protest, but Mr. Clarkson went on, "I'll accept no refusal!"

They departed for the gardens after dusk. The Thames was remarkably pleasant that evening with a light breeze that thankfully blew downwind of the sewage. Sarah greatly enjoyed the walk across the bridge. The summer heat of the day had cooled into a most wonderful balmy evening. At last, they approached the gate to Vauxhall. Reading *Evelina* may have given Sarah a general idea of what Vauxhall was, but the actual experience far dwarfed anything that could be put to pen.

They could hear the sounds of music long before they reached the main entrance that fronted the river and where admission was paid. Mr. Clarkson offered to pay for Sarah's admission, but she insisted on using her own coin. Upon entering the buildings, from the Turkish tent to the famed rotunda, everything was done in Rococo style. From there, they proceeded along the grove, where the supper boxes lined walkways on either side. In front of the boxes stood the orchestra building and a statue of Handel playing his lyre. As they proceeded along the Grand Walk, they came across a golden statue of Aurora and a life-size statue of Milton, but the statues, as lovely as they were, scarcely made any impression on Sarah. She was too taken with the lights.

After dark, Vauxhalls Gardens was lit by over fifteen thousand gas lamps carefully hung in trees. As a result, the rough painted boards and towers among particularly formal garden walkways were transformed into an enchanted kingdom that delighted and overwhelmed the senses. It was a spectacular effect, and one that Burney sadly had not done full justice to in *Evelina*, or so Sarah concluded.

Thousands of people were in attendance that night to admire the fireworks displays and the magnificent mirrors and chandeliers of the rotunda. An appearance by Aladdin and other figures from *Arabian Nights* would not have seemed surprising here. Fireworks exploded overhead with fantastic displays in red, yellow, and orange that lit up the sky like dragons. The famous Madame Saqui performed her tight rope act to universal applause. The attendees came from all walks of life. Some had the look of common tradesmen. Others were the most gorgeously and expensively attired fops among London. There were also a number of young female beauties from London's streets who would rush in upon gentleman in groups, pleading that the men should buy them some wine. Vauxhall and other pleasure gardens were always excellent places for prostitutes to find business, and all sorts of transactions could be conducted among the darker alleys. Unlike the literary heroine Evelina, though, Sarah was used to the sight of London's first working women and a great deal of other seedy things as well. Being less situated to be scandalized by anything she saw in the gardens, she was far more receptive to its enchantments and sensory delights.

"Extraordinary! It's like fairyland!" she blurted.

"That it is," Mr. Clarkson was pleased with her reaction. "Mind you, watch your pockets while you're here. The place gets all manner of thieves." Sarah reached for her purse and eyed the crowd with more suspicion. "I don't know about you, but I'm hungry. Shall we find something to eat?"

They went into one of the supper boxes, which was decorated with a painting of milkmaids celebrating the Rites of May. Her mind suddenly flitted back to the last such celebration she had celebrated in Greenberry over a year ago. It seemed both an impossibly long time and impossibly short as well. So much had changed.

"Like the painting, do you?" Mr. Clarkson jolted her from her reverie. "Every supper box here has its very own painting," he explained, "and there are fifty supper boxes."

"Perhaps I should try finding work here," Sarah mused.

"I think they're good on portraits for now," Mr. Clarkson replied, "though maybe they need someone to paint the stage."

"I think I'll pass," Sarah demurely replied.

Supper was ham, cold meats, cheeses, custards, tarts, and pudding—all of it served by quick, efficient waiters wearing livery and brass buttons. Both Sarah and Mr. Clarkson ate eagerly and drank wine and cider as well. As they ate, they witnessed a display of a hot air balloon arising overhead.

"I've heard of hot air balloons but I've never seen one before!" Sarah exclaimed. "It's so... oh, I can't even put it in words!"

"Charles Green, the aeronaut, does them all," Mr. Clarkson informed her. "He even takes passengers on his flights, but the cost is stupendous. I once tried arguing they should let me ride for free so I could write it up in The Courier, but they'd have none of it." Mr. Clarkson relayed gloomily before he cheered up to note, "They'll be showing the cascade soon."

"The cascade?" Sarah asked.

"You'll see," he winked.

In the woodland area near the centre crosswalk was a stage made to resemble a three-dimensional landscape depicting green hills and a miller's house with a waterwheel. The centerpiece of that stage was a waterfall. No, not an actual waterfall, Sarah dizzily realized, but the illusion of one - an illusion abetted with both clever lighting and even the sound of roaring water.

"How do they do it?" she marveled.

"It's a system of tin sheets on belts," explained Mr. Clarkson.

"It's remarkable to get such an effect with a machine."

"We're living in a new, modern age of invention," Mr. Clarkson agreed. "I should write a column about it!"

There was country dancing in front of the orchestra afterwards, but neither Sarah nor Mr. Clarkson had been given any instruction in dance, so they were content to look on at others for a time. The tone here was considerably less formal than that of the Mandeville's ball. The music was more raucous and ladies and gentleman's manners much freer with one another. Indeed, liberties that would have caused a scandal in Greenberry were regularly taken here without anyone batting an eye.

Eventually, Mr. Clarkson suggested they explore some of the darker walks away from all the light. They wandered along a mysterious little path, managing momentarily to lose the crowd. She felt his arm encircle her waist. She smelled his tobacco mixed in with his own masculine odor. They could still hear the revelry and the silvery sounds of an Italian concerto being performed.

The country air smelled fresh and sweet with the scents of trees, shrubs, and endless arrays of perfumed flowers. This, perhaps, more than anything else, was the key to the popularity of Vauxhall and other pleasure gardens. It offered a taste of nature in all its verdant, fecund glory in the middle of a metropolis, but it was a taste of nature that came with all the delights and temptations of a metropolis as well. The Garden of Eden with a taste of Sodom and Gomorrah. Sarah felt dizzy from all the night's wonders. It had been a feast for all the senses, unlike anything she'd ever come across before. She stumbled on something in her path, and Mr. Clarkson caught her by the arm, pulling her close to his chest, inches away from his face. It was not clear whether he leaned in first or she did, or if they both did so at the same time, but they kissed one another - her lips and skin smooth, and his face somewhat rougher with stubble. A whole new realm of sensation to explore. It was some time before they once more emerged in the open, lighted areas.

Sarah's Journal

Well, last night was interesting. It was very interesting, and while it is not perhaps lady-like of me to say so, not unpleasant. Not unpleasant at all.

I have at least the answer to one question, whether Mr. Clarkson harbors any sentiments toward me stronger than mere respect and cordiality. He does. I am also now well aware he would like more from me than friendship. Quite a bit more, it seems. A proposal now must be imminent, and I must confess I am not sure anymore it would even be truthful for me to claim I did not love him. It may not be a grand passion, but I certainly feel great affection and more than a trace of attraction to him. Perhaps that is what true love is? Comradery and attraction? No, the moment he proposes, I will say, "Yes, yes, yes!"

There is still the matter of the scars, but while I would inevitably have to reveal their presence, I need not necessarily disclose the cause. I could always claim to have suffered illness and been bled by a doctor the way Mr. Mandeville was. There's no one who could contradict such a story on my part. No one except... but I will not think of him. He is not part of my life anymore. I am quite sure he never thinks of me. It is all for the better that I forget him, too.

Addendum: It is not just Robert I have to forget. I don't know why, but last night, I dreamed of Adam. He was standing in front of me, but he was as cold and white as snow. He looked sad and grave as if he were angry with me for having forgotten him. I began to cry, and when I put my hand to my face, I found I shed tears of blood. I woke up then, in a cold sweat, and straight away found the pouch to pull out the razor. I clasped it in my hand and held it against my arm. I meant to cut myself. Just a small prick. Just to make me feel better. But I couldn't do it. I had come so far in London, and if I shed blood now, I felt it would all be for nothing. But I could not bring myself to put the razor blade away either. I just rubbed the metal against my skin over and over, like a talisman, for hours. I could not sleep, and finally, I had the urge to draw pictures of some of my scars. Of needles piercing skin. Of bleeding arms and limbs. I even drew a picture of poor, poor Adam that last time I saw him, bleeding in the snow. It was only after drawing all those that I could put the razor away and go to sleep, as it was nearly dawn. Now, as I look over those pictures again, they are not perhaps the finest detailed work, but they do have a certain power. Even if I could find buyers for them, though, I would not sell them. Perhaps I shall keep them with my journal?

Thirty-One

"Three may keep a secret if two of them are dead."
–Benjamin Franklin

Rufus Clarkson continued to call on Sarah, though, by some tacit understanding, they never discussed their woods sojourn at Vauxhall. Rather, they demurely continued to take tea together under Mrs. Mundy's watchful eye. One evening, he guided Sarah along a London walk that, by sheer coincidence, offered numerous cozy nooks to steal kisses in. It was in one such dark corner he told Sarah.

"You know, as of this week, The Courier turned ten years old?"

"Really? It's still young enough to employ a governess," Sarah quipped.

"Very amusing, but fact is we're having a sort of party to celebrate, and I was wondering if you," he gave an exaggerated bow, "would do me the honor of attending as my guest."

Sarah laughed and curtsied. "I'd be delighted," she said. "I'm afraid I don't have much experience at parties, though. In fact, I don't think I've ever attended one at all."

"Don't worry," Rufus Clarkson waved a hand dismissively. "This won't be some ballroom full of fops and snobs, like they've had at the Great House. No,

Old Boots just wants an excuse for a speech, I reckon."

"Old Boots?"

"Mr. Boots, founder of The Courier. He's worked in newspapers since he was this high," Clarkson held his arm about four feet above the ground. "The Courier is a lifelong dream of his, and he's put everything he has into it. Blood, sweat, and tears. Old Boots is the first to arrive in the mornings, last to leave at night, and often sleeps on the floor of his office."

"Well, he sounds quite dedicated," Sarah had remarked. "What does his family think of such hours, though?"

"Old Boots never had time for a wife," Clarkson had explained. "If you cut that man's arms, he'd bleed ink instead of blood."

Clarkson laughed, but Sarah, at that moment, had inexplicably flinched and murmured, "Everyone bleeds blood... everyone."

"But Boots is an all right chap," Mr. Clarkson continued. "He personally offered me a job here in London."

"So, I have him to thank for us crossing paths," Sarah mused. They had, by this time, arrived back on the street where Sarah lived. Sadly, once they returned to the coffeehouse, despite his best entreaties, Sarah remained adamant about admission to her room after dark.

"What would Mrs. Mundy say if she caught you sneaking out in the morning?" she protested.

"She'd probably inquire as to whether I gave satisfaction," he declared with an impish look in his eye, and Sarah gave him a playful swat.

"You're a cad. I don't know what I'm to do with you," Sarah laughed.

"Good question. You are still coming to the party at The Courier tomorrow, though, aren't you?"

"An evening surrounded by newspapermen? I could hardly say no, now could I?" Sarah returned inside and crept up the stairs, only to be stopped midway by the sound of Mrs. Mundy calling out, "Sarah? Is that you?"

"Yes, it's me," Sarah called back.

"And it's just you, isn't it?"

"Of course, it's just me. Who else would there be?"

"Just checking, my dear. Just checking. Not that I've been waiting up for

you or anything, love." Mrs. Mundy gave an exaggerated yawn, "Lord, it's late, isn't it? Time to get some rest."

For their momentous anniversary, The Courier's print boys had sorted through the pile of old editions and plastered the walls with some of their note-worthy articles over the years. The juiciest scandals, the broadest invectives, and the grisliest of murders. Lingering smells of paper and ink hovered in the air. Smaller desks had been pushed together to make a big banquet table in the middle of the room. The table groaned under its weight of cheeses, meats, puddings, and massive punch bowls. Instead of the usual din of the printing presses, there was a new kind of clamor, that of music. One of the typesetters' cousins played the fiddle attended along with a friend on the clarinet, both of whom had come for a nominal fee, and more importantly, the promise of a free meal.

It was a mostly male party but with a few wives present as well. The first hour featured mostly drinking, eating, private conversations where one had to nearly scream to be heard, drinking, an occasional impromptu jig in response to the fiddle and clarinet combination, and, of course, more drinking. Sarah was introduced to a great many colleagues of Rufus's. She heard more names than she could possibly remember while trying to pace herself on the punch. She ended up cornered by a Mr. Wilkie, who went on a long harangue about his own attempts at writing a novel and about the current state of newspapers and publishing. It seemed that other authors and their publications occupied a great deal of space inside Mr. Wilkie's head, and he was eager to share with any captive audience.

"And old Reverend Sidney Smith's at it again," he added one point. "Man's got a perfectly nice living, but he insists on writing all the time anyway, and he's got a new hobbyhorse every month! Sometimes it's women's education, sometimes it's slavery, and now it's mantraps."

"Mantraps?" Repeated Sarah who, for the first time since being cornered by Mr. Wilkie, was now paying full attention. "What does Mr. Smith have to say about mantraps?"

"He's against them, of course. Claims they're cruel and inhumane, and he's written a big, blistering article about them in the Edinburgh Review. He thinks parliament should ban them all – like that would ever happen! Every property owner in England needs traps to defend themselves from poachers these days."

"No, they don't," Sarah responded in a sharp tone. "No one needs those horrid things. Pheasants aren't worth human lives, and God bless Reverend Smith for saying so! It's a barbaric practice! It's pure evil."

"Evil?" replied Mr. Wilkie, not a little discombobulated by her sudden vehemence.

"Evil," Sarah repeated empathetically. "Damn things should all be banned at once." She took another sip of her punch.

Mr. Wilkie wondered at a seemingly genteel young woman who let the word "damn" pass her lips so easily. He found an excuse to slip away, leaving Sarah to herself in a corner. Sarah was not offended but simply sat alone, waiting for the return of Mr. Clarkson.

A little later, one of these fellows who'd been speaking the most, started clanging a spoon against his glass, "Quiet, everyone! Quiet! It's time to make a speech," and as if by magic, all other noise in the room dwindled into nothing, and everyone paid careful attention, even the wives. Sarah retreated to a corner of the room, unnoticed.

"Now, over ten years ago, I had a dream: to found a new voice of the people here in London."

This man, Sarah realized, must be Mr. Boots, who had founded The Courier and had hired Mr. Clarkson from York. She examined him with interest. He was a man of about fifty, wore a fierce expression, and had more hair in his eyebrows than on his head.

Old Boots had clearly enjoyed a great deal of the punch and was in excellent spirits that night. He gave a long and eloquent oratory of The Courier's history, how it had originated as a dream in his mind, of the long and arduous search for funds to found it, and of its desperate search for readers. He thanked numerous members of the room, from copy boys, who were, as Boots put it, "starting out just where I was!" He thanked typesetters for all their hard work. He had especially honeyed words to one gentleman who had been an early investor in The Courier. Then, he began addressing the various reporters, one by one, informing all and sundry of their biographies and what particular contributions they had made to The Courier's fortunes.

Mr. Wilkie's acknowledgement, Sarah noticed, was rather brief in comparison to the far more effusive way Boots described Mr. Clarkson. To Sarah, that seemed most appropriate. Old Boots expounded on fond memories of having stumbled on a York paper by accident, where he had found Mr. Clarkson's work, and of then writing to him with an offer of employment, which Clarkson had immediately taken. "And he's been one of the best newsmen London's ever seen!" Old Boots proclaimed grandly while Mr. Clarkson gave a not-very-convincing show of modesty. Sarah felt both bemused and proud at the same time.

"Thank you, all," said Mr. Boots as he looked ready to close his speech. "It's been a great ten years, men, and I can't wait for ten, twenty, thirty, or a hundred more!"

"Aye!" Mr. Clarkson, who had stood by Boots's side during the speech, raised his glass in the air, "May the sun never set on The Courier!"

"You should hope not, Rufus!" Boots clanged glasses eagerly. "The day we close shop, you'd have to go home to your wife!" Boots roared with laughter. Sarah did not believe her ears.

Surely, she had heard wrong? Or Boots was wrong? Her eyes fell on Rufus's face, and his stricken expression told her the truth. His eyes met hers, and he then knew that she knew. Without anyone else noticing, Sarah ran from the room. On the street outside, it was now raining very hard. Sarah had no parasol or any other protection, but she didn't care.

She walked madly for hours, getting more and more drenched, combing old alleyways and making her way back to the park where she and Mr. Clarkson had dined on meat pies that one day so many ages ago. It wasn't wise to stay outside and get wet, but she feared what she might do if she were alone at night in her little attic room and close to her pouch. There was also a certain strange comfort in feeling the rain beat down on her. The pressure was not unlike constant pinching with the added sensation of being pricked by ice. In fact, her dress became so damp that it felt as if lead weights had been sewn into her clothing. She welcomed the sensation eagerly. It was akin to walking out into the middle of a river or lake, she thought dreamily. The same sense of cleansing and purification. Really, why didn't people do this more?

Sometime after midnight, thoroughly drenched and exhausted, Sarah arrived back at the coffeehouse. Her dress sloshed water on the floor, and though she tried to tiptoe up the stairs as quietly as possible, Mrs. Mundy came out wearing a kerchief and holding a candle.

"My God, you look like a drowned rat!" Mrs. Mundy's verdict came. "Do you wanna catch your death of cold?"

"He's married," Sarah replied dully.

"What?"

"Mr. Clarkson... is... married," Sarah drew the words out and Mrs. Mundy took in a deep breath.

"Bastard!" was her next verdict. "Smooth tongue like that. Should have known he was a liar."

"He didn't actually lie," Sarah mused. "I never asked him whether he had a wife or not. He just failed to disclose that he did."

"He's a filthy dog is what he is, and if he ever comes by again, I'll be sure to crack something across his skull." Mrs. Mundy was indignant. "A dish, perhaps? No, I need my dishes. The poker! That'll show him," she proclaimed triumphantly.

"Don't do that," Sarah pleaded.

"But wait, you're still dripping!" Mrs. Mundy noted. "You best get out all those wet things now and warm up quick."

Sarah did go upstairs and undress down to her shift, but she didn't build up a fire in the stove to sit by as Mrs. Mundy had suggested. Instead, she laid in bed and brooded until eventually she fell into a restless sleep.

Sarah woke the next morning with a red, swollen nose and a throat that felt like it had been stuffed with cotton. All for the best, then, that she had no desire to go out or any particular appointments that day. She drank tea, stayed in her room, and on Mrs. Mundy's urging, took a dose of some vile tasting tonic from the local apothecary. She tried to sleep and sketch a bit from time to time.

That afternoon, she heard a commotion down below. She recognized the voice of Mr. Clarkson calling out, "Sarah! Are you there?" She did not answer, and then she heard Mr. Clarkson saying, "But I want to see her! To explain!"

Mrs. Mundy responded with a great deal of profanity and threats with the poker. A few minutes later, Mrs. Mundy came up to the attic, rapping once on the door by way of warning before walking in without getting formal permission.

"Is he gone?" Sarah asked, and Mrs. Mundy nodded. "Good. I'm not up to seeing him just yet."

"No need for you to ever see him again at all," Mrs. Mundy responded warmly. "Let me tell you, I made it clear he wasn't to come around here no more!" Then she hesitated.

"What is it?" Sarah asked.

"He gave me a letter," the words came from Mrs. Mundy's mouth slowly and grudgingly as she pulled out a sealed envelope. "Wanted me to promise to give it you. Don't have to read it if you don't like. We can just toss it on the dust heap," she added cheerfully.

Sarah weakly held out her hand and took the letter.

"Well, I've got business downstairs anyway," said Mrs. Mundy, but as she turned to leave, she looked back once over her shoulder. "Mind you, he's a newsman so he knows how to pretty things up in print anyway he sees fit. But whatever he's got to say won't change anything. A man can't have two wives, and that's all I've got to say about that."

Mrs. Mundy left and Sarah weighed the letter in her hand before finally opening it.

Sarah,

I don't know if you'll even read this, much less care. I wouldn't blame you if you didn't. But I have to at least try to tell my side of the story. What you heard last night is true, in the strictest sense, though maybe not so true in another. Many years ago, in my foolish youth, I made the biggest mistake of my life and married a woman who didn't suit me, nor I her. It was to the relief of both of us when I accepted the offer to live and work in London. We haven't seen each other in years, much less shared a bed. So, while law and church call me a married man, I can't say I think of myself in those terms at all. Truth be told, I wanted to forget I had a wife. I wanted to forget I'd ever been such a fool as to court that woman at all.

There is a child. A young boy who's being raised by my wife's kinfolk. I can't say I'm any part of his life or that he's any part of mine. My past never really gave me any trouble or disturbed my mind at all. At least, not until I met you. If only we'd met ten years sooner.

I know I should have told you this sooner, but in my defense, at first, I thought we were just friends, and by the time we weren't, well, I was too taken by your beauty and charms to do anything to that might change things between us. In my defense, I don't think anyone could blame me for wanting to be with you or clinging tightly to what we had.

I honestly say I never meant to mislead you or cause you any harm. I hope someday you'll forgive me, and please, please let me talk to you!

Sincerely,
Rufus Clarkson

Sarah's Journal

Mr. Clarkson is married. He has a wife and a son he never, ever sees. He did not see fit to tell me this himself. Had it not been for Mr. Boots's speech, I might never have known at all. When he writes that he did not set out to mislead me, I believe him. I do not believe that was his original purpose, but whether he meant to or not, the end result was a form of deception. How long did he think the charade could continue? He writes he did not want to give me up, but really, what future could we have had? Did he intend for me to be his mistress, or did he hope to practice bigamy with one wife in the city and another in the country? Or perhaps he wasn't thinking of the future at all. Perhaps he deliberately kept that out of mind and just preferred to "live in the moment," as it were. I could see that. For all, he's behaved very badly, but I cannot bring myself to hate him. In fact, I rather pity him, trapped as he is by his marriage that is evidently not a happy one. Obviously, things between us cannot go on as they have, but what to do next? I do not know.

I was not madly in love with Mr. Clarkson. I did not feel for him what I felt for another before him. Yet, this is still a great wound. We were not Romeo and Juliet, nor Lancelot and Guinevere, but I did think Mr. Clarkson and I, unlike those unfortunate characters, could have a happy ending. I did think there was a chance for the two of us to have a future together. The artist marrying the newsman. It seemed so appropriate, somehow.

And I see now how truly gratifying it was to finally have a man take an interest in me as a woman, to actually be considered alluring, to inspire temptation and passion. I've spent so many years being a sort of sexless, monstrous creature, fit only to be locked away in the schoolroom. It was pleasant to be attractive for once. Very pleasant. Even *now, I'm rather grateful to Mr. Clarkson for even if his intentions were, in fact, dishonorable. Well, at least he's the first man to even think me fit for dishonor, but I cannot be Lady Howard or Clair Clairmont. I won't. I'm no Frenchwoman, and the title of mistress is not for me. Perhaps I should speak to him again, but I'm not up to it right now. My head is ringing, and I feel feverish. For now, I must rest. Then, maybe I can think.*

Thirty-Two

"Right actions in the future are the best apologies for bad actions in the past."
−Tryon Edwards

An old friend of Dr. Healey's had invited him down to London for a visit. Because Greenberry, at that moment, was going through a bit of a slow patch, medically speaking – everyone in town that summer had been disgustingly healthy – Healey gladly accepted. He had, of late, for reasons he could ill-define, been feeling restless. He felt a journey to town would do him all the good in the world. He would come for a week, refresh his supply kit, and maybe even see a patient or two in London. He was not, of course, going for the sake of Miss Pole, now Miss Crow. *That would be ridiculous. To make a trip solely to see a woman whom he had not seen in months—a woman clearly beset by demons, and a woman who'd made no indication at all of wanting to see him?* No, Dr. Healey was far too sensible a man to do any such thing.

While in London, he did, indeed, call upon some old friends, the Fospers. Both Tim Fosper and his wife, Amy, were amiable hosts, though Amy Fosper had, of late, developed an unfortunate interest in finding Robert a wife. She was constantly asking about the young women in Greenberry. Having Robert strongly object that there was absolutely no eligible prospect for him in Greenberry at present, she had calmly offered to make introductions for him in London. He had to take a very, very firm tone with Mrs. Fosper to avoid that calamity. Mr. Fosper wisely refused to take any sides or even comment on his wife's matchmaking ambitions.

During a brief sojourn of good weather, Robert was able to roam through the city and the parks. By what was, of course, pure chance and coincidence, he somehow found himself one day on a particular street where Miss Pole – or was it Miss Crow – lived. From where Sarah's letter had been addressed. In fact, he could see the coffeehouse she had so visibly described right down the road. Robert stopped and thought. *Well, he wasn't in London to see Sarah, but now that he was here, perhaps he should pay his respects? If only to see how she was getting on? Their last meeting had been a rather bitter one. In the name of their onetime friendship, wouldn't it be proper to talk things out? For closure, if nothing else?*

He had to stoop to make his way into the dark, claustrophobic coffee shop. It was, he noted with dismay, a rather dingy little establishment that did not, to his mind, match the romantic description she had written to Elinor and Violet. He didn't mind for himself. Lord knows, as a poor student, he'd been in far grimier places than this, but was it a really suitable address for a gently born woman like Sarah? Of course, he remembered she'd been fine visiting in cottagers who lived in far more wretched and humble circumstances, but there was a difference between visiting and living in. Quite a comedown from Bromley Hall, he should think, but he'd never actually seen her room at Bromley Hall, had he? For all he knew, he thought with a start, this might be a step up.

There were a couple of tradesmen in a corner, drinking coffee and talking between themselves. On the other side of the room stood a shrewd-looking older woman whom he approached.

"Are you Mrs. Mundy?" he asked her.

"Who wants to know?" she eyed him suspiciously.

"I wanted to ask about a young lady I heard was at this address. Sarah Po— I mean, Sarah Crow."

"If you want a sitting done, you'll have to come some other time. She's indisposed at present," Mrs. Mundy retorted.

"I'm not here for a sitting," he explained patiently. "I'm here as a friend. An old friend."

Mrs. Mundy remained suspicious, "And whose name should I give her, old friend?" She delivered the last two words quite tartly.

"Healey. Dr. Robert Healey."

The woman's countenance changed dramatically, and she leaned in, speaking in a whisper, "You're a doctor? A proper one?"

"Yes. Yes, I am," he said, wondering both why she was so interested and what she would consider an improper doctor.

"Come this way, then," Mrs. Mundy led him up a flight of rickety stairs and to a door.

"Didn't want to discuss this downstairs, might be bad for business, you know? But thank God you're here," she told him as they entered the attic room.

A number of paintings and pictures lay on the walls and floor. There was an old easel with a half-finished street view of London and an outdoor market, but all Robert had eyes for was the narrow little cot and the still figure lying on it. Sarah was still and insensible, not unlike the day young Adam had died. He rushed to her side.

"My God, what happened?" he touched her forehead. "She's burning up with fever!"

"She was out in a storm for hours the other night. I told her to be careful of getting a cold, I did," Mrs. Mundy explained. "At first, it was just a red nose and a cough, and then she seemed like she was getting better, but for a few days, it's been like this. I didn't know what to do."

"Has she seen no other doctor?" he demanded. Mrs. Mundy shook her head.

"At first, I thought a little tonic from Mr. More around the corner would do the trick – always has every time I been ill – but she kept on getting worse, and I suggested a doctor, but she wouldn't hear of it. Worried about the cost, I reckon. Doctors are expensive, and it's so hard to find a good one these days anyway."

Robert, remembering the day of Adam Riggs's death, had another theory entirely for why Sarah refused to see a doctor, but there was no need to share that with Mrs. Mundy. Instead, he simply replied, "Well, I'm here now, and she's hardly in a position to refuse to see me."

Instead of waiting for an answer, he rested his ear against Sarah's chest and listened. "The infection's settled in her lungs," he announced.

"Oh, dear Lord," Mrs. Mundy groaned. "Should we call Father Gorman?"

"Father who?"

"Father Gorman. He's a priest Sarah's been talking to."

"Sarah's talking to a priest? She's not even Catholic!" Robert was stunned. Mrs. Mundy just shrugged.

"I guess she had things she needed to say," was her reply. "But you know, this might be her last confession or chance."

"I didn't say she was dying!" Robert yelled, and Mrs. Mundy looked shocked. Robert reminded himself of the need to be professional. He took a deep breath and spoke more calmly.

"Her condition is serious, very serious, but it is not invariably fatal. The next twenty-four hours will be critical. She'll need someone by her side," he took off his black coat and folded it over a chair.

"Shall I get you a dish?" Mrs. Mundy asked.

"What?"

"A dish for when you bleed her," Mrs. Mundy noted. "Unless you're one of the ones who does leeches. Nasty things, though," she shuddered. "I think I'd prefer the knife to having those slimy gibbers sucking on me."

"There will be no knife, and there will be no leeches. There will be no bleeding at all. That's the last thing she needs any more of," Robert said that last bit almost under his breath, and Mrs. Mundy looked confused.

"Run along and get me some tea," he told her. "We are going to have a long night ahead of us."

Mrs. Mundy turned to go and then suddenly stopped and addressed him, "By the way, are you married or not?" Before a stunned Robert could reply, she muttered, "Oh, nevermind, that's not the problem, now is it?" And then she was down the stairs before she could explain her meaning.

Robert sent word back to where he'd been staying to inform them that he was out on a case. Sarah lie mostly quiet and still. On at least one occasion, he had left the room to let Mrs. Mundy help Sarah up to use her chamber pot. Mrs. Mundy managed to induce Sarah to take a few sips of water the few times she was conscious. Even then, she seemed unaware of her surroundings. Robert found it very difficult to see her in such a state. He tried to smother his feelings under professional duties. He checked her pulse and monitored her respirations. No change. He pressed damp cloths to Sarah's forehead to help control her fever. Sarah's condition remained the same. No better. No worse.

Day made its way into evening, and Robert called for candles. Mrs. Mundy was worried enough that she produced them without even thinking of the cost, and hovered for a moment in the room, listening to Sarah's shallow breaths.

"You're sure you don't want me to send for Father Gorman?" she asked, and Robert gave her a fierce glare that sent her away from the room. Never had the subject of a priest angered him more. He delicately pulled back Sarah's sleeves and found no signs of fresh injury. That, at least, was some small consolation.

Too often there was nothing to be done for his patient but wait. To pass the time, Robert explored the little attic. He noted the meagerness of Sarah's wardrobe and possessions, but the place was filled with pictures, and even by candlelight, he found them interesting to examine. He was especially curious of one of a woman in a green dress that seemed somehow to have stepped out of a stained-glass window. Sarah also kept a number of books on hand. He perused the titles.

It was only then that Robert found the journal. It posed quite a dilemma. A man cannot simply read a girl's private journal to assuage his own curiosity, no matter how curious he might be. And Robert admitted to himself he was quite curious, indeed. But there were other circumstances here, were there not? Here, he had a patient who obviously suffered afflictions that were not physical in nature, but which might well have contributed to her physical condition, and if the pages of Sarah's journal could offer insight into her present illness, shouldn't he, as her doctor, read them? Purely so he could better treat her, of course. After all, it is not typically proper etiquette for a man to touch and examine a woman to whom he's not married either, but every physician had to do it. No, he decided, he had a professional duty to read the journal which superseded the normal rules of behavior.

Reading the first account of Sarah cutting herself as a child made him blanch at first. Somehow, the image of a sad little girl taking a blade to her own skin seemed worse than any of the gory spectacles he'd seen in medical school or in practice. He felt he could not read on but found himself doing so anyway, much as a person seeing a terrible accident in the street cannot bring themselves to look away.

Thankfully, it wasn't all blood and horror. Indeed, Robert found himself smiling from time to time at Sarah's tales of her schoolgirl days. Inside that section, he found a folded-up page and opened it up to see the portrait of "Sarah Crow." He studied it for a long time and wondered what sort of person would draw themselves in such a light. When reading of the pouch, he felt a sudden, mad desire to find the damned thing right away and burn it, only to have to remind himself that it was far too late at night to be searching through Sarah's things. He read with relief of how she had for a time stopped using the pouch in her final year at Weberley, and then, with pain, how she had taken it up again once she'd arrived at Bromley Hall.

He'd never been a superstitious man before, but between Sarah's relapse and Adam's death, he couldn't help but wonder if the great house was a cursed manor in one of those ridiculous gothic novels. He was decidedly indifferent to the comings and goings of either the Servant's Hall or the Mandeville family and found himself hurrying impatiently through those pages. Any mention of the poor Riggs family brought a note of dread. He had a moment's amusement when Sarah wrote that it seemed as if Alicia feared her. Unlike Sarah, he immediately thought he knew why that was. Lord, at first, he'd almost been frightened of the dark, silent Miss Pole, too.

He did not bother to read the letters from Geraldine or Clara, but noted to keep them aside with their addresses in case there was anything he might have to notify them about. No need to look for any clues to Aunt Penelope or Uncle Harold's whereabouts. It was all too clear, he reflected darkly, that they didn't give a damn, and perhaps that's why Sarah had come to such a state.

When he came to the point in the narrative when his own name was mentioned, Robert hesitated. The only thing more ungentlemanly than reading a woman's private journal without her permission is reading whatever she's written about you personally, and unlike other parts of the journal, there could be no justification for understanding her present illness or knowing who to notify.

Then again, he was curious to know what she truly thought of him. Paradoxically, though, the very fact he found himself so interested in the matter was perhaps all the more reason not to trespass on Sarah's thoughts on the matter. After all, whatever her sentiments toward him personally, it was fair to say they had no bearing on her scars or her sickness. He went back and forth over the matter for a long time. His curiosity at odds with his sense of rightness.

No, he resolved. He would not further invade her privacy any more than needed. Certainly not for such selfish considerations. Could he just avoid every page he was mentioned? But he wouldn't know if he was mentioned unless he read the section. Finally, he decided to skip over anything else she'd written about her time in Greenberry and peek ahead to events in London. He became acquainted with Father Gorman through a description he read, and he found the priest's cavalier attitude towards Sarah's hobby surprising. Then again, there probably wasn't much that could shock a priest. He rather felt grateful to the man, in fact, for recommending Sarah write a journal. Anything to keep her away from that damned pouch.

Much of the tales of London were entertaining. Indeed, at several points Robert laughed aloud when reading of how some of Sarah's sittings had went. And it was with considerable relief he read that Sarah had not cut or pricked herself since her move. In that light, even finding sketches of bleeding wrists and open wounds seemed a queer sort of blessing. Better she commit that sort of thing to the page then her own body.

There was, however, the disagreeable matter of how much Mr. Clarkson featured in the narrative from that point on. The matter of their evening at Vauxhall, in particular, was especially difficult to read, and while the disclosure of Clarkson's country wife did, in fact, make him quite indignant on Sarah's behalf, and his letter inspired Robert's scorn, he could not help but feel a twinge of satisfaction as well. Given Sarah's current condition, though, that satisfaction was brief indeed, even though she had not been in love with the newspaperman, the disappointment had still clearly come as a crushing blow, and one that had contributed to her present illness. She may not have resorted to the pouch, but hadn't spending hours outside in the rain been another form of self-harm? Possibly even a more deadly one.

No. It would not be deadly. She would live. She had to.

Thirty-Three

"To sleep, perchance to dream: ay, there's the rub;
For in that sleep of death what dreams may come."
–William Shakespeare, *Hamlet*

At first, there had been the tiger. She had been in a cool, dark forest under the light of a full moon. Tree branches tangled in among themselves to make secretive shapes. Shadows seemed to dance. The only source of illumination had been the tiger, whose dazzling orange stripes had shone as if lit by candles from within. Then the tiger had dissolved into a shower of fireworks, and the dark woods seemed to melt away.

She was at the sea once more. The sun shined brightly over the waters, creating little pools of light. The air was fresh and briny. It was so welcome after London's soot, and she inhaled it deeply. Everything was bathed in light, yet the sun did not cloud her eyes. At first, she believed she was somehow back in Weberley, but when at Weberley had the sky been this blue? Or the waters this luminous? Even the foam seemed whiter and pearlier than ever before, and at Weberley, it had been the sound of gulls, but here, she heard the caws of crows. What would crows be doing at the seaside? There they were! There were seven crows: six black and one snowy white. The white one turned to her, and its eyes were the same azure shade of the sky and waters. She started to approach it, but all seven birds then flew away.

"Sometimes they're friendly. Sometimes they're not," she heard a familiar voice behind her, and she turned around.

"Adam," she said wonderingly. It was definitely Adam, though somehow different. Perhaps it was because he was cleaner. Or perhaps because he no longer had that lean and hungry look that been his wont in life. Or maybe he looked different because everything looked slightly different here. Things seemed sharper, more in view, somehow, than they normally did—like a drawing where someone goes over an initial rough sketch with ink, tracing out all the fine details and adding shading. Everything was somehow heightened.

"You know, I never saw the sea before," Adam commented as he looked out on the horizon. "Never saw anything beyond Greenberry at all, really. It's right pretty, it is. The sea, I mean. Air smells nice, too. I see now why genteel folks always holiday here."

"Is this a dream?" Sarah wondered. Adam didn't answer. She took off her glove and reached down to the pebbles at her feet. She could feel the stones, feel the dampness upon them. She lifted her finger to her mouth and tasted salt. If this was a dream, it was far more vivid and real than any she'd had before. She suddenly noticed her skirt and hem. She was wearing an unfamiliar gown. An Indian muslin in sea foam green that matched the waters themselves. Simple, but the material was far finer than any she'd ever worn before, and shorter sleeves than she'd ever worn before that showed smooth, white skin, unmarred by any scars. Wonderingly, she ran her hands over her own arms as another possibility came to mind.

"Adam, if we're both here... Adam, does this mean I'm dead? I don't feel like I'm dead," Sarah mused.

"That's because you're not. Not yet, anyway, but if you're here, well, you must not be doing so well," he confided.

"Then am I about to die?" she asked tentatively.

"What are you asking me for? I still haven't figured out all the rules here myself," Adam gave her a smile. "It's not the way Reverend Graham made it sound at all. Bit of a relief, really. Never fancied the idea of playing a harp – or fire and

brimstone neither."

There was a sudden chorus of caws in the distance. Sarah looked in the direction they came from. The crows had settled on a rock with the snowy white one right in the middle. Just beyond the crows and rocks lay an old stone building with a thatched roof that looked familiar. She peered at it closely. Could it be?

"Is that what I think it is?" Sarah asked. Adam smiled and said nothing, and Sarah began to walk toward the structure. The sand beneath her feet turned to grass, and then into a familiar road leading through an even more familiar front garden. It was the country parsonage of Walnut Hill, where she had spent her childhood. Ivy crept along the familiar stone walls. Ordinarily, peonies and marigolds grow in summer while roses only grow in autumn or spring, but here, they were all abloom at once and the fragrance was overwhelming. The crows had now flown to the roof of the house to keep vigil. Sarah stood outside the old oak door for a moment before making a single solitary knock. The door swung open. Here was her family's old parlor in the parsonage. There were the old, shabby, and yet comfortable furnishings. There was the old wall with the crack in it.

There was her family. Not as they had looked in their terrible, final days on the sickbed, but as they were before. Her father was in his old blue waistcoat with kind, grey eyes permanently lined with merriment, his hairline somewhat receded, but his smile friendly and warm. Little William was in a blue suit with his brown curls running unruly and wild. He met her gaze with his clear blue eyes and stuck his tongue out between his teeth. And there was her mother, of course, wearing brown muslin with her white cap and apron. Not unlike Sarah herself in appearance, with dark hair and pale skin, but her mother had always been far prettier. Her mother was smiling, but her dark eyes were misted over with tears. Sarah embraced her and smelled homemade bread.

"Am I here to stay?"

"Not yet, Sarah," her mother spoke. "Not yet."

She bolted upright. She was no longer at the parsonage. Here were the familiar walls and ceiling of Mrs. Mundy's attic. Here was her cot. It had all been a dream after all. But wait... here was also Robert Healey? He was by the bedside craning his face at hers, anxious with concern. *How could he be here?*

"Sarah, you're awake! Thank God, thank God." Just like her mother's had, his eyes, too, glistened with tears.

"Oh," said Sarah. "So, you're here, too." She stretched out her hands and cupped Robert's face, feeling the stubble and makings of a beard.

"What are you do–" Robert began to ask, but before he could finish, Sarah had stopped him with a kiss. A long and hungry kiss. And while Robert Healey had neither initiated nor expected it, he found himself returning it for a moment or two. Sarah's practice with Mr. Clarkson had taught her a thing or two, and tongues tasted and tangled with one another. Finally, Robert managed to pull himself back.

"Don't," he gasped. "I mean, we can't."

"It's a dream. I can do anything," Sarah sighed.

There was a sudden bang, and there was Mrs. Mundy standing in the door.

"You're alive!" she crowed. "I mean, you're awake!" She hurried to Sarah's side by the cot, "You gave us quite a scare, you did, Miss Crow. You've been out for days. Thank heavens the doctor came to call."

Sarah's sleeves had come somewhat undone and her arms, and scars, were exposed, but Mrs. Mundy either didn't notice or pretended not to.

"Robert– I mean, Dr. Healey came to call?" Sarah repeated, stupefied. "I'm awake."

"Of course, you're awake. That's the whole point!" Mrs. Mundy shook her head.

Sarah's head thudded against the wall behind her while scarlet points arose in her cheeks.

Robert loudly cleared his throat before saying, "I think our patient could use some fresh water, Mrs. Mundy. And some food as well."

"Of course," and Mrs. Mundy left. When she did so, Sarah covered her face with her hands and gave a deep moan.

"It's all right," Robert said.

"No, it isn't!" Sarah spoke through clenched fingers, her face still covered. She now realized that the bedclothes felt damp and smelled musky. They'd been soaked in sweat. "How are you even here?"

"I happened to be in the neighborhood, and so I came to pay my respects. When your landlady learned I was a doctor, she immediately asked me to treat you. I've been here since yesterday."

"But why?" Sarah uncovered her face and peered out with her dark eyes that looked all the more oversized than ever in her face having not eaten in days.

"Why did I treat you?" he sounded incredulous at the question.

"Why did you come to see me?"

There was a long pause, and Robert looked uncertain.

"I don't know," he said finally. "I just didn't want the last time we ever spoke to be, well, the last time you and I did speak. Sarah, why did you run?"

"I didn't run. I gave Mrs. Mandeville plenty of notice, and then I relocated. There's a difference," she sounded defensive.

"You know what I mean. And why did you start calling yourself 'Miss Crow?' Was it to make sure no one could find you?"

"No!" Sarah was shocked by the very question, and Robert gave her a skeptical glance. "Really, Robert, if I was trying to disappear, I wouldn't have written to anyone about where I was, now would I?"

"Then why the name change?" he asked again.

"Many artists and authors work under a nom de plume you know. It's quite the custom."

"Sarah." One word that somehow said so much.

Sarah hesitated a moment before speaking slowly, "I wanted to change things, Robert. I wanted to change a lot of things. So, I guess I thought changing my name would be a good way to start."

"Like cutting yourself." It was a statement, not a question.

"Yes, like cutting myself. For what it's worth, I haven't done so once since I came to London."

"You have no new scars," Robert noted.

"No. I've been seeing a priest as well. Father Gorman."

"Mrs. Mundy mentioned him," Robert replied, carefully.

"And I've been ever so busy with clients as well."

"Not all of them human clients," Robert noted. "The girls shared your letter to them with me about Lady Fowler and Jeanne Marie." The corners of his lips twitched.

"Yes, well, believe me, Jeanne Marie was an absolute angel compared ⸙

some of the models I've had to work with," Sarah rolled her eyes.

"I imagine," Robert chortled. "That awful Burns family! It sounds like their son ought to have a leash and muzzle on him."

"Wait, how do you know about the Burns?" Sarah asked.

Robert was nonplussed, "Well, your letters."

"I never wrote about the Burns family to the girls. I only wrote about it in my journal..." realization struck Sarah. "You. Read. My. Journal," her voice was like broken glass.

"Parts of it," he admitted, raising his hands as if about to deflect a blow. "I made a point of not reading anything that took place in Greenberry after my arrival."

"That's not the point! That journal was private!" Sarah's lips and fists were clenched in rage. She spat the words out between her teeth as she borrowed a phrase from Geraldine, "You bastard!" Then she collapsed into a fit of coughs.

"Perhaps I am. Be that as it may, you're still weak to do anything about it. I'd recommend resting for a little while first. Once you've gotten your strength back, you can expound on all the various deficiencies in my character."

Sarah's only response was a seething glare.

"A little help with the door, please!" Mrs. Mundy's voice could be heard from outside. Robert let her in. Her arms were laden with a heavy tray carrying an earthen brown pitcher sweating water, and some chipped white and blue mugs and plates. There was also half a large loaf of brown bread, a hunk of cheese, and a little butter knife. Robert helped her array the tray on the cot before Sarah.

"Mind if I join you?" Mrs. Mundy perched herself at the foot of the cot before getting a response and grabbed a crumb of cheese off the tray. She then looked around.

"Did I miss anything?" she asked.

Thirty-Four

"Healing is a matter of time, but it is sometimes also a matter of opportunity."
—Hippocrates

Sarah's original intention had been to have Mrs. Mundy show Robert out. However, she had become distracted by the contents of the tray. Finding that she was really was quite parched, she first drank most of the pitcher. Then, finding she was famished, she devoured some hard bread and cheese. After having been fortified by food and drink, Sarah had hoped to have the necessary strength to throw Robert out. But instead, once she'd had her fill, her eyelids felt unaccountably heavy and she was asleep once more. She awoke hours later, when it was nearly dusk, only to find Robert already gone. According to Mrs. Mundy, he'd gone back to wherever he had been staying. This was clearly all for the best, but Sarah felt something strangely resembling disappointment anyway.

The next day, however, Dr. Healey – presumably fully recovered from his vigil – was back to check on his patient and accept Mrs. Mundy's offer of some tea. Robert might yet have been thrown out, but he made a brilliant, even inspired, tactical move. He behaved as though it were a perfectly normal follow-up visit and that nothing unusual had happened the day before. No mention wa made of the journal or the kiss. Or scars. His manner was professional, yet also friendly and jocular. Robert Healey, while Irish by birth, had apparently adopted the English practice of reticence, at least in this instance. Sarah was both grateful and instinctively wary, lest the whole thing turn out be some sort of trap.

Robert offered news about events in Greenberry and stories about his friends in London. His conversation was lively and amusing. It was a welcome distraction from the otherwise not exactly enthralling scenery of the little attic and coffee shop. By now, Sarah could get up, clean and dress herself, and move around a bit. She was under orders not to make any sort of exertion, which included going outside. No one, of course, had the power to keep her from her sketchbook. Robert noticed she'd begun a new, particularly intricate drawing of a family of four: husband, wife, daughter, and son. Both the wife and daughter looked oddly familiar, with dark hair and deep-set eyes.

"Oi," said Mrs. Mundy, "whose family portrait are you doing now?"

"My own family," Sarah answered to Mrs. Mundy's surprise, though Robert had already guessed. "We never had a portrait done, so now I'm doing one for them while their faces are now fresh in my mind once again."

Neither Robert nor Mrs. Mundy bothered to ask Sarah what she meant by having her family's faces fresh in her mind again. There seemed a tacit understanding that the answer wasn't one they needed to know. Before leaving, Robert had one request.

"Can I be introduced to Percival and Peck?" he asked.

"Who?" This came from Mrs. Mundy.

"Pigeons," explained Sarah.

"You named the bloody pigeons?" Mrs. Mundy shook her head. "You know, you've always been a bit peculiar, dear, but pigeons? Filthy things, they is! No better than flying rats."

"Percival is actually quite handsome," Sarah interjected.

"So I read in your letters. It's why I'm anxious to meet him," Robert pro-d solemnly. Mrs. Mundy wore an expression of befuddlement mixed with that somehow the young folks were having a go at her. Upstairs, Robert vent with a handful of crumbs. Soon, they had coaxed both Percival n the windowsill. There was a disagreement between the two over the last and biggest crumb. Percival, being the larger of the two, felt that gave him rightful claim, yet scrawny Peck showed unexpected perseverance and ferocity. He won the crumb, and Percival was left temporarily sulky before gathering up his dignity and proceeding to preen himself as if nothing had happened. Sarah and Robert both had a good laugh.

"Elinor and Violet will want to hear all about this when I go back," Robert mused. Sarah gave a mild start. She had somehow in the pleasantness of the day's events forgotten that Robert would eventually be leaving London. Much less that there was a point when she had been anxious for him to do so, but now having been reminded of just how amiable Robert could be as a friend, the thought of him going away again seemed a gloomy one, particularly when she no longer had Mr. Clarkson's companionship.

"Oh," she kept her tone as light as possible, lest she seem too interested, "when will you be going back to Greenberry once more?"

"I'm not exactly sure, but probably soon." *Was there a hint of regret in his voice?* "I can't abuse old Fosper's hospitality forever, and it wouldn't do to leave Greenberry without its only doctor indefinitely."

"No, of course not. Well then, when you do get back, please give my warmest regards to the girls."

"I will," said Robert. "The girls miss you, you know." He looked her directly in the eye and said intently, "You are very much missed back home." He put special emphasis on that final word. Long after Robert had left for the day, Sarah found herself pondering the true meaning of his words. Was Robert saying he had missed her as well? And what did he mean by "home?"

Technically, she was already at home. Admittedly, there was a certain temporariness to her current living arrangements, but hadn't that been the case always? As a girl, her family had never owned Walnut Hill. It had merely been a temporary residence for them as long as her father had lived and occupied his position. The Parsley School at Weberley had, by definition, been a way station until she was old enough to make her own way in life. Bromley Hall had never been her home, that had been obvious from the very moment she had arrived. No, Robert must have been talking about his home in Greenberry. Unless, could Robert have meant that he considered Greenberry itself, if not the hall, to be Sarah's home? B why would he think that? Assuming, of course, he thought anything. She might be reading far too much into his choice of words.

And shouldn't she be angry at him right now? In fact, she really ought to be in a furious, uncontrollable rage at him for reading the journal, but she wasn't. Why not? Perhaps because, as her doctor and the man who'd examined her and the first man to ever see her scars, they were already beyond most of the normal formalities. It wasn't, after all, that her thoughts about cutting would have been any surprise to him at this point. Perhaps she ought to be offended at the idea of him reading about her and Mr. Clarkson, but found herself rather indifferent on that matter as well. The whole thing now seemed like a dream and hardly relevant. If Robert, or anyone else for that matter, had been scandalized by the affair, she could honestly say she couldn't care less, but judging from his reaction so far, he didn't seem scandalized at all.

Finally, of course, there was the matter of what she had written about Robert himself. He claimed he hadn't read any of it, but there was always a chance he had or that subsequent journal entries might have given him some insight into her feelings. Of course, whether he had read anything incriminating or not, kissing him certainly had been a far greater giveaway than anything she had ever written. However, he was behaving as if that had never happened at all. Sarah found herself missing the company of Geraldine and Clara to discuss the matter fully, and this thought prompted her to write brief missives to both of them, summarizing Mr. Clarkson's marital state and her recent illness, but stressing that she was no longer in any danger. She asked Mrs. Mundy to post the letters for her.

Thirty-Five

"Every man is surrounded by a neighborhood of voluntary spies."
–Jane Austen, *Northanger Abbey*

In the meantime, Robert Healey had surprised his hosts. First, with the fact that he had taken on a surprise patient in London. Second, that he had stayed at that patient's bedside all through the night. Third, that he was visiting this patient on a daily basis, even after the crisis had passed. Fourth, that he did not seem to expect any kind of payment from the patient in question. This prompted a number of questions about the identity of the patient and how exactly Robert had come to treat this person.

"Well, I know her from Greenberry," Robert explained.

"Her?" Mrs. Fosper asked. Her husband wisely elected to stay silent through all this.

"Sarah." Mrs. Fosper's eyebrows went up and Robert realized his mistake. "I mean, Miss Pole was the former governess at Bromley Hall. You've heard me mention Bromley Hall?"

"We have," Mrs. Fosper conceded, "but you didn't say anything about consorting with the governess there."

"I wasn't consorting," Robert attempted to correct her.

"How would you even make her acquaintance? I thought governesses were supposed to stay in the schoolroom," Mrs. Fosper went on and gave Robert a queer sort of look.

"Well, she used to assist me in Thomas Mandeville's bleedings," Robert explained. "She wasn't squeamish, like some of the servants."

"So, she was just assisting you with some bleedings? That was all?" Mrs. Fosper looked skeptical.

"Well, she did assist with another procedure on one of the servants once, and when we had the injured traveler," Robert grimaced remembering the injured traveler in question. "Also, we did sit beside each other in church sometimes," Robert admitted. "And sometimes around the town or around the estate, when she was taking the girls on rambles."

"Sounds like you saw quite a lot of each other," Mrs. Fosper concluded. "And now you're calling on her in London! How old is Miss Pole, would you say?"

"I wouldn't know," Robert answered sharply. "She hasn't told me her precise age, and it would hardly be polite for me to ask would it?"

"Is she an old hag?"

"No."

"Is she middle-aged then?"

"No," Robert admitted.

"Would you say she's about your years then?"

"Actually, she's almost certainly younger," Robert noted with a start. "She was still at school only two years ago. Though, with her manner, she seems much older than her years."

"Uh-huh," Mrs. Fosper noted. "Could you describe her appearance?"

"No, I could not," Robert replied through clenched teeth. "And you are he nosiest, most meddlesome busybody I've ever met!"

Mrs. Fosper was unrepentant.

"If Miss Pole's feeling up to it now, tell her that she is invited to come and anytime she likes," she continued.

" is?" Mr. Fosper spoke for the first time.

"ost certainly is," Mrs. Fosper declared.

Robert fumed about it for some time afterward. Honestly, why is it that anytime a single man spent any time in the company of a single lady, idle tongues conceived of intrigue? *Really!* It was almost enough to make him stop checking in on Sarah altogether. But of course, he couldn't let Mrs. Fosper's ridiculous notions get in the way of his concern for his patient's welfare. In that spirit of defiance, he decided to check in on Sarah once more.

Sarah's Journal

When Robert came to visit today, I surprised him by asking him to take me for a walk. For a moment, he seemed flustered, asking if anyone would get the wrong idea. Whatever that might mean. As I pointed out, there is no one to get any sort of idea but Mrs. Mundy, and she was busy with her customers. He laughed a bit at that. I told him to wait outside.

His eyes grew wide when I came out carrying the pouch. He knew what it was all right. Not surprising if he's been reading this journal. Clearly, he was curious, even anxious, to know why I was carrying it, but showing enormous restraint, he didn't ask. I walked with him to a bridge overlooking the river. I did not hesitate more than a moment.

I stretched out my arm as far as I could and threw the pouch into the water. It sank from view. For a moment, I felt quite overwhelmed as if having made some heavy exertion. I had to sit down and catch my breath. Robert was quite solicitous and seemed almost ready to carry me home, or at least call for a coach. Eventually, I was able to convince him I really was fine and could walk home, but he seemed to hover over me every step of the way, as if fearing I might need his arm at any moment. It was only once we'd returned to Mrs. Mundy's and took tea that he spoke about the pouch itself. He said he was proud of me for ridding myself of it. I must admit, I colored a bit at that.

So, the pouch is gone. We must wait and see whether I will miss it or not.

It's been three days since my last entry. So far, I don't miss the pouch.

In fact, I've never felt freer. Though, perhaps that's because the heat is finally breaking in London. Robert is coming to tea today. He does that every day, and I can't wait to show him the latest picture I've started working on. I wonder what Robert will think of it.

It is of a crow. A scarred crow, who's clearly been hurt and injured, but the scars have healed, and the crow now spreads its wings, ready to soar into flight. The crow is stronger for having survived such injuries. Not weaker. No, the crow is not a symbol of death.

The crow is a survivor.

The crow lives.

Epilogue

The town of Greenberry was impatient when the town doctor extended his trip to London. They were surprised when Dr. Robert Healey returned from London a married man. They were even more surprised to learn that the new Mrs. Healey was none other than the former governess at Bromley Hall. Robert and his bride had first made a visit to a Reverend Stamford and his wife, Clara, at their parsonage in Wiltshire. There were rumors that she had been an artist in London for a time and was continuing to send pictures there even now. Elinor and Violet Mandeville were delighted that Sarah would now be living near them again. Hugh Mandeville was somewhat less pleased, but had the conciliation of knowing he was under no obligation to see the town doctor or his wife socially, nor did the Sir John Tudbury; his son, or daughter-in-law, call on a town doctor socially. They had always called on doctors in London anyway, so there was no professional relationship either. For that matter, Dr. Healey himself never seemed to miss treating any of the Tudbury's either. The Ambrose family, who were known to invite Robert Healey to dinner or tea from time to time, had never had any professional former relationship with Sarah at all, so there was no awkwardness there. Prett quickly, the delicate question of the social standing of the doctor's new wife settled in, but one peculiarity remained. The new Mrs. Healey made a point of calling on and regularly visiting some of the poorest households in the area. She would often bring along her sketchbook, and at Nellie Bloom's request, she did a drawing of Gertie the goose, bedecked in the best of finery. But she called most often on the humble dwelling of Mrs. Riggs, to whom she gifted a miniature portrait of Adam. The portrait brought tears to Mrs. Riggs eyes.

"But why did you paint him in front of the sea?" she asked.

"An artistic liberty," Sarah replied.

"A what?"

"Nevermind, but be certain, Adam's in a better place now. He's at peace." Sarah told her earnestly.

In time, the Healey household became three instead of two. The baby boy was christened Adam.